The Hanged Man

The Hanged Man

A ROMANCE OF 1947

Hilda Dunn

CREATIVE ARTS BOOK COMPANY
Berkeley ∾ California

Copyright © 2001 by Hilda Dunn

The Hanged Man card from the Tarot Classic Deck reproduced by permission of U.S. Games Systems, Inc., Stamford, CT 06902. Copyright © 1971 by U.S. Games Systems, Inc., Stamford, CT. Further reproduction prohibited.

No part of this book may be reproduced in any manner without the written permission of the publisher, except in brief quotations used in articles or reviews.

For information contact:
Creative Arts Book Company
833 Bancroft Way
Berkeley, California 94710
1-800-848-7789

The characters, places, incidents and situations in this book are imaginary and have no relation to any person, place or actual happening.

ISBN 088739-324-1
Library of Congress Catalog Number 99-68405

Printed in Canada

I do not find
The Hanged Man.
                —T. S. Eliot, *The Waste Land*

Chapter I

> Madame Sosostris, famous clairvoyante,
> Had a bad cold, nevertheless
> Is known to be the wisest woman in Europe,
> With a wicked pack of cards.
>
> —T. S. Eliot, *The Waste Land*

MADAME SOSOSTRIS WILL READ YOUR TEA LEAVES
SANDWICH, TEA, AND YOUR FUTURE — 99¢

The message on the door was hand lettered in purple Crayola on the kind of white cardboard that comes in new shirts. Kate Clark read it with her red mouth open. The noonday sun was behind her and she felt a trickle of sweat negotiating her backbone. She was hungry and thirsty, and she guessed at the thin sandwich and lukewarm tea, clogged with superfluous leaves, that would be offered inside. Nevertheless.

Her entrance startled a bell and she paused for a moment on the threshold, then closed the door behind her. The room seemed meant for a small store, but the display windows were heavily curtained; it was very close and dim, lit by a dangling bulb to which a strip of sticky fly-paper had attached itself. A bilious yellow lowboy, supporting a feeble and noisy fan, and four small oilcloth covered tables with pairs of rickety ice cream chairs made up the furnishings.

A gas company calendar with a color print of a kitchen stove shimmering under a palm tree hung from a nail that had pierced the wall with some damage to the plaster. The date had been circled with the same aggressive crayon: August 22, 1947.

A very young, fair, and greasy girl appeared in a doorway to the rear. A loose sundress of no particular color was cinched at her waist by an exhausted white organdy apron, and a morsel of the same fabric was bobby pinned to the top of her head.

"Cream cheese or jelly?"

"Could I have both, please?"

"Twenny-five cents extra."

Kate nodded assent and the waitress withdrew into the back where she could be heard opening a refrigerator. The tea had evidently been standing on a warmer. A meager lunch was soon produced.

"Y'all leave yer tea leaves," the girl instructed. "Madame will appear when she gets the 'fluence on her."

Kate finished quickly, and was as quickly aware of an atmosphere of sinister solitude. An amateur of *frisson*, she had time to observe how well the fan masked the noises of the street. A monstrous black roach traversed the yellow lowboy with the deliberation of a hearse.

Madame Sosostris swept in, and closed the door behind her without turning round. Ample reason for delay was visible on her rather splendid person, for she was bedizened with such a myriad of twinkly, jangly, gaudy trifles that Kate asked herself wryly which one could be the "'fluence."

She was not young, not at all, but her posture had some of the elastic grace of youth and her unpainted features were large and fine. She sat down opposite Kate and gazed at her with vast dark eyes, the irises flecked with gold. Her gaze was solemn, but not unfriendly. Above all, there was no hint of the perfunctory. She waited a full minute before speaking.

"I do not see everything," she began gravely, "but sometimes I see more than one wants to know." Dramatic pause. "It is for that reason that I have left Europa. It is for that reason that you see me in this place." A glance neither sad nor contemptuous acknowledged the dreary improbability of her setting. Her accent was heavy, but not easily placed.

"My dear child, I have a message for you. For you particularly. Pay attention to what it is I say. I am your friend. I have been a mother."

Kate nodded.

"You are now interesting yourself in your past. That makes well. The past is always only the past. To know it may sometimes poison one's happiness for a time. But it is only the future you need fear to know. For when one *knows* that an event will happen then it *must* happen. One has taken on some of the purview of God."

She paused to allow Kate time for reflection, then continued. "You need not hear me out. You may content yourself with your delicious refreshment." The irony in her voice was not quite imperceptible.

Kate was hooked, and knew it. And Madame Sosostris knew it. Kate's serious manner was offered as a tribute to her remarkable interlocutrix.

The fan groaned. Madame Sosostris should be in New York, thought Kate. Or Miami Beach, if she likes the heat that much.

When the seer's gaze had rested long enough on the future she turned her attention to the thick white teacup, cupping it exquisitely in long jewelled fingers.

"Some people do not understand why Fate hides in a cup of garbage," she began. "They do not comprehend the role of the tea leaves. They think that they too can read them, and see a dog, a letter, a snowstorm. They do not see, as you see, that the reading is a skill very few have."

"But I *wanted* you to see a journey. — And a tall man. He doesn't have to be dark."

"You are planning a journey. I know as much. Nothing will happen to prevent your journey, my child. You are one of many, many people who now take such journeys. No more the troop ships and the U-boats. Now it is time to see what persons and places the war has left behind. You are going back into the future."

Madame Sosostris entertained another pregnant silence, and Kate, against all the lessons of experience, jumped in to help her.

"You're right! I *am* going back. I wasn't born here." She clapped her mouth shut, furious with herself. Let them flounder. That was the first thing one learned to do with fortunetellers.

The sibyl shrugged. "To be sure you will find out things you do not know about your family, back there. In families the characters are mixed. One does not need special powers to see such things. I too have had a family in another country." A deep sigh followed.

With the ease of habit Kate's imagination roughed out a scene. In the heart of a dense forest a clearing, ringed with gypsy wagons, flickered within the fitful glow of a campfire. The tea leaf reader, young and incredibly lovely, danced a wild flamenco while her various relations tinkered, banged tambourines, or smoked pipes in a rich chiaroscuro.

The woman went on. "I do not interest myself in those facts that are essentially the same for everyone. I leave that to the novelists, and the newspaper employees who write the Daily Horoscope. But I advise you not to suppose that everything is as you imagine it to be. I think you like to believe your own fictions. It makes your life more interesting but it will not always be wise."

The great eyes were kind. There was no mistaking that look: friendly. Within the thicket of lashes — which were perhaps, after all, just slightly Maybellined — the gold flecks rang true. Kate had seen plenty of fool's gold in tearooms.

"But Madame — come on. *You* must know..." Here a glance at the cascade of beads, the glittering arms... "you *must* know it's not so simple as 'believing your own fictions.' Romance is where you find it. Paris is in the heart. 'Things as they are, are different on the blue guitar.'"

Madame Sosostris clearly liked the last bit.

"Exactly so. You have the predilection to be attracted, yes, charmed, by certain things. You are the little niece with the legacy, is it not so? What else is required to make the story? The lonely house on the moors? The cousin with the mysterious past? The gorse bush? Ah, we do not forget the gorse bush, because it blooms in the kissing season. After all, it is not clear in which month you find the hero. Or is he the hero? If I tell you that, then I seal his fate as well as yours."

Kate's eyes shone. Why on earth was this artiste in Titus, a town that woke up every blessed summer morning and drank its Dr. Pepper in the steaming midsection of Florida and told itself how lucky it was not to be in a New York heat wave?

"Oh, Madame, that's *great*. But planning ahead now, what about telling me one fact. One true fact."

"One does not say the 'true fact.' If something is a fact, it must be true, no?"

"Thank you for pointing that out. Your English is very good." The compliment was accepted with dignity. "However I haven't really had a fortune, you know." Kate leaned forward and looked into her cup. "Your girl puts in too many leaves. What about getting out your 'wicked pack of cards'?"

"The cards, yes. We will speak of one card only. Now you must pay very careful attention to what I say." Her voice had darkened. Her expression was serious, even ordinary. "It is very important that you do one thing that I ask you. It is a matter of life and death." Something in Kate's face made her add in a rough whisper, "It is absolutely necessary."

"I understand."

"You will give him this message: 'I do not find the Hanged Man.'"

"Give who? I mean give whom?"

"You will meet him, and you will know. Get it right. Agreed?"

"Oh, *yes*."

"I do not expect you to make a mistake. But — if you find that you have made a mistake after all — do not explain. Laugh, but never explain."

They looked at each other soberly.

The clairvoyant picked up the cup again and said in an offhand way, "I see a journey, a letter, a snowstorm, a tall man — he is fair the tall man."

She stood up. "In Egypt, you know, one reads the coffee grounds. My own grandmother did so."

Kate fished in her handbag and produced a two-dollar bill. Madame Sosostris pocketed it without comment.

Kate had opened the door onto the bleached and blinding street when she heard a taffeta rustle behind her.

"My dear child, do not forget that which I have told you."

"'I do not find the Hanged Man.'"

"Do not let your fictions deceive you. I am your friend, but I shall be far away." She looked worried.

"I'll be okay," said Kate.

"I suppose so. Well, one makes do."

The door closed behind her. There was nothing at all to show what sort of place it was except that white cardboard, stuck on the door with masking tape.

Chapter II

> The Law is the true embodiment
> Of everything that's excellent.
> —W. S. Gilbert, *Iolanthe*

Outside, on Fruit Street, the glare bounced off everything that couldn't hide in its own thin shadow. Next door to the Tearoom lay the Wishy-Washy Launderette, sporting a Back at Two O'clock sign on the glass door. Next to that slumbered the Helpy-Selfy Superette. And next door to that a well-baked lemon stucco office building was garnished with big metallic numerals: 123. Kate took an envelope from her handbag and looked at the upper left corner. Partridge, Partridge, and Rand, Attorneys-at-Law, 123 Fruit St., Titus, Florida.

Her $21 Bulova watch offered 1:27 as the approximate time. Time to grab one of Ed's Chilidogs before her appointment. Ed's place was across the street and sported a limp blue banner that proclaimed: It's C*O*O*L Inside. That proved to be an exaggeration, but the dog was delectable.

Fortified, she presented herself at the law office and was shown into the inner sanctum, where she sat face to face with Sumner Partridge, Sr., in an atmosphere so relaxed the ceiling fan seemed to be the only thing working. On the wall behind her uncle's lawyer, between a stuffed tuna and a group photograph taken in front of the state capitol, a framed motto asserted itself: Time is the Lawyer's Stock in Trade. Kate made a mental note of it.

Mr. Partridge, who had been perusing some documents, leaned back in his swivel armchair. Five fingers met five fingers. One bore a heavy emblem ring.

"To be sure, Miss Clark, you are free to dispose of your late uncle's property as and however you may choose now or at any future time… It is yours absolutely. But…"

The door to the outer office had been left ajar and a brisk young woman with a pencil behind her ear swept in without knocking. "Mr. Partridge, that woman is on the telephone. *I* cannot speak to her again. *I* have work to do."

"I thank you, Olive," said Mr. Partridge, and turning to Kate, "Excuse me, ma'am."

Kate had already identified Olive according to the typology of the Hollywood film. She was the bright and breezy office factotum, the Roz Russell/ Eve Arden girl Friday, the iron hand in the sandpaper glove. Mr. Partridge, played by Edward Arnold with a southern accent, allowed her to think herself the power behind the throne. In reality, he wrote the script and cast it to his own specifications.

As melted butter into a large order of hot grits, the mellifluous Partridge voice poured into the telephone. The stifling air was not soothed. Indifferent to the fan, it seemed to concentrate apprehensively. There was a flash, and a growl. The thunderstorm that pounced on Titus every summer afternoon had arrived in good time. The windowpanes went blind, and Kate shivered.

Sumner Partridge, Jr., immaculate in a seersucker suit and cat-footed in white bucks, came through the door and stopped short.

"I beg your pardon. I thought Dad was alone with Miz Furbush." He nodded at the phone while running an eye over Kate. She twinkled. She always hated it when she twinkled. Anybody would think she was a star.

Mr. Partridge put the phone back in its cradle like a Russian violinist parking his Strad. "Yes, Sumner?"

"Seems there's more to that deceased Gurney account than his lawyer was told. I'm going to stroll over to the bank before the county probate officer decides to go on a fishing expedition. Any instructions?"

"Call your mother. She's havin' a catbird because you didn't tell her your girlfriend Lenabelle was comin' down from Savannah."

"I forgot." Sumner was grinning.

"And don't speak to Olive except to bow. She's on the warpath. Leave the door."

The Partridges smiled at each other with mutual satisfaction, then Mr. Partridge turned his attention back to Kate.

"Now ma'am, to business. As I was sayin' there are no strings on this nice little property. No trust fund, nothin' of that sort. In this regard your uncle acted as he felt your father would have wished him to. You may convert the whole of it to cash within six months."

Kate started to shake her head, but Mr. Partridge was riding an incoming tide. "*But...*" The thunder sounded retreat, and a few words were lost. "... not to do it. Unless I am more mistaken than I usually am this little portfolio will greatly appreciate in value durin' the next few years. Meanwhile, perhaps you could use the income?" A sharp glance through Country Lawyer spectacles underlined the question.

"Well, I *am* usually pretty broke. I live in Barnaby's Boarding House in New York. It's rather well known. It's for beginning theatre people, but most of us have to have other jobs. I work at Hamburger Heaven, but I had a part in 'The Flies' downtown."

"Ah, yes, Off Broadway." This was unexpected. "What part was it?"

"I was one of the flies." Mr. Partridge looked respectful, and Kate warmed to him. "It does have a lot of class."

"Miss Clark, class often needs cash. There will be about $1000 left in your uncle's bank account after expenses. You may have a use for it." Kate thought of her prospective journey, and was glad she hadn't to ask for money from that little portfolio Mr. Partridge was so fond of. "I take it you agree with me about the securities."

She nodded.

"We'll draw up a list of the number of shares of each stock to be transferred to your name. You'll find the certificates in your uncle's box at the bank, I presume. I have a listin' Trixie can work from for now, just leavin' a few blanks until you get back." His mellow voice became a shade less mellow. That shade made the difference.

"Trixie," he just barely called.

Trixie, thought Kate.

Trixie was candybox pretty, with auburn hair, hazel eyes, and a mouth at whose shape art and nature had contrived with something near the same intention. The ceiling fan drew up and diffused a powerful whiff of Fabergé's *Straw Hat*.

Enter the flighty, flirty steno. Kate would bet that she and Olive were hired as a set.

The list didn't really amount to much. Though Kate had begun to picture herself as a madcap heiress, Hepburn style, with a beret and maybe a pet cougar, hers seemed to be, after all, a very *little* portfolio.

Still, nothing at Partridge, Partridge, and Rand, or in Titus either, was rushed through. There was still time for the sun to spread itself on the sill before Trixie headed for her typewriter, casting a backward glance at the stocking seams which beelined up her shapely legs.

"Whatever else is in your uncle's safe deposit box is now your property, Miss Clark. Take this authorization over to the Central Florida Guaranty Trust and they'll make it available to you. I don't know what you'll find. If there were anythin' of real value besides the stocks I think I'd know. Still, no man tells his lawyer everything." He handed Kate an envelope. "If you come back here before five we can sign Trixie's final list and you'll be finished."

He glanced out of the window at a bright spread of cloudless sky.

Kate hesitated, puzzled. "But what about the house? I mean my uncle's cottage on Snake Lake?" She feared being misunderstood. "I mean I don't need it or anything. It's just… well, isn't it mine? He hadn't anyone else."

"There was a lady your uncle wanted to remember. He altered his will the week before he died. I suppose he didn't have time to tell you. He could hardly have thought you would have any use for it."

"A *lady*? Kate turned pink. "Of course I don't want it, Mr. Partridge. I just never guessed."

The lawyer looked mildly disapproving, though of what wasn't clear. "Everything but the house and its contents is yours, ma'am." He paused, then said firmly, "Your uncle was a very sick man, Miss Clark. Don't you go blamin' him." Kate opened her mouth to remonstrate, but Mr. Partridge raised a hand. "Are you meanin' to tell me that old lizard Flossie duPage didn't give you an earful the minute you got off the Jacksonville bus? She was prowlin' around out to Snake disguised as a raccoon the whole month of June."

Kate shook her head. Flossie duPage was the proprietress of Mrs. duPage's Comfy Guest House, hard by the bus station. "She just sat on the porch fanning herself with a fan that said Property of Sinkhole Baptist Church. She didn't even show me my room." The Partridge mouth curled. "It *was* very hot," she added.

"It's always very hot in August. That old crow was after Albert Clark herself but he was harder to grab than an armadillo."

"It's okay, Mr. Partridge. There's probably a letter for me at the bank." She stood up and made for the door. "His wife died quite a while ago," she added apologetically.

Mr. Partridge smiled at her kindly. "Flossie duPage wasn't so bad once. She got herself widowed unexpectedly. Made her tougher than a boiled owl."

In the outer office Olive was fuming into her typewriter, a half-eaten sandwich in her open drawer. Trixie was stopping a run in her stocking with pink nail polish.

"I'll see you later," said Kate.

Olive sent up a smoke signal.

"Y'all have fun now," advised Trixie.

Kate Clark was an orphan. Her Australian mother had died young and her father, who had sent her to his brother in America when war broke out, had disappeared in the chaos of Dunkirk. When she arrived in Florida in 1939 she had been a gawky English schoolgirl with unravelling braids, an outgrown gym tunic, a marked accent, and a teddy bear. Of these attributes only the teddy bear remained. No one now would have said she was not American, least of all herself.

Nevertheless in her heart was a dream of Home, a longing for a background with names and faces. A box of letters from her cousin Sally Bell was proof that it existed, and all the proof there was — for no one else had ever written after her father disappeared. Uncle Albert said there wasn't much family. It would be up to James and Doris, Sally Bell's children, and to Kate herself, to do something about it.

Alone in the cool basement of the bank, she solemnly opened Albert Clark's safe deposit box. Like the average magic casket, it contained three envelopes. She opened the one with her name on it first.

Fair Albion
June 15, 1947

My dear Katherine,

    Sumner Partridge will have explained my financial arrangements to you. The shop did better than we hoped so you need not be quite penniless. I am the more glad of that as my dear brother had nothing to leave you.

    Your Aunt Ada and I both felt that we were very lucky to have had you with us. I'm afraid we were rather dull for such an imaginative young person. Never mind. You will be able to go to England now and visit Cousin Sally Bell. She was always the liveliest of our lot when we were young. Do you know she boasts of being the first woman in England to wear ankle socks?

                    God bless you, my dear.
                      Your affectionate uncle,
                              Albert

P.S. Please tell Sally that I tried to help James. I shan't be coming to the bank again.

    The postscript was written in an unsteady hand. She read the letter again, but could conjure up no mention of the mysterious lady.

    The second envelope was large and brown. It contained proofs: Uncle Albert's discharge papers from the Northumberland Fusiliers in 1918, his marriage certificate, and a document attesting he had become a United States citizen on November 8, 1933.

    The third envelope was long and heavy. Inside was a thick parchment, folded twice. When Kate opened it a name in Black Letter seemed to jump out: Oswald Clark Birkie. Cousin Sally Bell's maiden name had been Birkie; that much she knew. She began to read.

    "He whom this scroll commemorates, at the call of King and Country, left all that was dear to him..." It was signed George Rex. When she tried to replace it in the envelope she discovered a small object loose inside.

    It was a gold locket, no bigger in circumference than a dime and threaded on a gossamer fine chain. Inside was the tiny photograph of a young woman with fair hair piled high. Opposite the face a name had been engraved in letters not quite too small to read — a name elegant, romantic, aristocratic: Ilse von Elfenstein.

    A magic casket might have topped things off with a sere and yellow leaf. Uncle Albert's box included a small stack of certificates, held together by an elastic band. Kate pushed the buzzer and asked whether she might have a large manila envelope, big enough to hold everything.

She ran into Sumner Partridge, Jr., in the Central Florida Guaranty Trust's revolving door. Trapped in the same plate glass wedge they were precipitated into the bright wide street.

He raised his straw hat. "I declare, Miss Clark," he said in a southern gentlemanly manner, "you'd do well to wear a sunbonnet yourself if you plan to spend time in Titus in August." His friendly gaze traveled down from her curly head past her sharkskin skirt with the reversible pleats and when it got to her spectator pumps a message embedded in the sidewalk in metal studs seemed to inspire him.

"Could I persuade you to join me for an ice cold Dr. Pepper?" She hesitated. "Well, how about a Tom Collins? A beer? There's such a thing as orange juice around here once in a while. It's fairly cool in the hotel bar, as I suppose you know."

"I'm not staying at the hotel. I'm at Mrs. duPage's Comfy Guest House." She smiled. "Anyway I don't frequent bars by myself."

"Very wise," he said, steering her easily across the street to the pale and shuttered Titus Hotel. Seated in a dim booth, she was soon sipping ice-clogged claret lemonade. Sumner had a beer.

"I have to be back at your father's office before five," she said.

"And so do I! Obviously the Fates conspire to keep us together. But why did they lead you to the duPage Mausoleum?" He stopped, abashed. "Look, I'm truly sorry. I forgot for the moment why you are here. My dad handled your uncle's estate."

"It's okay. Your father directed me to Mrs. duPage's. I wrote and asked him about an inexpensive place."

Sumner smiled at her. "But your uncle must have left you something? It didn't all go to Madame X?"

"Maybe you can tell me who she was. My uncle never said a word about her. I was awfully surprised."

"Damn handsome woman, not that anybody got much of a look at her. But your English uncle was no Ronald Colman. I'm afraid I'm being terribly unprofessional. It must be your eyes."

"Maybe it's *your* eyes," said Kate. "I'm still wearing my sunglasses."

"So you are." He reached over and took them off, very gently. "What do people call you when they want to be very friendly? Katherine? Star Eyes? Cupcake?"

"Kate."

"Just plain Kate?"

"Uh huh. What's wrong with that? What do they call you?"

"Sumner."

"Just plain Sumner?"

"It's not all that plain, do you think?"

"I suppose not. It sounds like a Famous Fort."

"You have to meet my cousin Sumter."

Men like Sumner Partridge, Jr., Princeton types with lines that spread out like ivy and black knitted neckties, usually made Kate nervous or cross. Sumner himself did not, and she was having fun.

"I knew that! I even went to school in the South for a while."

"So did *I*. Talk about Fate."

"But we didn't meet."

"We went to different schools together. What about another drink? It won't be any cooler outside."

She shook her head, and a voice at the bar was suddenly audible.

"Thought Hogie was about ta move his tackle store in that empty place on the corner of Fruit 'n' Billings?"

"Yeah, he is," said the bartender, drawing a cold beer from the tap.

"Well, somebody else moved in last night. They got a card stuck on the winda. Some kinda Tearoom."

A grinding groan signalled the nickelodeon's successful ingestion of a coin. There was a flat plop, and instead of the bartender's answer Kate heard a low voice crooning, "In a small cabaret there's a lady they call the gypsy. She will look in the future…"

What if Sumner Partridge knew all about Madame Sosostris? Kate took a deep breath and said, very fast, "I do not find the Hanged Man"

"I knew you were a damsel in distress," he said, unpocketing a very well-ironed handkerchief.

"It's just something in my eye." She squinted dramatically.

"Allow me," said Sumner, leaning across the table, but Kate pulled an upper lid over a lower and said, "Gone."

Sumner looked at her eyes, and looked at his watch. "How long are you staying in town? Would you like to have dinner and go to an air-conditioned movie?"

"I thought your girlfriend Lenabelle was comin' down from Savannah." She smiled a little smile. "Your mother is havin' a catbird."

"Oh, damn. I forgot. It's the whole week-end shot."

"I'm leaving on the bus for Jacksonville at 6 a.m. Then I get the train for New York. Thank you for the drink, though."

"I come to New York now and then. How about if I call you there?"

"Sure. I'm going to England for a few weeks very soon though. You could leave a message. They specialize in messages at Barnaby's."

"Give me your number. I must see you again. After all you borrowed my second best handkerchief."

"No I didn't. You put it back in your pocket."

He felt the pocket. "Oh, well, wouldn't you like to borrow it? In the Old South, you know, a lady must have a handkerchief. Kleenex won't do at all. And since you've lost yours…"

Kate shook her head.

While Sumner paid the bartender Kate surreptitiously looked at her eyes in a dim mirror by the door. A black cat, cheerfully sinister, leered at her from behind a potted palmetto.

Back at the law office, departure was in the air. Sumner disappeared quickly. There were no changes in the list, and when Kate had signed it Mr. Partridge shook her hand and wished her bon voyage. Olive and Trixie whisked out together.

Kate set out for Mrs. duPage's Comfy Guest House. As she approached the corner of the street her heartbeat thickened. She looked for the card on the Tearoom door but it had been removed. Instead there was a big yellow sign with blue lettering:

OPENING MONDAY
HOGIE'S TACKLE HEADQUARTERS

Chapter III

"Didn't you hear me say 'Feather'?" the Sheep
cried angrily, taking up quite a bunch of needles.
—Lewis Carroll, Through the Looking Glass

Madame Sosostris was putting her cards on the table. Over and over, each time more frantically, she spread them out on the oilcloth for Kate to see: the Fool, the Hierophant, the High Priestess, and all the others of the Major Arcana. Each time she murmured in despair, "I do not find The Hanged Man." The young waitress, now with bright red fingernails and a sultry pout, brought Kate's sandwich on a tray with a tiny locket. Kate picked it up to take a bite only to see thin hairy black spider legs protruding between the soft white slices of bread. A scream seemed to stick in her throat, to strangle her with bony fingers. There was a smell of oranges.

"I think she must be having a bad dream," said a matter-of-fact voice. "You know Ruggles always twitches like that when he's having a bad dream. Sometimes he barks."

"Well, she ain't barked yet," said someone else. A hand made itself felt on her shoulder. "Wake up, sister. Take a look at Carolina in the morning."

Kate's eyes opened on a landscape more bizarre than any her dreaming fancy had shown her. Naked trees like bleached bones stood in a wide red river; there was no green at all in the landscape — it seemed not to belong under the blazing, but still recognizable, sky.

"Have an orange," continued the man who had awakened her. "We've got a sackful my sister-in-law gave us. I wouldn't mind living in Florida if I had a big fan. And a boat."

"Ruggles wouldn't like it," said his companion, a plump little woman with a pink enamel flamingo pinned near her heart. "He likes New Rochelle. All his friends are there."

Kate smiled somewhat ruefully at the couple facing her. She had pounced on the first forward seat in the coach hoping that the one that faced the rear of the train would stay empty and serve as a footrest. Exchanging her ticket for more luxurious accommodation was an idea that had not stopped to be entertained. One could only be extravagant with money one had earned. Uncle Albert's spirit might grow restless, otherwise.

The train had proved to be more crowded than the one she had come south on. "Lot of Floridians taking vacations up north to get away from the heat," said the man, holding out an orange in his hand. Kate thanked him and began to peel the fruit into a paper bag. She got out a limp Hershey bar and offered to share it.

"I know it's a mess, but chocolate and oranges are awfully good together."

"I was just saying to my husband," said the flamingo pin woman, "that Ruggles, our poodle, often has bad dreams. Do you have a dog, dearie?"

"No. I'd like to, though. I live in a boarding house in Manhattan. It's for actors." So who cares? she asked herself tolerantly.

"Oooooh. That's very thrilling, I must say. You don't *look* like an actress. My favorite actress is Bette Davis. She really *acts* every minute. Not like some of them. Some of them you don't know what they get paid for."

Her companion gave a leering snort.

Kate ventured upon a new subject. "Did you happen to visit an alligator farm while you were in Florida? My uncle who lived in Florida was a great admirer of alligators. He felt that they were exploited on those farms. Do you know that there are people who can hypnotize alligators just by tickling them?"

"You don't *say*," said the woman. "Did your uncle keep a pet alligator by any chance?"

"Oh, *no*. He wanted them kept in their native habitats. He was very active in the Alligator Protection League."

"You don't *say*. I suppose he wouldn't think much of my taking one of those baby 'gators home now."

Kate shook her head.

"Well, I got to admit I got one. I'm going to give it to the zoo in White Plains when it gets older. I thought it would interest Ruggles, you know. But then I heard people flush them down the toilets and the sewers are all full of big alligators."

The man looked at Kate. "Don't mind her," he said.

There was a silence, and Kate fished out *Murder First Class*, a slim volume she had picked off the rack in the Jacksonville station. On the cover a red train streaked across an Alpine trestle while in the foreground a young woman in a trench coat stared aghast at the smoking pistol in her hand.

Later in the day, when the train had stopped at Raleigh, Kate put her book down to consume a ham sandwich and a cold drink from the candy butcher. The man opposite had disappeared, but the woman with the flamingo pin was clearly in gear for a chat.

"Do you have family in Florida, dearie?" she began.

"I lived in Florida with my uncle when I was younger. He moved there after the First World War. He died last week, though, so I haven't anyone there any more."

"Oh, I *am* sorry. You went down for the funeral, I suppose?"

"Well, no." She flushed slightly, feeling stupid, annoyed, and awkward. "I was the only living relative he had in this country, and he'd asked not to have a funeral. He always hated fuss."

The woman's eyes opened rather wide.

"Look at that spotted pig!" The train was already in the outskirts of the town and Kate was pointing at an animal that was in a yard backed up to the tracks. "Or is it a rocking horse?"

"Well, maybe he didn't have a funeral, but they'd of had to do something," said the woman, undiverted.

"He asked to have his ashes thrown into the lake," said Kate. "Lots of people like to do things like that."

"Well, I never heard of anybody's uncle doing it. Besides, who was to do it if not you, you being his only relative and all?"

"I don't know. I wasn't asked. I respected his wishes. I'd really rather not discuss it." Kate picked up her book again.

"Well, I guess it's none of my business." The woman was smiling at her in a conciliatory way. "Did he leave you his house?"

It was Kate's turn to open her eyes rather wide. "What house?"

"Didn't he have a house?"

"Not any more. He had a cottage on a lake."

"If he had a house he shouldn't of sold it. My sister says it's crazy not to keep a house in Florida if you can. The prices go up every day. It's like the Boom. Of course, that was before your time." She got some pink yarn out of a shopping bag and started knitting furiously. The color matched her flamingo brooch, and the click of the needles blended in with the clatter of the train. She smiled again and Kate felt more cheerful.

"What are you making?" she asked politely, closing the book around her index finger.

"A sweater for my dog Ruggles." She looked up. "Oh, there you are, Harry. Could you get me a drink?"

Harry looked none too agreeable but he went away and returned with a paper cone full of water. "You'll have to put down your knitting unless you want me to pour it down you. These cups don't last worth a damn."

"I think I'll stroll a little," said Kate.

She stood at the rail at the back of the train for a long time, watching the flat countryside recede into the diminishing daylight. She thought back to Sumner and the gypsy and forward to England and Sally Bell. When a cool moon the color of lemonade appeared she heard the clearing of a throat.

"I'd like to help you watch that moon, miss." It was a sailor in summer whites, his middy hat resting on a set of alarming red eyebrows.

"Oh, no. But thanks." She started back through the rear coach, swaying a little, smiling a little. Some people were smoking and playing gin rummy on makeshift trays; some were trying to make children comfortable for the night. Almost everyone was tan. People with tans didn't look so tired.

When she came to her own seat again she hesitated, for her companions were not there, but she felt restless and kept on, bumping and jostling. Six cars forward was the dining car, nearly empty and in some disarray. The waiters were clearing away where they could, crumbing the glossy white tablecloths and emptying ashtrays into a bucket. With the lights above and the carpet below, with the bud vases in their gleaming holders on each table, each with a single rose, above all with the rocking darkness clinging to the windows and making mirrors of them the scene had a theatrical glamour that made Kate stop and stare.

A pretty woman with frizzy hair and a sleeveless linen dress was counting out bills onto a waiter's tray. At the table beyond her were Harry and the woman with the flamingo brooch.

Those two were engaged in such earnest low-voiced conversation that Kate had not immediately recognized them. Harry was facing her, wearing glasses and pouring coffee with thin nervous fingers. He looked angry and defensive. The headwaiter bustled in, and, seeing Kate, said in a loud voice, "The dining car is closed, Madam."

Harry looked up quickly and his expression changed to bland recognition. His companion stood up, spilling her handbag to the floor. Kate moved to help her to retrieve the contents and noticed among the welter of cosmetics, cough drops, pill boxes, combs, notebooks, change, tickets, hairpins, scissors, and thread a small suede bag of an odd but familiar shape.

"I'm always telling Fan she needs one of those Efficiency Experts to sort out that pocketbook." Harry looked at Kate's outsize handbag with a mocking smile. "Bet you could go her one better if it came to that."

Kate was silent, puzzled.

They overtook her before she got back to her seat, the three of them making a little procession through the rackety cars. Seated again, Kate opened her book. The woman called Fan took out her knitting and set furiously to work. Harry began picking his teeth.

"Me and Fan thought we'd find you in the dining car," he began. "We hoped you'd join us for a piece of pecan pie. They have excellent pecan pie. It's a southren specialty, you know."

Kate looked up. "It's too sweet."

"Whipped cream goes good with it," he continued. "Kind of cuts it. What's *really* too sweet is this dessert I once had at a Greek wedding. Balaclava, it's called. Full of honey."

Fan knit on, looking cheerful and vague, and making no effort to join in.

Harry spoke again. "Would your uncle's place be out to Snake Lake by any chance?" Kate put her book down and looked at him in amazement, but he continued without a break, droning on with the natural persistence of a cicada. "I just ask because my brother-in-law says that's the best place for fishing in central Florida. Yep, there's a million lakes around there but Snake Lake, that's a big one. Deep. I wouldn't swim there if I was you. Not unless you are particularly good at tickling alligators." He smiled ingratiatingly.

"I thought your brother-in-law lived near Tampa," said Kate. If this was a game, they could all play it.

"He loves fishing. I guess your uncle fished some?"

"Look, Mr. . . ." Kate began.

"Feather," said Fan, not looking up. Kate noticed that her knitting had been distributed on two more needles.

"What?" asked Kate. "I mean I beg your pardon."

"Feather! Harry's name is Feather."

"But then isn't *your* name Feather, too?"

"Well, I suppose it is in a way. But I hate being called Fan Feather, if you know what I mean." She paused. "'Sally Rand lost her fan, give it back you nasty man!'"

"Don't mind her," said Harry.

Kate waited a little. Harry and Fan looked at her with noncommittal good will. Mr. and Mrs. Saphappy America. Apple pie and cheese. Let's face it. Everybody has a right to act serious once in a while. Harry and Fan probably had troubles she couldn't guess at.

"My uncle didn't like to fish much," she said gravely. "He just liked to sit on the porch and watch the lake. It *was* Snake Lake, though, where he had the cottage. He lived in Titus until he retired. He was a haberdasher, like President Truman."

"If you wasn't to the funeral I suppose you went to see about the cottage and all like that. Sad." Harry sighed.

It was too much. She returned to her book and ignored all further remarks. After a while the lights were turned down and the passengers slept or dozed. At some point she was aware of the train standing still, and she looked out of the window and saw the Washington Monument, an illuminated finger admonishing the zodiac.

At some other point, she was aware of her handbag being replaced on the seat next to her.

"Sorry, dearie," whispered Fan. "I knocked it off the seat when I went to the lav."

Chapter IV

> But then she had a devil of a spirit
> And sometimes mixed up fancies with reality
> —George Gordon, Lord Byron, *Don Juan*

There was a letter from England on the mail table at Barnaby's. Another George Rex, thought Kate, glancing at the stamps. The envelope was addressed in Cousin Sally Bell's bold but tidy hand. Stuffing it into her handbag, Kate made for her room.

MaJa, her roommate, was lying face down on her bed in a black and white two-piece bathing suit. She had propped the window open with a coat hanger and was reading *Cold Comfort Farm*. "Hot, what?" she asked in an imitation English accent. Her name was really Mary Jane, but upon arriving in New York from Wisconsin she had decided to give it some oomph.

"Must be one of those heat waves they keep talking about in Florida," replied Kate, plopping down on a bulging overstuffed chair and draping her legs over the arm.

"So give me the blow-by-blow," demanded MaJa, turning languidly onto her left hip and supporting her head with a long bent arm.

"You won't believe everything I have to tell you. But first, any calls?"

"Well, Mrs. B. called at this very room to say that if you don't pony up she's going to give your part in the Irish stew to somebody else. And Hamburger Heaven called to see if you could work the first shift tomorrow."

"What, me, the little heiress with the gorse bush, wait on table?"

"Your uncle left you a gorse bush?"

"Haven't you ever read *Jane Eyre*?"

"Sure. That wasn't a gorse bush. It was a horse chestnut."

"Same difference. Listen, MaJa, Uncle Albert did leave me some money. It was awfully nice really. I mean it seemed he was very glad to leave it to me. He wanted me to be able to go back to England and see Cousin Sally." Kate sighed. "Oh, Maj, sometimes I think about what it would have been like if my father hadn't gone to Dunkirk in his little boat. They asked everyone to go." She paused and looked at MaJa. "I guess I told you a million times."

"A googolplex," said MaJa kindly. "Have a cookie." She nodded at a shoebox on the table.

Kate sighed again. "I wish *I* had a big family." MaJa was the youngest of five, and was always getting food parcels.

"Well why don't you get married and have a passel of brats? Everyone's doing it. There's going to be a Baby Boom."

"I have to think of my career."

"Buzzing around the stage giving everyone a headache is some career."

"Jealousy is a terrible vile passion, MaJa."

"Okay, how about going to England and looking up your relations then? Did you get your letter? I meant to bring it upstairs."

"Yes, thanks. I'll read it in a minute." She held up the little locket. "What do you think of this?"

MaJa fingered it. "Teeny-weeny. Who's Ilse von Elfenstein?"

"I can't imagine. It was in the safe deposit box with my uncle's papers."

"Maybe some robbers broke into the bank and things got put back into the wrong boxes."

"Maybe somebody broke into your head and put things back into the wrong hemispheres."

"Go ask your cousin. She'll probably know. Sounds like her speed, what with playing early Beethoven on the pianoforte and all that stuff."

They both laughed. Speculation about Cousin Sally Bell was a popular topic.

"Okay, so now you're an heiress," said MaJa. "Are you being pursued by handsome fortune hunters yet?"

"Maybe. Are there any Cokes downstairs?"

"Cash only. Svengali ate all the Eskimo Pies yesterday and Mrs. B. suspended the honor system."

"My treat, dearie. You go fetch. I'm bushed." She tossed MaJa a dime.

Kate took off her wrinkled dress and put on ragged blue shorts and a polka dot halter, then went down the hall to splash cold water on her face. A sign on the bathroom wall read: Twelve Other People Use This Room.

When she got back there were two cold bottles on the table with straws poking up.

"Ah, your Moonbeam McSwine outfit," said MaJa, who had taken the upholstered chair.

"Ay washed me 'ands and faice." Kate picked up her drink and sat down on her bed, resting her back on the grey distempered wall. "I met a man."

"Was he a lawyer?"

"How did you know?"

"Elementary, my dear Clarkson. You went to Florida to settle some old family estates and you came back with the promise of a gorse bush. You have an ink stain in your ear and your suitcase is tied up with red tape."

"It was going to pop. I have to get a new one to go abroad."

"Well, is he handsome? Tall? Presentable?"

"The law is the embodiment of everything that's excellent."

"Tell me more."

"Well, he's the son of the lawyer my uncle had and he's a partner in the firm. He's very smooth, but funny — like Cary Grant. He took me for a drink and he wanted to take me to dinner, but he couldn't. I think he really likes me, but on the other hand it doesn't seem very likely." She paused. "He's very good looking and Ivy. I mean you know the type I usually draw."

"Watch out. Maybe he's after your money."

"Oh, it's just peanuts to somebody like him. I bet those lawyers make more in a year than Uncle Albert made in his whole life."

"Sure, but what if he knows something they didn't tell you, being on the inside? Maybe you're the heiress to the whole von Elfenstein principality in southern Prussia and when Germany gets stitched up you'll be sought after by crowned heads."

"Since when do you know anything about Prussia?"

"Well, tell me this dreamboat's name anyway."

"Sumner Partridge."

"Probably an alias."

Kate groaned. "Well, listen to this. It wasn't Sumner Partridge who was interested in my inheritance. It was this crazy couple I met on the train coming back. They were really a pair of fruitcakes. Harry and Fan. Doesn't it sound like a vaudeville team? They even had a poodle named Ruggles. Fan was knitting him a pink sweater." She thought a minute. "At least they said they had a poodle named Ruggles."

"Well if you told them about your inheritance the least they could do was tell you about their poodle."

"But I didn't tell them about it. They asked questions about my uncle and his cottage and the lake and whether the cottage was mine or not. It was as if they were really trying to find something out." MaJa was looking mildly amused. "Well, it was funny," Kate squeaked. "I mean it *wasn't* funny."

"'Hamlet and His Problems,' by T. S. Eliot. English II. Objective Correlative," said MaJa.

"You mean my emotion is in excess of the facts as they appear?"

"Some people *are* terribly nosy, Kate. I mean you know how nosy some people are. Didn't you ever get the third degree from Mrs. B.?"

"She has a vested interest in me. Anyway the funny part was I saw them in the dining car when they didn't know I was there. They were like two different people. She dropped her handbag on the floor. There was a suede bag inside — a little suede bag — and in the middle of the night when I realized that she had been into *my* handbag I also realized what was in that little suede bag."

"Aggies?"

"A gun. A little gun. A Mauser or a Derringer sort of little gun."

"Kate, you know about guns the same as I know about Prussia. It was probably a patented juice squeezer or something. Did the little suede bag say Souvenir of Florida on it?"

"It was a gun. I think so." She was serious. "I never told you Uncle Albert had a gun. I found it in his desk when I went down for that wedding. It looked brand new."

For the first time MaJa too looked serious. "Did you say good-bye to these not so funny people? Did they ask you where you lived?"

"Why bother? I'm sure she went through my bag. I was very cool. At Penn Station Harry offered to help me with my suitcase, which anyone could see was ready to burst. I said that my fiancé, a city detective, was meeting me under the clock."

"So they didn't wait?"

"They vanished in a puff of steam."

"What do you make of it then?"

"I'm trying to fit it in with what the fortuneteller told me."

MaJa laughed. "The fortuneteller! Spare me the fortuneteller. Boy, they heat up the kettle the minute they hear your dainty dogs hit the pavement. Ah declayah if it wan't a southern fortune telluh with a crystal ball in the icebox and a wig made of Spanish moss. What did she tell you? To beware of pink poodles?"

"She advised me not to believe my own stories. She seemed to think that I was inclined to see Romance and Adventure all over the place."

"Just the kind of girl who drops in on fortunetellers. You do spin a good yarn, Scheherazade, but I don't really think you can see through little suede bags after all."

"MaJa, you know those x-ray machines they have in the shoe stores? You push a button and see the bones in your toes? It was like that the way I saw that gun."

"Kate, baby doll, I love you. Don't stay in England too long 'cause I might be in the big time when you get back. I've got an appointment in one hour with a man who says the harpist is quitting in Phil Spitalny's All-Girl Orchestra."

"Oh, is that thing next to your bed a harp? I thought it was a clothes horse."

MaJa made a parting raspberry as she went out with a towel and a terry bathrobe.

Kate got out Sally Bell's letter and moved back to the chair. It was lumpy but she liked it. I'm no Prussian princess, she thought. I could sleep on a can of beans.

She slit the envelope with an orange stick, took out two sheets of ruled paper, and began to read.

Quo Vadis
35, The Oval
East Tinkham, Kent
Tuesday

My Dear Kate

I am answering your letter by return post though I doubt you will get it before you go to Florida. The postal service enjoy one tea break after another whilst the public suffer. Once upon a time one could chuck a letter out of the window of a morning and have it delivered in Glasgow before the shops shut. Which they generally do.

So poor old Albert has gone off all on his own. That wife of his was a proper stick. But what can you expect of someone named Ada Annie? I wish he had found it possible to come back to England once in a way, but there you are. Nothing rum about his not wanting you to have the worry and sadness of a funeral. Very considerate, was our Albert.

I don't suppose I ever mentioned James's plan for popping off to Florida, never having regarded myself as part of that vast network for disseminating English family news that seems to have spread into every corner of the globe with the seeping tides of Empire. (The Empire's had it, by the by. High time. I never saw any reason why the Hottentots should have to drink afternoon tea.) At any rate, that's off now I suppose. James's wartime experiences seem to have rattled him a bit.

We are all in a tangle at home at the moment what with James pacing the lounge and Doris having left Felix and moved back to the family seat. It's a semi-detached, after all, with one bath and two W.C.'s. They are certain to both depart suddenly one of these days. Dear old Fred's no bother, as long as he has his garden and his comics on the wireless. In any case, there is a place just for you here, as there has been every blessed minute since I put you onto the boat train, your eyes all glassy wet, all those many years ago. Come as soon as ever you can, my pretty dear.

A friend gave me two tickets for a concert at the Albert Hall last night. It was Dmitri Bolonsky, the legendary Russian whom no one has heard since before the war. He is very soulful and Slavic with great hands that come crashing down on the keys in an apocalyptic manner. Not exactly my style, I must say, and I was chagrined that Doris wouldn't go simply because she hadn't any more ration for chocolates. James likes large music (ugh! Wagner!) but had an engagement so I took poor Fred.

Your affectionate cousin
Sally

Kate read Sally Bell's letter three times. Had Quo Vadis been Pomfret Castle it could hardly have intrigued her more. Imagine calling your house Quo Vadis! But then, Uncle Albert had put a sign over his cottage door, done in twigs and shells: Fair Albion.

Chapter V

> There lies the port; the vessel puffs her sail
> There gloom the dark, broad seas
> —Alfred, Lord Tennyson, "Ulysses"

Thin paper ribbons pretended to hold the ship to the land, a multi-colored web now at full strength. Kate leaned on the rail and mouthed another exaggerated "Good-bye" at MaJa, who certainly knew how to hold the other end of a yellow streamer without looking silly.

The pier was full, but the man at MaJa's elbow seemed to be crowding her even more than was necessary. That sort of thing often happened to MaJa. However, this was not one of those times. His gaze was nailed to the ship's rail and he was simply moving toward MaJa to avoid the stolen kisses of a small poodle in a pink sweater being held within range of his left ear. Yes, a poodle in a pink sweater in the arms of a small thin man in a soft felt hat and glasses.

It was hard to be sure at that distance, with such a crowd of faces. Kate put the end of the yellow streamer between her teeth and got a midget pair of opera glasses out of her bag. It was Harry all right, Harry and Ruggles. Ruggles was wearing his new pink sweater. Like almost everyone else, Harry was holding the end of a streamer. Kate tried to connect Harry's streamer to some hand at the rail but it was hopeless in all the criss-cross confusion. A lot of streamers were randomly connected anyway, and a lot went to upper decks.

Putting the glasses away, she tried to alert MaJa by improvising a message in mimic semaphore. MaJa responded with an alarming Harpo Marx impersonation.

The *Queen Victoria* emitted a deep and pregnant hoot. Fore and aft massive ropes were unwound and tossed aboard. An officious red tugboat, dancing among discarded banana peels and Cracker Jack boxes, signalled readiness to escort the big ship safely out of the harbor. The shore shifted, the paper streamers snapped, a cheer went up, and the crowd on the pier soon turned into little dots in a half tone engraving.

Freed at last from the pain, pleasure, or boredom of saying good-bye, most of the tourist class passengers dispersed. Some headed for their cabins to unpack or to size up fellow occupants. Some made for the purser's office to leave passports, make inquiries, change money. Dollars bought a lot of large notes and heavy coins and Americans loading their pockets emitted synthetic groans. Quite a few people sought immediate relaxation in one or another of the public rooms.

Kate lingered at the railing, wondering at the spell cast on familiar landmarks by the fading light and by the sense of darkness rushing toward them from the open sea. A ferry slid by like a cockleshell and there was some waving. The Statue of Liberty was beautiful and brave.

"Not bad," said a voice. She glanced at its owner, who was resting one elbow on the rail and looking more at her than at the spreading wonders of the harbor. His attitude made the remark ambiguous.

"To what do you refer?" she asked primly.

The speaker smiled innocently, but his black beard mitigated the effect. "Oh, I see what you mean. 'Breathes there the man with soul so dead he never to himself hath said — hmm, not bad?' As a matter of fact I was referring to the way the half-light bouncing off the water makes everything seem passing strange. What *do you* think?"

"It does look like a different world. I thought it was because I was starting on an enchanted voyage." That was not what she meant to say.

He looked interested. "Do you think it could be the difference between the poet and the painter?"

He certainly didn't look like a painter. In that beat up leather jacket there was something tough about him. "Are you a painter?" she asked.

"Not really. Why is your voyage enchanted? After all, you brought it up."

"I didn't mean to. It was because you said 'passing strange.' Have you travelled a lot?"

"Most able-bodied men of my age have travelled a lot, of necessity," he answered in an offhand way. "I take it this is your first visit to Blighty."

Kate laughed with pleasure. "'Off we go to Blighty, Early in the morning, See the little choo-choo, Standing on the line.' My mother used to sing that to me years and years and years ago."

"Was your mother English?"

"I was born in England. My parents are dead and I was sent to America to my uncle."

"I'm sorry. It must have been when you were quite young, though."

"Not so very. My father's boat was lost at Dunkirk. It was before that."

He looked grave.

"Oh, well," she said quickly. "I don't know why I'm *telling you*."

"Because I asked. Have you family in England?"

"Some cousins. What about you? You're certainly not English."

"I spent the war in England. Funny how you get attached to London, what's left of it. The Germans creamed a lot of swell pubs. The night they got the White Bulldog I decided to bomb Hamburg." He looked sad.

"People like me just saw it in the movies," she said. "Were you in the Air Corps?"

"RAF. Look, how about going for a drink in the bar? Maybe we'll attract some kindred spirits."

"What makes you think that you and I are kindred spirits? I've never spoken to a man with a beard before, except at Christmas."

He surveyed her affably. "It's okay to flirt with me, as long as you're just practicing."

Kate was furious. "If you're anxious to organize your social life I suggest you look elsewhere. I belong with the clean-cut Coca-Cola year-at-the-Sorbonne crowd."

"Ah, but a shipboard clique should be mixed. Take it from an old hand. A pretty girl is a must, and you're the first one I've spotted."

Kate stared fixedly at an inbound freighter, draped in fairy lights against the thickening dark.

"I apologize. You are a pretty girl, and I am an awkward flatterer. Come to the lounge and let me buy you an orange squash. I suppose you've forgotten how to make change of a pound note. I can teach you."

Mixed emotions whirled like garments in a washer. Then Kate settled for, "I haven't forgotten. I've got it all down to the farthings. I want to stay here anyway, but don't let me keep you. All the girls will get picked up by somebody else."

The bearded man sighed loudly. "What shall I tell the others?"

"Which others?"

"The kindred spirits who are hanging around waiting for us to appear."

Kate was getting chilly.

"Oh, *all right*. But I warn you you'd better produce them. I have no interest in a *tête-à-tête*."

The lounge was crowded, but Kate's companion found a fair-sized table occupied by a cheerful looking man with ruddy cheeks and crinkly hair. "Excuse me, my name's Sam Gordon. Mind if we sit here?"

"Not in the least. I'm Joe Collins. My wife's gone to powder her nose."

"This is..." began Sam, leaving Kate to fill in the blank.

"Kate Clark. How do you do?"

Joe Collins rose briefly. "Americans? Or need I ask?"

"Yes and no," answered Sam. "You sound like an Australian."

"Can't be helped," he said with a grin. "You'll be welcome as springtime in England but I'm just another ruddy colonial."

"Why should they like Americans better than Australians?" asked Kate indignantly.

"Nothing personal. They really look down on the lot of us. It's the almighty American dollar brings stars to their eyes."

"I take it you're not on a pleasure trip?" asked Sam.

"Damn right. I have a grant from the Nuffield Trust to look round the new Health Scheme. I'm interested in socialized medicine. I'm a doctor."

Sam looked at him with friendly interest. "Can I get you another drink? What about you, Kate? You don't have to have squash." He started to get up. "Shortage of waiters."

"I beg your pardon. Aren't you a friend of Geoff Weston's? I was at school with him. I'm called Tony Smith." The voice, cultivated as a three hundred year old lawn, belonged to a fair man in a well-worn Harris Tweed jacket. He was addressing Sam Gordon, but he was looking at Kate. And Kate was looking at him. A violin, a bass viol, and a piano had materialized at the top of the room, and this miniature orchestra suddenly struck up "My Heart Stood Still" in a cheerful tempo. Kate crossed her fingers and willed Sam to give the correct answer.

"Not exactly," answered Sam. "Knew him slightly during the war. Have I met you? My name's Sam Gordon. Care to join us?"

"Thank you very much," said Tony, still looking at Kate. "I thought I had seen you together at Lord's. Perhaps it was someone else."

"Us guys with beards all look alike. I'm off to the bar. What do you drink?"

"Nothing just now, thanks," said Tony, offering a battered silver cigarette case with a crest. Alice Collins came back with a well-powdered nose and they all introduced themselves and each other. The Australians were very natural and friendly. Not that Tony wasn't. But his friendliness had about it a kind of subtle courtesy that Kate felt she'd only heard of before, and never understood. He must be an English Gentleman.

When Sam came back he looked at Kate's shining eyes and his face assumed a slightly sardonic expression.

"Weston wasn't in my squadron. Anyway, his *esprit de corps* didn't extend to the transatlantic riffraff as a rule." He spoke blandly. Joe Collins looked amused.

"Geoff's a bit shy, actually," Tony replied pleasantly. "It puts people off sometimes. He was my senior at school and jolly kind to me. I had been brought up by my aunt in remotest Scotland and was as green as grass."

"Oooo," said Kate, marvelling at the way he said *grahss*. "Why don't you have a Scotch accent then?"

"Scots. The accent's liable to have to do with the sort of school one's family goes to." He smiled and she felt he was leaving out something she would have to learn. "Your own accent's rather different from Gordon's you know. American accents are something of a mystery to me."

"Oh mine's early London mixed with central Florida and the whole thing washed off at the American Academy of Dramatic Art."

"Surely you're not English?"

"Yes. I was partly a war orphan. I was sent to my uncle in America while kids could still be sent."

"At least you weren't a war bride."

"We *think* she's detached," said Sam. "But I saw her first."

"What's a semi-detached?" asked Kate, ignoring Sam. "My cousins live in a semi-detached."

"It's two houses joined with a common wall," said Alice Collins.

"Like Siamese twins," added Joe.

"Will you excuse us both?" asked Alice. "I'd like to write to the children before dinner. Maybe we'll see you later on."

Sam and Tony both stood up, and Sam said, "We'll be around here somewhere. Like to hear the whole truth about kangaroos."

Kate, Sam, and Tony found they were all on the second sitting for dinner. Sam looked at Tony, and said casually, "You have the advantage of me, as they say in the old country. You're rather tall for the RAF."

"I was in the army, actually."

"Where abouts?"

"North Africa. Then Europe."

"Get into Germany?"

"I was a prisoner there for a few months."

"Oh. Where?"

"Silesia. Place called Kahlberg."

"Yeah, for officers."

"That's right." He turned to Kate. "This must be a frightful bore for you."

"Oh, no," she said eagerly. "My cousin, where I'm going to visit, was a prisoner in Germany." She turned to Sam. "He was a pilot too. In the RAF."

"What's his name?" asked Sam. "Maybe one of us met him. The world got smaller."

"James Bell."

Tony looked blank, but Sam was interested. "I remember him from the early days. Heard he was shot down. He got back all right then?"

"Yes. I don't really know much about him. His mother writes to me. She said he had been thinking of going to Florida."

"There's always a lot of that after a war," said Sam in an indignant tone. "You fight and die for your country and then they don't want you any more."

Kate laughed. "I guess that's what happened to Uncle Albert after the other war." She became aware of someone standing behind her chair.

"May we join you? Heard a couple of American accents over here. My name's Tom Burrows. I come from Toledo, Ohio."

"Have a seat, Tom," said Sam. "And the lady too. Room for everybody."

Tom Burrows looked like an ad for Macy's Big Man's Shop. He set a half empty beer mug on the table, and pulled out a chair for his companion. "This is the Dragon Lady," he said. "We're not really together. We just happened to team up to get the lay of the land."

Kate noticed that the attention of Tony and Sam had shifted to Tom Burrows' acquaintance. She was interesting all right, with exquisite Oriental features, blue-black hair, and a knotted string of pearls that looked soft enough to melt. Her smile was remote.

"Mr. Burrows and I met at the purser's office, and he offered me a drink. When we had exhausted our mutual interests we began to examine our fellow passengers." Her accent was French.

"Yeah, turns out the lady's not too interested in rotor detents, which is what I'm going to Europe to peddle," said Tom Burrows, who didn't sound as cheerful as he looked.

There was a silence, into which Tony politely moved. "What *are* rotor detents?"

"Please," said the woman languidly. "Not again. You will doubtless have many opportunities during the voyage. I'm Lisa Dragonette, by the way. Soon I must go upstairs to dress for dinner."

"Too bad," said Sam. "You lend class to the joint. Upstairs you'll have to compete with Paulette Goddard and Lady Tingley-ffinch."

Tony looked surprised. "The passenger list is not available yet, surely?"

"Not for the general public," answered Sam. "There's an early edition for us international jewel thieves. Speaking of upstairs, by the way, what's somebody who went to school with Geoff Weston doing down here with the *hoi polloi*?"

"I'm the younger son of a younger son. Lady Tingley-ffinch is a friend of my aunt's, however. I shall be obliged to go up and bend the knee at some point." Tony looked rueful.

Lisa Dragonette smoked a Turkish cigarette in a long black holder. Sam looked at her rather often. The talk was desultory and she soon excused herself.

"Who's Lisa Dragonette, if anybody?" asked Sam immediately.

"I haven't a clue," said Tony.

"Gorgeous dame," offered Tom Burrows. "Seemed kind of sour when I didn't recognize her name. Sounds phoney."

Somehow they were a shipboard clique already. As a matter of fact, Kate knew who Lisa Dragonette was. "She's a theatrical designer from Paris. She did the sets for *Pink Gardenias* on Broadway."

"I saw that," said Tom, starting to hum the hit tune.

"She's pretty famous," said Kate.

"Such is fame," said Sam with a grin.

"Well, you're probably not very interested in the theatre," she said rather grandly.

"Just your average rogue and peasant slave," he replied.

"I say," offered Tony, "let's not talk about the theatre. I saw a play once. It was about a damnable chap from Glamis whose wife kept washing her hands. Didn't care for it. Scotland's not like that, you know."

Kate's eyes told everyone that Tony was divine. Aloud she said, "I'm off to change my face before dinner."

"It looks all right the way it is," said Tony.

But Kate stopped at the perfume shop to buy a new lipstick anyway.

Deep inside the great ship the grid of corridors seemed to turn into a labyrinth. Kate turned and turned again but the numbers on the doors wouldn't match the one on her key. She wished she had paid more attention when the steward had shown the way in the afternoon.

She saw the flash of a white jacket whisk around a corner. Somewhere a door closed, shutting in laughter. The quiet seemed bizarre. She quickened her steps, hoping to find someone to ask.

She made another turning, from a long corridor that ran fore and aft to a shorter, cross corridor. It was blocked. The body of a woman was lying across it, with the grotesque abandon of the unattended dead. She had a flamingo pin on her lapel and a brightly printed rectangle in her hand.

Fan.

Chapter VI

> Those are pearls that were his eyes.
> —William Shakespeare, *The Tempest*

Everything everywhere stopped, but only for a moment. Like a thief, a magpie, a child, Kate bent down, snatched the pasteboard card from the limp hand, and shoved it into her pocket. Then she turned and ran. Doors slid past like blank pages. She turned and turned again.

Somewhere, coming closer, someone was whistling "Slave Bracelet" from *Pink Gardenias*. She collided with Tom Burrows at the next intersection.

"Hold it, honey. You won't be late. First sitting just got dessert. Hey, wait, what's wrong?"

"Oh, please. I saw a body in one of the corridors. It's a woman. She's dead. I don't believe it. It's true though. Nobody could look like that who wasn't dead. But I don't believe it. Oh, please, come with me and look. Then we'll find help. Oh, *please*."

She began pulling on his arm. "Take it easy," he said roughly, then, less roughly, "Just take it easy, will you?"

Together they went back the way she thought she had come. The corridors had come to life. People were talking, laughing, going in and out of cabins. They smelled of face powder and shaving lotion. There was no outcry, no panic, no hint of anything out of the ordinary.

Tom Burrows had taken hold of the situation, and his size was reassuring. He kept on whistling and saying "Steady," as they explored the monotonous rows of transverse corridors.

"Sure it was on this deck, kiddo?"

"Of course I'm sure. This is my deck." She opened her hand and showed her cabin key.

"Well, I say we've covered the whole damn place. You're on the wrong side. What do you want to do? Just keep cool. The woman probably fainted and her friends took her to her cabin. Maybe she went into insulin shock or had a stroke or something. I bet a buck they handle these things very quiet on ships. They want to keep everybody in a good mood."

"Tom, it was just *minutes* ago. They'd have to get a wheelchair or something. It's just not possible. Besides..." Kate was cold and trembling.

"Honey, I don't for one minute suggest that you imagined it. You just panicked and got some part of it wrong is all. I mean be reasonable — without the old *corpus delicti* you're no place. I suggest you fix your face and we'll meet outside the dining room. What's your table number?"

"I'm going to the purser's office. If you want to come along, okay. Otherwise I'll see you around." She disengaged herself from his arm and seized a railing for support. Maybe it was getting rough now that they were really out on the ocean.

"Would Tom Burrows, of Toodleooo, Ohio, desert a lady at a time like this? You haven't even got your sea legs yet, for Pete's sake. Let's go to the main office. They'll tell you not to worry. That's what the English always say — 'Not to worry.'"

"Not to worry, Miss Clark," said the First Officer in a soothing voice. "If someone is missing we ought to know it by tomorrow. Have to be jolly careful on a ship, you know. Can get into no end of rows with indiscreet inquiries. Now you say the woman you saw is in her forties, smallish, plump, light brown hair. And her Christian name might possibly be Frances. All that should make it very much easier."

"I think you should take a close look in the corridors. Maybe there's something there, some clue."

"Well, of course we'll have the cleaning personnel take a special look round when they wash the lino down there. We're not Scotland Yard, remember. I must impress upon you most seriously — and upon Mr. Burrows as well — the importance of not talking about this affair to anyone else. Doesn't do to get the wind up people on a sea voyage. Always some imaginative types on board."

"All right, then. Thank you. But you really have to tell me anything at all you find out that fits in with what I saw." The First Officer nodded a little too reassuringly. "Otherwise," said Kate firmly, "I'll tell my friends about it."

"You have other friends aboard ship, do you, Miss Clark?"

"New friends. Mr. Burrows knows them too. The dead woman wasn't a friend. Just a woman I saw on a train."

"Oh, right you are. Rum go. Well, cheerio then. We'll be in touch in any case. If you're late to dine just say you were detained over a passport mix-up. The purser will vouch for you. Eh, Andrew?"

Tony and Sam were both waiting outside the dining room after dinner. Chance had seated them at the same table and they had arranged for her to change places with a silent Lithuanian starting the following morning.

"What about me?" asked Tom, striding across to join them. "My table's split between college kids and a pair of Limey old maids just waiting to see me eat peas off my knife."

"You've got to be cool as dammit with them," advised Sam. "They're just going to mash theirs onto the backs of their forks along with potatoes and gravy. What kind of way is that to treat innocent peas?"

"It's all very well for you to talk, but I'm going to be bored stiff." He sounded aggrieved.

Tony looked bored already, but Sam said affably, "I'll see what I can do tomorrow." Then he turned to Kate. "What kept you? Your face doesn't look like anything in particular. In fact you look rather pale under all that war paint."

"Oh, nothing much. They misplaced my passport. Then I got lost looking for my cabin. Tom found me."

"That's the trouble with these monster ships," said Sam sympathetically. "Go Canadian Pacific next time. The *Empress of Canada*'s about the right size." Tom looked at him sharply, but he didn't seem to notice. "How about a stroll on deck before we establish a beachhead in the lounge? We have to find a snug spot. There's bingo and horse racing in the main saloon."

"We shall want warm things," said Tony. "May I see you to your cabin, Kate? Perhaps we could all meet on deck in ten minutes."

Kate yawned.

"You want sleep, Kate. Just sit here on this convenient bench and I'll get your coat for you."

"Thanks a lot, Tony, but I bunk with three old ladies. They'd have a fit if you knocked. They're probably asleep already."

"Lousy luck," said Tom. "I've got a cabin to myself, practically. It's a two-bunker and I've barely met my pal. He plays cards. Offered to deal me in but I know a shark when I see him brush his teeth."

"I'm in with some young Texans bound for Edinburgh Divinity School." Kate looked dubious but Tony went on. "They are extraordinarily pleasant, actually. I mean to introduce them to Sam. He's so jolly Biblical with that beard."

Kate looked at Sam who was looking rather wicked. "Come on, Kate," he said. "Let's get the show on the road. It's opening night."

Identical pictures of Fan's body, sprawled grotesquely across the narrow corridor, seemed to be pasted on the insides of Kate's eyelids. When she closed her eyes she got a stereopticon view of the scene, an image that lent depth to the corners beyond the corpse and opened unseen possibilities. The vision was no friend to sleep.

Fan was dead. If she should meet her on deck it would mean the ship's officers had rigged up an imposter in order to calm her nerves. *Not to worry.*

It was an odd assortment of kindred spirits Sam had managed to assemble. Kindred spirits? Lisa Dragonette and Tom Burrows? Joe Collins and Tony Smith? But what about Kate Clark and Tony Smith? A shipboard clique should be mixed, Sam said. Well, there was no way he could have masterminded the whole scene. He had recruited *her*; the rest were pure chance. Would they hang around together the whole way to Southampton? If only Tony Smith would...hang around together...

She closed her eyes again, wrapping herself in that thought as if it were an encircling blanket. And then the corridor reappeared, with strange angles and shadows. Someone was hidden in the picture!

She sat up, bumping her head on the ceiling. She was in an upper bunk. Very quietly she pushed the button that turned on her reading light. She slid her hand under her pillow and took out the card she had taken from the lifeless hand of a woman she had once met on a train. It was proof of passage, a message left for her alone. It was a card from the Tarot pack — The Hanged Man. She must tell someone — who?

Toward morning she slept; she missed breakfast.

The sky was grey flannel and the sea was dyed to match. The wind was more bold than fierce. In the afternoon Sam organized a shuffleboard game, issuing orders about hats, sweaters, and windbreakers. Kate begged off and established herself on a deck chair in a secluded corner. She had an old travelling rug that had been Uncle Albert's and a paperback copy of *Bubu of Montparnasse* for camouflage. She meant to stay awake, and managed to do so for about ten minutes.

"Beg pardon, miss." She sat up with a twang of nerves. "Mr. Finney sends 'is compliments, and would you be so kind as to step up to the purser's office as soon as possible?"

"Oh. Oh, thank you very much. Yes, of course."

"That's all right then," said the steward in a manner Kate found somewhat enigmatic. Maybe it was a trap.

She got a mirror out of her handbag and combed her hair, with some help from the wind. Then she made her way inside.

In the office she found several persons in uniform. The young officer she had spoken to on the previous evening was holding an American passport in his hand.

It seemed a woman had turned up missing. She had not slept in her cabin nor appeared for any meals. She couldn't be found on deck or in any of the public rooms. She had not visited the infirmary. Her name was Frances Birdsill, and she came from New Rochelle, New York. He opened the passport and showed Kate the photograph.

It was Fan, looking vague and jolly.

Kate looked up at them and nodded. They all believed her now. Even the captain, a majestic and immaculate figure in whom Kate imagined she saw one of those legendary admirals of the recent war. No more "Not to worry."

Their main concern, however, was not justice but peace. It was essential to avoid a panic on the ship. There were always people whose imaginations were overstuffed with homicidal maniacs. It was the greatest good fortune that a young woman of Miss Clark's obvious intelligence had been the unfortunate...but what about Mr. Burrows? Better say nothing more even to him for the present. Let him suppose that she had come to believe that she had made a mistake. She could dissemble in the public interest. Her passport identified her as an actress.

"But...?"

Ah, of course, meanwhile they themselves would be conducting a discreet but thorough search. They very much doubted that an object of human size could have been dropped overboard without attracting attention. The woman's cabin mate, a stranger, had not seen her since New York, and had been told that an emergency had caused her to disembark at the last moment.

"But what...?"

Should His Majesty hear of the incident he would be very distressed. His Majesty was not very well. Kate would naturally not wish...She was a British subject, after all. When they found the late Mrs. Birdsill, Kate would be summoned. Thank you very much. Good-bye. Cheerio. Stiff upper lip, you know. Smiles. Everything all right? Anything you need? Try to enjoy yourself then, eh?

The door closed behind her. *Let's be British*, she and MaJa used to say to each other at moments of crisis.

It was a relief to think that forces had been set in motion. Oiled wheels were turning. She should have told them everything, of course, but she wanted to deliver the gypsy's message first. Madame Sosostris had said it was a matter of life and death.

What if Fan's life and death were not the ones she meant?

Heading back for the Tourist level, she started down a flight of steep stairs and met Tom Burrows coming up. This time he wasn't whistling "Slave Bracelet." In fact he looked quiet — a big quiet American, anyone would have said. The sight of Kate seemed to activate hidden springs of affability. "Hi there cutie pie. Wondered where you were hiding since lunch. Been up to see how the other half lives? Or did the executive suite have some news for us?" The last question was rather sharp and Kate took note of the pronoun.

"I guess they feel the same as you, Tom. I should have tried to help whoever it was instead of going all girlish panic. I was just curious to try another deck."

"And what did you see?"

"I saw the sea." They were at eye level, and she looked at him in what she took to be a saucy manner. "And where might you be going, since it's okay to ask? Off to look up Lisa Dragonette? I can warn you they're on the lookout for class crashers."

He looked sheepish. "She's a knockout all right. Reminds me of somebody. I don't know why she picked on me, or wanted to mingle with the two-pant suit crowd downstairs."

"If you ask me we're a pretty motley crowd. Anyone would fit in."

"Yeah, I guess you're right. I think she'll be down to take another look at Sam anyhow. C'mon, let's get down off this ladder before we hit an iceberg."

Kate followed him down the stairs. "Why do you think she's interested in Sam? I'd think she'd be more attracted to somebody like Tony Smith."

"Yeah," he said.

She turned slightly pink.

"Ever been to the races?" Tom went on. "Sam's a dark horse. I got a funny feeling he's a real dark horse."

"That's not a mane, it's a beard." Tom seemed so familiar, somehow, that she felt almost carefree again. "I'll tell you what then, Tom. If she does come back we can watch and see whether they exchange any Meaningful Glances."

"Hey, great." He squeezed her arm. "How about a spot of tea or a short beer? Maybe we'll find the rest of the gang."

"Funny how we got to be a gang in one day."

"Gotta work fast on ships, kiddo. *Tempus fugit*."

"They go too quick."

He looked puzzled. "Who does?"

"Flies. You can't time flies."

Tom made a little circle with his finger at the side of his head. "Anything you say. The customer is always right."

"I'll have to find out what rotor detents *are* before I place an order. I would love a Coke, though. But if we meet anyone let's not drop any hints. I mean let's not act as if we know anything special."

"Afraid Tony's going to get jealous?"

"Oh, you know what I mean."

She didn't really think he did, but he said, "Okie-doke. Do you mind waiting a second while I pick up something from my cabin?"

"Not at all. Is it on the way?"

"It's right here. Wanna come in? I don't suppose the shark is at home at this hour."

"I'll wait in the corridor."

She found a place to lean opposite Tom's door. She was wondering where he had been going and whether or not to give him the Message when her eye was caught by a small white speck lodged against the doorframe. The floor was shining clean.

She picked it up. It was a tiny fake pearl. She held it in her palm, looking at it.

When Tom came out he said, "What's that?"

"An aspirin," she said, closing her hand.

"Awful small aspirin," he said suspiciously.

"It's a half," she said. "I only have the first half of a headache. Let's get that Coke."

"Coke and aspirins..." he began.

"Phooey," she answered.

She started to button her coat as if to muffle the beating of her heart. She'd seen a pink enamel flamingo more than once. The first time it had had a seed pearl eye.

Chapter VII

Strangling is a very quiet death.
—John Webster, *The Duchess of Malfi*

The second full day at sea passed unremarkably. The air was clear, sunless, empty, cold. Apart from the dislocation made by the ship, a trifling affair out here in the great northern waste of water, the waves continually disposed themselves in solemn ranks. Kate, Tony, Sam, and Tom played bridge in the lounge with Kate's lucky deck.

"Are you fond of toffee, Kate?" asked Tony.

"Oh, yes please," she answered. "How did you guess?"

"The cards are rather sticky."

They smiled at each other for longer than the joke required. Tony's charm was so very easy that some hint of tension, of seriousness, was hardly noticeable. But for Kate, as the long sea hours went by, that hint made the difference between being merely charmed and something more exciting.

Between rubbers they walked the deck, holding on to each other and laughing when the wind took a swipe at them.

In the afternoon they decided to take in the movie: *The Secret Life of Walter Mitty* with Danny Kaye. Tony found it "amusing." Tom pronounced it, rather sourly, "a riot." Sam declared that he preferred to act out his fantasies, jumping like a monkey to grasp a pipe running along the ceiling of the corridor.

"Wotch wot yer a doin' of, mite," shouted a voice.

Sam dropped softly. He had a way of moving very quietly. "Sorry about that," he said. "Got carried away. My mother wouldn't let me walk home through Prospect Park after the Tarzan movies for fear the cops would nab me for swinging on the trees."

"I didn't know you were from Brooklyn," said Kate, unreasonably surprised. "You might have told us."

"I like to keep a few conversational gambits in reserve. Don't pretend you've told us everything there is to know about Kate Clark. You've told us practically nothing about your theatrical career, for instance. Of course *I* couldn't care less but I suspect that Tony here is mad about actresses. His kind always are, secretly."

"I say," said Tony. "You might have kept it dark. You make me sound like one of those frightful loose-limbed asses in the picture papers."

"Oh, are you a loose-limbed Englishman?" asked Kate. "I've forgotten so much about England. My cousin Sally Bell says I'm coming home to England but it feels like going abroad to me. I don't know. I feel ambivalent."

"The best cure for that is a drink," said Tom. "And as the sun is way the hell over the yardarm, or whatever they say, why don't we turn into our neighborhood saloon before the shoe factory gets out?"

They found a table near the bar, and Kate asked for ginger beer. Sam suggested she try a shandy gaff.

"What is it?"

"Lemonade and beer. Prevents scurvy, always a danger on these long sea voyages. The English love it." He smiled encouragingly.

"One thing about it," she said after a few sips, "it's probably not addictive."

Sam and Tony were nursing pint mugs of beer. Tom had taken to drinking straight whiskey.

In the evening the Tourist lounge was a scene of merriment. Each round of a competition between a Scots baritone and an Irish tenor — the object being for each to sing an ever more sentimental ballad about his homeland — was greeted with wild applause. Persons who had been holding themselves aloof were drawn into the genial camaraderie of their neighbors.

The group that Kate had begun to think of as the Basic Four had been joined by Joe and Alice Collins and the conversation was thick with boomerangs and the habits of wallabies when Lisa Dragonette appeared in the doorway. She was wearing her pearls and a slink of blue satin. The blue was the color of the sky just before they switch the stars on.

The noise level fell perceptibly. Sam got up and escorted her to their table. He ordered her a gin and It and introduced her to the Collinses. Then he inquired in a polite tone, "What brings you to the lower depths, Miss Dragonette? You cut a wide swath in that costume. But don't worry. The vulgar plebs are too dazzled to swarm up the companionway and demand their cut of the caviar."

She smiled. Her teeth were exquisite. "Do please call me Lisa, all of you. You are very amusing, Sam. There is no one amusing in the First Class. It is like a morgue."

"I want another drink," said Tom.

"I've met Lady Tingley-ffinch," said Tony, "but what about Paulette Goddard?"

"I told you about Tony and actresses," said Sam to Kate, *sotto voce.*

"She took one glance, and developed a dreadful *migraine*. For myself, I prefer to seek out interesting people." Lisa didn't look at anyone but Sam. In spite of her better judgement, Kate found herself exchanging a glance with Tom Burrows.

"Madame," began Sam, "I'm sure I speak for the whole gang here when I say how much we appreciate the honor you do us. Thanks to you, our table is the synopsis of all eyes."

"I rather think that's not quite right, old man," said Tony languidly.

"What, Mr. Interlocutor," answered Sam, looking at Tony with exaggerated surprise, "you can't mean that there is anyone here who does not appreciate Miss Dragonette's — Lisa's — seeking us out like this on a quiet Sunday evening?"

"On the contrary. It's merely your diction I question. Perhaps it's an American usage?"

"Don't pay attention to Christopher Anthony MacLeod-Smith, Lisa. He has the preoccupation of his class with linguistic trivia. At his school it was probably considered bad form to use 'synopsis' at all."

"You are a gentleman?" asked Lisa, looking at Tony.

"Only officially," answered Tony. "I'm a notorious cad in my personal life."

"This conversation's over my head," said Tom. "Let's get back to the Australian bush."

Joe Collins liked to tell stories, and he did it well. His wife provided suggestions from time to time. They had lived for some years in the outback, a vast remote desert area where Joe had provided the only medical care within a thousand miles. In that inhospitable land non-native inhabitants were very liable to be fugitives of some kind, criminals or draft evaders.

"I thought everyone in Australia was descended from a crook anyway," said Tom.

Joe threw him a glance of cold appraisal, and Kate, who felt that Tom hadn't really meant to be offensive, jumped in with, "Oh, Tom, you know what the frontier's been like. You're from Ohio."

"Ohio hasn't been the frontier lately, kiddo," answered Tom. "Used to be I guess. Sorry if I said the wrong thing."

"There aren't enough frontiers around to accommodate all the fugitives and crooks the war generated, anyway," said Sam. "Some of them must be mingling with the crowd." He smiled at the Collinses, then turned to Lisa. "Where were you during the late uproar? Indo-China?"

"Paris," she said, not elaborating. "And you?"

"Up in the air."

"I was in the U.S. Army in the European theatre," offered Tom. "I entered Germany with Patton."

Sam looked interested.

"I told Lisa." Tom sounded defensive. "You fly boys are such hot shots I didn't think an infantry captain would cut any ice."

"That's hardly fair to Sam," said Tony in a bored voice.

"Tony seems to have been in the British army," said Sam pleasantly. "He's cutting a lot of ice, not to mention mustard."

Kate looked at Tony, found him looking at her, and began to slurp up the melted ice at the bottom of her glass with a wilted straw.

Tom suddenly flashed an affable smile. It didn't ring quite true but there was no malice in it. "I apologize all around, folks. Guess I been pretty obnoxious for no good reason." He looked around the table and added, "I'm just sore cause all the good-looking women seem to be taken." The remark fell rather flat.

"It's an optical illusion," said Sam, imperturbable. "Who wants a nightcap? The crowd's thinning out and I have to see Lisa home."

"Shall we take a stroll on deck, Kate?" asked Tony.

"I'll join you," said Tom.

Kate lay awake for a long time puzzling about Tom. One thing she knew. It was with Tom she had searched for the body, and with hardly a moment to spare.

She slept for nine hours. They had closed the dining room when she arrived for breakfast.

Several hours earlier the body of the woman called Fanny Birdsill had been found by an official, but surreptitious, search party. It was in the bottom of a lifeboat and had been covered with a tarpaulin. Rigor had passed.

"Fits the girl's story all right, sir," the First Officer said grimly. "The police will have to be notified."

"It's done," answered the Captain. "Scotland Yard have been asked to come aboard at Southampton. Nobody allowed off until after questioning. I daresay New York's provided some info already. Woman's a U.S. citizen. Not our show, I shouldn't think."

"Here's Russell. What's the gen, doctor?"

The ship's doctor looked at the Captain, who gave a go-ahead nod. "Confirmation will have to wait for the official autopsy, of course, but I can say that the deceased suffocated. Appears to have been strangled with a thin cord of some kind. No noise if it's done quickly."

"Damn risky for somebody, just the same. And where the hell was the body all this time? The lifeboats were searched first. Excuse me, Sir," added the Purser.

"The answer to that one's obvious. Plenty of passengers have trunks in their cabins. Someone waited his chance and got the corpse out before it began to stink." It was the doctor speaking, very cheerfully. Up to now he had been regretting his decision to go to sea.

"What happens now, Sir?" asked the First Officer. "Do we notify the girl?"

"I think we have no choice, Mr. Jones. She'll cut up rough if word leaks out." He looked distressed. "Rather a nice girl. It's a pity." Then he added, "She needn't identify. Obviously the passport woman."

Once more Kate was asked to say nothing and so for a few hours she said nothing. However, by midday the *Queen Victoria* was like a monstrous humming hive into which an unforseen object had been thrust. No one seemed to know how the rumors started but by tea time some of them were so alarming that the Captain decided on a statement. Passengers were gathered into manageable groups and told some bare facts: A woman had died under unusual circumstances but there appeared to be no cause whatever for alarm. The police would be coming aboard at Southampton so disembarkation would be slightly delayed.

Everyone was asked to co-operate by carrying on the normal recreations of life at sea. Anything out of the ordinary should be reported, as discreetly as possible, at the office. Members of the deck crew and service personnel were privy to no more information than anyone else, and should not be harassed.

For the rest of the voyage all but the most blasé passengers were clearly simmering with excitement. Trade in the bars had never been better. The public rooms were always packed, the decks after dark virtually deserted. On the whole the atmosphere was cheerful. After all, it was an adventure. Suspicion rested now here, now there — on those who were solitary, or disagreeable, or had beards.

"Were I you I'd visit the barber," said Tony to Sam pleasantly.

"Too late," answered Sam. "Just the sort of thing to rouse suspicious cops. Somebody would tell them." He turned to Kate. "Now tell us again, Kate, exactly what this woman said to you on the train."

They were bundled up in deck chairs drinking morning bouillon, and for once Tom was elsewhere. England was less than a day away.

The three of them had been reviewing the previous evening's events in the lounge. Joe Collins had entertained the gathering with a learned dissertation on the physiological merits of strangulation. "With a good grip on a thin strong cord, just about anybody could do it. Of course shooting, stabbing, blunt instruments, poisoned chocolates — they all have their advocates in the medical profession." At that point Lisa Dragonette appeared, stunning in a grey wool dress and a green silk scarf, professing a curiosity — a very mild curiosity — to hear what was being said among the tourists.

Among the passengers, Kate's story was known only to Tom, Tony, and Sam — Tony because she chose to tell him and Sam because he asked her what she knew in such an off-hand easy way that she simply blurted it out. Furious with herself, she wondered whether Tony had said anything to him. They seemed to hit it off extremely well. She was grateful to Tom for his silence. He might have purchased considerable popularity by retailing the details of his meeting with her in the empty corridor.

By this time Sam had heard everything she chose to reveal and heard it more than once. With Tom out of the way she was concentrating on wishing that he would remove himself. The voyage was almost over and her Shipboard Romance, which had seemed promising last evening, was stalled again.

She answered his request rather glumly. "Oh fudge, Sam. You've heard it all already. What's it to you, anyway?"

"You ungrateful child, I'm simply trying to help you get your story straight for the police. They're going to go over you with a vacuum cleaner unless someone else turns out to smell really fishy."

"Lady Tingley-ffinch smells fishy," put in Tony. "She spends half her life in a trout stream."

"But why on earth should they?" asked Kate. "It's not as if I knew the woman. She didn't even give me her right name."

"Look, it could be that New York has already wired them the vital information they need. If so, you're home free. But chances are good that you will be all they've got. They'll turn your mind, such as it is at your tender age, inside out. You've heard of Scotland Yard, I presume?"

So Kate told her story again. She said nothing about the pearl, although she meant to give it to the police.

Of the Tarot card, she would say nothing to anybody. Madame Sosostris had trusted her. She must deliver the message. But she just couldn't go around babbling it to every man she met, could she? It had to seem right. Madame Sosostris had implied as much.

Chapter VIII

> Lingering tones of romance, touched with a hint of mystery.
> —Bergdorf Goodman Advertisement, *NY Times,* 5/5/81

While the corpse was keeping cool under a sheet in an improvised morgue, the costume balls, decreed by custom for the last night at sea, went on as usual. In the Tourist saloon the music was professional enough but the costumes ranged, with few exceptions, from makeshift to marginal. Nevertheless, the effect was appealing.

Joe Collins was there in a white lab coat with a stethoscope around his neck; Alice wore jodhpurs and riding boots. Tom had on an Ohio State sweatshirt with VARSITY in big letters across the back. Sam's only concession to the occasion was a black half mask in which he looked moderately diabolical.

Tony surprised them all by appearing in immaculate evening dress. Standing near the entrance he raised a monocle to his left eye and surveyed the scene, scanning the colorful assortment of ingeniously contrived flowers and ballerinas — crepe paper had been supplied on request — moving around the floor. There was a sprinkling of military uniforms, the most splendid being that of a Polish cavalry officer in full fig.

To her black velveteen slacks and matching lambswool sweater Kate had added a crepe paper tail and prick ears with pink linings. She was standing with Sam when Tony strolled over and bowed.

"Madam, will you dance?" he asked.

"I'd love to," she replied, "but you must watch out for my tail."

"I expect you'll have to hold it over your arm, as if it were a train."

"I'm afraid I'd need to practice that. I've never had a train."

"Perhaps you could tuck the end into your pocket, if you have a pocket in those smashing trousers."

"That sounds discreet."

They danced to "Falling in Love with Love" and then to "Stardust". Tony danced well, holding her with a formal ease that she supposed must be European. Sleek and elegant, they were observed with some envy, and for a time Kate was sought as a partner by several men she had hardly spoken to. Tom seemed to be very much taken by a peroxide blond in a shedding grass skirt. Sam was leaning against the bar watching the revels through his black domino. When she found herself dancing with Tony again the room had become much more crowded.

"Speaking of pockets, where do you keep your monocle? You don't just have it dangling on that cord like a skate key."

"Oh, it tucks away."

"Is it just for show?"

"In any event, I don't wear it every day. It's not like Sam's beard."

"Oh, *Sam*." Forget about Sam.

He smiled. "As you like. But don't be too impressed by my accent and my dinner jacket and the rumor of my formidable aunt in the highlands. I'm an ordinary sort of chap really. No glamour."

"That's for me to say." She looked at him and colored slightly.

He smiled again and held her closer. "I rather suppose you don't know that 'glamour' is a Scots dialect word. Sir Walter Scott introduced it into literature."

"Oh, *Tony*," she murmured, and then, in what she hoped was a more casual manner, "I bet there are a lot of glamourous costumes up in the First Class tonight."

"If you look carefully as we turn round you'll see a sample on the floor."

Lisa Dragonette was dancing with Sam. She was wearing a heavily embroidered silk sheath with a mandarin collar and deep slits on either side of the hem. Her almond eyes were outlined in black pencil; her tiny feet were shod in silver sandals with improbably high heels.

"The Dragon Lady," breathed Kate appreciatively.

Lisa and Sam were very close, barely moving in time to the music. They were not speaking. Lisa's heavy blue-black hair rested against Sam's beard.

"She's really a very talented woman," Kate said.

"One can see that straight off," answered Tony.

"I mean in her work as a designer. I don't know what she did in Europe but she had an enormous success in New York with *Pink Gardenias*."

"I think rather a lot of people let themselves go aboard ship. It's like being suspended from real life for a while, especially if one's on one's own. Friendships are made that couldn't happen anywhere else." He spoke gravely.

He's warning me off, thought Kate. Oh, what if he's *married*? Aloud she said, "That's part of the fun. Nothing seems quite real."

The music stopped, and Kate said that she was thirsty. Tony saw her to a table where the Collinses and Tom were sitting with two American students with crew cuts, one of whom was extolling the virtues of Mothersill's Seasick Remedy.

"Whiskey's the best thing for *mal de mer* — right, Joe?" asked Tom amiably.

Joe flashed a grin, and Kate said, "I didn't know you knew French, Tom. Maybe you're the one who's a dark horse."

Tony looked from Kate to Tom, and at that moment Sam and Lisa appeared. Tom looked at Lisa and said, "Oh, I was in France for a while. They gave me the Crock de Goo." He drained his glass. He seemed to be in a much better mood.

Kate said she'd have an orange squash, and Lisa asked for her usual gin and It. Tony excused himself, saying that he wanted to go up and speak to Lady Tingley-ffinch, now that he was presentable. His aunt would make no end of a row if she found that he had not done so.

Maybe she'll have a catbird, thought Kate wryly.

"Do you think the police will keep us long?" Lisa asked languidly. "I am anxious to get to London."

By tacit agreement everything to do with the crime had been off bounds among them all evening. The American students noticed Joe's raised eyebrows and closed their mouths quickly.

"I'm sure they'll do their best to accommodate the more distinguished passengers," said Sam. "If any of them have seen *Pink Gardenias* you'll be out in a flash."

"Oh, but it hasn't opened in London yet." She gave him a small pearly smile. "You're teasing me, Sam."

Emboldened, one of the Americans asked Lisa to dance, promising that his friend would take charge of her drink. Joe and Alice stood up together, and Sam turned to Kate.

"What about it, Rat? Shall we cut a rug?"

"If you're trying to play Joe College, your usual role of cynical soldier of fortune suits you better. I'm not a rat anyway. I'm a cat."

They stood up. Sam led her in an undistinguished fox trot, looking at her in what appeared to be a friendly manner. "So that's how you see me? World weary and devil-may-care?"

"I said that's your role."

"But the real me is idealistic and home-loving?"

"Oh, let's not talk about you. What do you think of Lisa Dragonette, if there's any more to it than meets the eye?"

"If you're referring to our performance on the dance floor I assure you that's all her doing. It's like dancing with Chinese wallpaper."

"Well, there's enough room between her and Dink Stover to play ping-pong."

"Chinese game. Look, Cat, I'm supposed to lead."

"Well, then, I wish you would. You're a natural leader when you're organizing people to do things they'd rather not do."

"There's gratitude for you. How would you have spent this voyage if I hadn't taken you in hand? Dancing with Dink Stover yourself, finding out all about his career options, hearing how he won the Big Game."

Kate caught a glimpse of Lisa's frozen face and smiled.

"Ah-hah!" pounced Sam. The music had stopped but he made no attempt to release her. "You must admit that ours is an interesting group."

"Okay, you win. I'm glad you knew Tony's friend."

"*Knew* is hardly what they call the operative word." He steered her into a new dance and began humming "Mam'zelle".

"Your humming isn't much better than your dancing."

"You should hear me when I'm alone. Seriously, though, Kate, any friend of the Honorable Geoffrey Weston is probably out of your league. Don't be offended." He sounded apologetic, but Kate was outraged.

"What business is it of yours? What do you know about anything? How come you and Tony are so thick? I suppose he asked you to speak to me."

"He didn't and I assure you he wouldn't. Your name has never been mentioned when you weren't around. I know who Geoff Weston is and I know Tony's type. It's possibly a good type but I don't know what it's good *for.*"

He was so matter of fact that Kate grew calmer. "Oh, you needn't worry, Sam. I'm not really such a complete idiot. Do you know if he has any family besides that famous aunt?"

"He hasn't mentioned any to me, but I gather his aunt is in the classic mold — cousin-german to the Loch Ness monster only the sightings are more frequent."

"What's cousin-german?"

"Old French."

"Wow, we're certainly a cultured crowd all of a sudden. I didn't know you knew any old languages."

"I'm a dark horse. *Equus Tenebrus*, as they used to say at the Hippodrome."

"That's what Tom said."

"What did Tom say?"

"That you were a dark horse."

"In what connection?" Sam sounded interested.

"Oh, just something to do with Lisa only having eyes for you. Which can hardly be called a secret at this point. Tony says people on ships form unlikely attachments." She made her voice cool.

"I'll tell you what. Let's all meet on deck at midnight. In masks, of course. We'll see who ends up with whom. But first, we may find ourselves in different places in the morning. You will probably have the star part, with Tom coming on for a soft-shoe. What are your plans after disembarking? That is, assuming you aren't whisked off to the Old Bailey in a sealed van."

He saw her face and looked chagrined.

"I'm a helluva wise guy, Kate. Look, you're obviously not a suspect. I hope you don't mind my wanting to know where I can get in touch with you. You may even be glad to see me, after a while."

"I know I will, Sam. If you have any paper I'll write it down for you. Cats have to travel light. Come on, let's sit down."

The ball went on. In a euphoric glow of fleeting romance, couples circled the floor like figures in a dream. It was well past midnight, the beat was slower, the dancers had the air of wind-up toys that would soon run down.

The sinister climax of the voyage seemed to have been forgotten, at least by the remaining celebrants. Tony had come back, and Kate turned blissfully in his arms. They didn't speak; no one was speaking above a whisper. She noticed the Polish officer was dancing with a tiger lily whose petals were drooping all around her. Tom Burrows had both arms around his blonde friend's waist. She had lost most of her grass skirt; her white legs were like summer clouds.

When the band packed up the last dancers wandered off in pairs to search out corners in which to pass the little time they had left together. Hardly any of them would ever meet again. Even those who had no other ties would exchange a postcard or two and then forget.

Kate and Tony agreed to a stroll on the deck. He waited for her outside her cabin while she stealthily got a warm jacket, leaving her tail and ears behind.

Outside it was clear that they were nearing harbor. Other seagoing traffic was visible on either side of the ship and sometimes there was a ghostly hoot. The wind was warmer and smelled of earth. There were stars.

They leaned on the rail.

"I recommend the stars," said Tony. "One doesn't see so many in England during the autumn."

"I don't believe it's always pea soup in London."

"Shall you be stopping in London, Kate?"

"Sort of. My cousin lives in a suburb in Kent."

"I shall be coming up to London soon. When I do I'll order stars for us. One can still order things in London."

"I'm so glad." She didn't say about what. "But where will you be that you'll come *up* from?"

"It doesn't matter actually. London is always up."

"Not on the map."

"No one lives on a map." He got out the silver cigarette case and opened it. Kate said idly, "Is that your family crest?"

He passed it to her. "Souvenir of Germany. I acquired it during the war."

"How did you get it?"

"It was left lying about." He smiled. They all seemed very reticent about their war experiences — Tony, Sam, even Tom. Maybe James Bell would be more forthcoming.

"Did I tell you that my cousin was a prisoner too?"

"You mentioned it. There were rather a lot of us at one time or another you know."

"Yes. Tony, wasn't it all awful?"

"One did one's duty. It's over now."

"Why doesn't anyone want to talk about it?"

"There are those who talk of little else." His tone suggested that those who did were not gentlemen. He threw the end of his cigarette into the sea. "I must be off very quickly in the morning, Kate. I'm being met at Southampton by my aunt's ghillie. You'll be on the telephone, I presume?"

She nodded.

"I'll write the number and your cousin's name in my pocket diary."

"What if the year ends?"

"Bags of time." He sounded amused.

"Shall we go inside where there's more light?"

"I'll manage. My eyes are very good."

"Both of them?"

"Ah, you like that monocle."

While she wrote the number Kate came to a decision. Her heart felt suddenly like an endangered balloon. It had been so much easier in the innocent languor of Titus, before Fan.

"Tony!" She spoke peremptorily.

"What's amiss?"

"I do not find the Hanged Man." This time she enunciated every word. His face was in shadow. "What does it mean?"

She sighed. "It's from a poem by T. S. Eliot."

"Oh, the bloke that's talked about for the Nobel Prize."

"Yes, that's the bloke."

"Didn't he write 'Let us go then, you and I...'" He took her hand.

"But the evening is not spread out against the sky," she said feebly.

"It's the dawn that will be spread out all too soon." He drew her away from the rail, back into the shadows.

She was standing with a wall at her back, her eyes closed, and Tony's hand gently moving the blown hair away from her mouth when she heard a familiar voice. It was too close for comfort.

"Damn it all! Why is there so much rope around here? It isn't a sailboat." It was Sam.

Tony moved back, taking her hand again. Kate, her eyes wide open, saw at the other end of the area what Sam must also plainly be seeing. A big man lighting a woman's cigarette, a cigarette in a long holder. Tom Burrows and Lisa Dragonette, after all.

"Sorry. I seem to have stumbled into *A Midsummer Night's Dream*," said Sam, nodding at Kate and Tony affably. He raised his voice. "Lisa, I believe you have forgotten our assignation on the poop deck."

"Sam, you are absurd." But she sounded relieved as she moved to his side and took his arm.

Tom turned and Kate could see that he looked puzzled. But when he saw them his cheerful manner came on strong. "Curses! Foiled again!" he said. "Well, I gotta meet my date. She went to put her running pants on."

For Kate and Tony, the magic moment seemed to have passed, blown back out to sea on the offshore breeze that came from England. They said goodnight rather formally at her cabin door.

Chapter IX

> A principal fruit of friendship is the ease and discharge of the fulness and swellings of the heart, which passions of all kinds do cause and induce.
> —Francis Bacon, "Of Friendship"

By the time the *Queen Victoria* docked the stars were long gone, the morning mist had settled over the harbor, and the C.I.D. men were in possession of sufficient information about Fanny Birdsill to justify a self-confident manner. She'd had a couple of convictions for smuggling, and was widely suspected as a con artist who spent a lot of time working the transatlantic passenger routes. She was married to an inept small time crook named

Harry Feather. They were U.S. citizens, and were not wanted in Great Britain, either dead or alive.

It wouldn't have taken the great Scotland Yard to figure out that Fan's untimely demise probably had something to do with some criminal activity in which she had been involved, something with higher stakes than usual. The police officers who set up headquarters on the ship examined the passengers with the educated hope that they might smell out some pre-certified rat.

They had very nice manners.

They questioned Kate very politely, but naturally they were curious. Her story, though it lacked the gypsy, the (presumably) cryptic message, and the Tarot card, was still interesting. They heard about Fan and Harry on the train and they became interested in Uncle Albert.

"Can you tell us exactly what your uncle left you, Miss Clark?"

"Just...money. Not enough to worry about either."

"Just money — in what form?"

"Some stocks, and $1000 in the bank."

"What sort of stocks would those be then?"

"Oh, I see. You're thinking of the lost emerald mine in Venezuela or something. Nothing doing. It was all stuff like AT&T."

"What was your uncle's business, Miss Clark?"

"Men's furnishings."

"You knew of no sidelines?"

"Oh, no. It was a small store, and he worked very hard until two years ago. Then he went in for alligators. You know, natural history."

"I see. You were his sole heir?"

"No. He left his cottage to a friend."

"His name?"

"It was a lady. I don't know her name." The police officer looked exceptionally blank, so Kate added, "He was a widower."

"Thank you very much, Miss Clark. Most helpful." He picked up the seed pearl from a small box on the table. The flamingo brooch had not been on the victim's body when it had been taken from the lifeboat. Too bad. This way it could be almost any lost pearl. Imitation pearls were common as fleas on dogs. But that didn't mean that they wouldn't explore the area in question with very particular care.

Kate was obviously an alert observer. She must notify them immediately should anything out of the way strike her. They took the Bells' address, and reminded her that she must register with the police the following day in any event. She was free to go. She closed the door behind her.

"What do you think, Alec?"

"Bit wet, in my opinion. Nice girl, though."
"I daresay. Umm."

> On Board the Southampton Boat Train!
> October 12, 1947

Dearest MaJa, actress comma harpist

I am actually abroad. Everything is strange, wonderful, and dimly familiar. Picture me (in my grey suit, very chic) next to the window in one of those trains with compartments off corridors and windows that let down with leather straps. The man opposite me is wolfing caramels and reading *The News of the World,* MaJa! I can see the back — it's all about some boy scout leader who sold nude photos of his wife to the troop. Outside is very misty and spooky but occasionally you get a glimpse of a castle or a pub.

I suppose you know about the murder on the *Queen Victoria* — you may know even more than I do by this time. The victim was a known crook, I hear. But the interesting thing about her is that she was the woman I told you about from the train — Fan! Now do you believe me about the gun? You were standing practically next to her husband and dog Ruggles on the pier. I almost flipped when I saw them. Ruggles was the one in the pink sweater.

I was the one who found the body. I don't want to tell anybody why I think so, not even you, but I think I was meant to find it. I don't know how or why, but it's because of the gypsy. MaJa, those fake gypsies in those chintzy tea-rooms are always so very very bad — utterly bored and artificial. Only somebody with a passion for false futures would listen a minute to them. But Madame Sosostris was different. She was real. She trusted me. Don't laugh. She didn't trust me because she saw straight into my true and trustworthy heart. She trusted me because *she had to trust me.*

There is more to this whole business than just some squalid Thieves Fall Out. I am being used, that's clear. Of course it looks fishy because I just fell heiress — but to what? No, it's my theory that I happened to stumble into some plot quite by chance. I certainly don't want to obstruct justice but I just have a feeling that I can do something useful. She knew I was coming to England so I'm going to see what happens.

Oh, by the way, I'm madly in love. His name is Christopher Anthony MacLeod-Smith. Sounds bad, doesn't it? I mean can an orphan whose only relatives live in a semi-detached find happiness with a man with a voice out of Debrett's and manners you wouldn't even notice if they weren't so exquisite? (I always wondered what exquisite manners were.) Well, think of Our Gal Sunday. Of course if his aunt — he has an aunt, that's all I know — even got a whiff of my cologne she'd start roaring and thrashing her tail. (I believe she's very fierce.) Well, let her. Let her send some old family retainer with a blank check to recover his letters to me. I will splendidly toss check *and* letters into a blazing fire conveniently located nearby. That will show them all.

Just because I'm being flippant doesn't mean my heart is not involved.

15 minutes later

I just went to walk up and down the corridor and think about Tony Smith. That's what he's called for short. I looked out of the window while I was at it. There's a whole real England out there. It's not just a scrim or a movie set. People live in the houses, even very old ones, even ones with thatched roofs. Children and dogs watch the train go by and where they are is real life. We're just a clackety sausage full of strangers from the ships.

Ah, the ship. Of course finding that body thrown down like a beanbag was a nightmare, but otherwise I had a ball. Paulette Goddard was on the ship, not that I saw her. But guess who else from the wonderful world of make-believe? Lisa Dragonette, the stage designer. She's supposed to be checking out the sets for *Pink Gardenias* before it opens in London. Don't ask me why. She's absolutely gorgeous — golden skin and slanty eyes. Like butter almond ice cream. She also has tiny feet, not that I see anything wrong with big feet. She used to come down from the First Class to have some fun. I guess it was pretty dead up there if you'll pardon the expression.

It looked very much as if the kind of fun she came down to have depended on this character Sam who used to be A Yank in the RAF. (He calls it Raf, as in raf! raf! said Spot.) He had a *black beard*. I don't know exactly what she saw in him — I mean imagine kissing someone with a beard! Of course he does have a certain *raffish* charm but he's a rotten dancer. However when he danced with Lisa Dragonette they just oozed around the floor like a pair of fatally poisoned caterpillars.

It ill becomes me to complain of Sam Gordon though. It was his little clique I was part of — without him I might not even have met Tony. There was also a salesman from Toledo. I don't think anyone really liked him much but somehow he seemed to be part of the group, a big part, size 44 maybe. He liked Lisa but she spurned him so he took up with a big blonde in a grass skirt (or part of a grass skirt) — there was a costume ball — Tony wore a monocle! There were also some great Australians, a doctor and his wife. Quite a cast of characters.

I wonder if I'll be met in London. I'll mail this. Please, please write. Tell me everything. What calls did I get? Did I hear from Sumner Partridge, not that I care? He's just the understudy. Are you still working? Here's my address in case you lost it:

    c/o Bell,
      Quo Vadis
        35, The Oval,
          East Tinkham,
            Kent, England,
              Europe.
                Love,
                  Kate

Amid clouds of smoke and steam and a whole divertimento of squeaks, groans, and exhausted expirations the train settled into its slot in Victoria Station. Kate had two big suitcases, and a struggle. As she clambered down she spotted Tom Burrows hopping out of the train farther forward. He should have been helping her after all they'd been through. Somebody should have been helping her. Where was Sam? She had nothing but the Tarot card to show for all the excitement.

A porter spoke to her in what sounded like a foreign language. She nodded. He hoisted her bags onto a cart and rushed off, leaving her to pant after him. They swept through an iron gate and into a great crowd of meeters, parters, shouters, greeters. The station was a vast cold cavern, full of damp and noise.

A small woman was looking at her. She was wearing a squashed green hat, a large raincoat, brown Oxfords with Cuban heels, and orange ankle socks.

"Kate?"

Kate nodded, breaking into a happy grin.

"My dear, you're so desperately like your poor father. I'm your cousin Sally Bell."

Chapter X

> It's a regular joint.
> —W. C. Fields in *The Bank Dick*

"You are taller than I expected, though," said Sally, standing on tiptoes to kiss Kate's cheek. "I can't think why your generation are all so much taller than ours. They say it's milk. Where is your luggage?"

"It's gone with a porter. Do I really look like my father?"

"Desperately, my dear. I said to Fred 'How on earth shall I know her? I expect she will look like a film star.' And there — we never arranged to wear chrysanthemums or whistle the Troll Dance or anything. But then the moment I saw you, bang, Clark written all over you. Doris is like her Grandma Bell — bit of a dumpling, but James is all Birkie, like my poor brother. Where did your porter get off to? Our train to East Tinkham leaves from King's Cross. I suppose if you've much in the way of bags we ought to get a taxi. The underground is grand though. Pluto's realm."

"They're very heavy, I'm afraid. Someone suggested I bring a canned ham and some salmon. I think the porter would suppose I wanted a taxi."

"Come along, then. We'll be off to the taxi place. You needn't give the porter more than a bob. Do you know what a bob is? Here's one. I do so love English money. It must be dreadfully dull having dollars and cents all in decimals. And other countries are just as bad — well, not drachmas, for instance, or zlotys. But I don't care for those little Swedish things that sound as if you'd got indigestion rather suddenly. Marks, there's another dull one. But then if you don't count music everything German is apt to be dull — or ridiculous — churches like cream cakes!" Sally paused for breath, and went on. "James doesn't agree of course. No more did my brother Oswald who was killed in the Great

War. James is very much like him."

The porter had deposited Kate's bags in a monstrous black taxi. When they were settled Sally stretched her legs and gave the driver instructions to go round by Buckingham Palace. The sun was putting in a brief appearance and Kate was trying to see every possible thing. "Oh, is that...?" she began.

"I see you are looking at my socks," said Sally with evident satisfaction. "Quite the thing to wear, my dear. You won't do well in those thin stockings here. First thing you know, bang, you've a ladder. Mending's a bother and you'll certainly not get any more very readily. Of course I was wearing ankle socks long before the war. I was the first woman in England to wear ankle socks, you know. 'Prove it,' says Doris. 'Well, just look around,' say I. 'How many women do you see in ankle socks *even now?*'"

Kate had ten pairs of new nylon stockings in her suitcase. She smiled cheerfully and asked, "Does the Union Jack flying mean the King's at home?"

"Wouldn't you like to pop in for a spot of something? Sherry and biscuits would be the thing about now, I expect. Never mind, pet. We'll have some butter to our bread when we get home. And some fish paste. And I've some lovely tomatoes, grown by Fred. He does wonderful things in that little garden, does Fred. I'd be very surprised if the king had better tomatoes than Fred's. Not but what he wouldn't deserve them, mind. Been a splendid king all through the bombings and the worries and never meant to be king at all. That Edward and his moon-faced American woman. A proper bad lot, in my opinion."

There was a wait at King's Cross so Kate, famished, ate a thin slice of cheese inside an enormous dry bun. "Are many things rationed?" she asked.

"Meat, eggs, cheese, shoes — not that you'll be needing any shoes immediately I don't think. Anyway, most things. And the rest very scarce. Country folk do better. They get the odd rabbit, not to mention sub rosa odds and ends. This Labour government's very busy and it can't be watching every blessed pig and hen in England. It's quite all right, though. There's plenty of bready sausage. We won the war — that's the main thing I always say. Shouldn't have liked the Nazis in their disgusting liver-colored uniforms tramping all over the place. They say Hitler liked the English. Rot! He only met fools and knaves, say I. He wouldn't have liked *me*, and I'm typical English, absolutely typical."

Kate smiled at her and said, "The cheese was good, what there was of it." Sally was gazing pensively at a fat man with a cello case. "I'll just go over and see whether there's anything about the murder in the newspapers." Sally looked vague. "Don't you know about the murder on the ship? That's why the boat train was late."

"Oh, was that why, pet? I didn't think much about it. When they said it was late I rang up Doris and we got into such a row about Graham Sutherland I had to think Early Music for quite a long time to calm my nerves."

"I wouldn't get very far thinking Early Music, I'm afraid, Cousin Sally," said Kate. "I know quite a lot of poetry, though."

"It doesn't matter. The main thing is to have inner resources. I have inner resources."

Kate bought several newspapers, and she and Sally read in companionable silence once they had boarded the train. For some reason, details about the murder were rather meager. It sounded like a routine gangster crime: the New York police had provided several leads and an arrest was expected shortly. Sally was reading about the ballet.

"You know the English ballet is having a splendid renaissance, don't you, my dear? Who would suppose the English could dance, living as we do on steamed pudding? But I think the Muses touch down now here, now there, just as it strikes them. Terpsichore has landed. Who can say? One day one of them may even visit America."

"I assure you the arts are flourishing in the New World, Cousin Sally. The ballet, for instance, is packed every night and there are some wonderful dancers."

"Pooh! The Americans *buy* talent. Ours is indigenous."

Kate was about to remonstrate when Sally sprang up and started struggling with the bags. "We shall have to get them off ourselves, my dear. Oh, there's our Doris. Just bang on the window, will you Kate? She can pop on and lend a hand."

Doris was a robust young woman with bangs and a dirty raincoat. "Leave loose, Mum," she said, taking one suitcase away from Sally. "Hallo, Kate. Can you manage the other? Right-o. Have to look slippy or we shall find ourselves off to Kings Colly in a trice."

When they had squeezed into Doris's little Morris Minor Kate asked where Tinkham was, if this was *East* Tinkham.

"Oh, Tinkham's just a dot. They chuck off the mail without stopping. Generally bag a cat or two in the process. *East* Tinkham's got all sorts of amenities in the way of pubs and car parks."

"We do have the park, my dear," said Sally. "That's a genuine amenity."

"Not the whole of it, Ma. It's 1500 acres."

"That sounds awfully big for a park," said Kate.

"It's jolly. Certainly the local high spot," said Doris. "The King left it to some local nabob and when his lot ran out the public got it — on condition it be left intact and only used for recreation."

"Which king?" asked Kate.

"Was it Henry the Eighth, Mum?"

"Do watch what you're doing, dear. You nearly ran over Reginald Budge, and he's a very nice child." Sally spoke calmly.

Quo Vadis was spelled out on a neat little plaque on the front gate. Its mirror image, the other side of the semi-detached, was called simply Hilda. Both sides had little front gardens full of late-blooming roses. Doris unlocked the door and they deposited the bags in the hall.

"Now, then," said Sally, "on with the kettle. Kate's had nothing but that blash they sell in the station for ever so long. Oh, fancy. There's an air letter come for you this morning, pet. Postie knocked on the door instead of just popping it through the slot. "' 'oo's Miss Katherine Clark? Anyone belonging 'ere?' he said. 'Mr. Dobbins,' said I, drawing myself up, 'you can see that the letter is very clearly and properly directed to this address. That is all ye know on earth, and all ye need to know.' With that I took the letter and I shut the door. Of course I shall tell him about you in a day or two. I did rather want to spring you on the neighborhood myself."

"Oh, great, thanks. It's from my best friend. Do you mind if I read it?"

"My dear child, you must do exactly and precisely as you wish in this house," said Sally.

"Better look sharp in the bathroom of a morning," said Doris.

Sally gave Kate a kiss. "You are to be quite quite at home in every way, pet. And I'm not at all the motherly sort, so you needn't let *that* bother you. Isn't that so, Doris?"

"Indeed it is," said Doris. "If James and I hadn't got her brains we'd never have thought she was our mum."

"Get away with you, impudent scamp. Now then, Kate, sit down and read your letter in peace. There's a sunny window at the back."

MaJa's letter was brief. It was dated the very day Kate had sailed.

> Dear Kate
>
> So guess who was sitting in the parlor having coffee with a captivated Mrs. B. when I blew in? Sumner Partridge, Jr. He is divine. Why didn't you tell me? Mrs. B. agrees, and she's seen them all. You know she once had supper with John Barrymore. Anyhow S. P. was looking for you. Something about a handkerchief. He's coming to England so I gave him your cousin's address. I hope you don't mind that I had dinner with him. We went to the Roman Goldfish and had saltimbocca. It was incredible. Write me everything.
>
> Love
> MaJa
>
> P.S. There's something about your uncle, too.

Doris had slapped a cloth on a round table by the fire and Sally came in with a big steaming brown teapot and a blue striped milk jug. Soon they were sitting down, talking and eating.

"The bread looks awfully healthy," said Kate, spreading a grey slice with butter.

"It's very nutritious," said Sally firmly. "That's the bread we've been living on all through the war."

"In other words," said Doris, reaching for the strawberry jam, "it's the bread of affliction. I happen to think that white bread is one of the landmarks in the rise of Western Civilization."

"I don't see, my dear," offered Sally, "how you and Felix get on so well. His tastes in food are so, well, *wholesome*."

"Well, there are other things in life besides putting on the nosebag, you know, Ma." Doris threw Kate an amused glance.

"What about another cup?" said Sally.

After tea Kate and Doris carried the bags upstairs. "You'll be sleeping in here, that is if you can dislodge the cat. Salammbo! Buzz off!" The cat was enormously spread on a narrow bed of Spartan appearance. "Can you imagine calling a basically decent animal Salammbo? That's Mum for you. Gives the cat no end of side. She thinks she's only answerable to the moon."

"But whose room is this?" asked Kate. "I hope I'm not in the way."

"It belongs to James when he's here. I was going to go back to chez Felix, but when James decided to decamp I thought I'd stay long enough to see what you were like." She smiled. "Sorry about that. Tact's not my line. Ask anybody. You seem all right, though. Tell you what. I'll take you to my studio one day and show you some paintings."

"I'd like that a lot. I wish James had stayed too though. Will I see him at all?"

"If I were you I'd go to Moon Croft and face him in his lair when you get a bit jaded with London."

"What's Moon Croft?" The name made her heart beat a little thicker.

"Oh, we own an old farmhouse up on the Yorkshire moors. Grandpa Birkie bought it to retire to. It's rather romantic country if you're keen on wind at all. It had been called Upland House for at least a hundred years but as soon as Mum got hold of it she re-christened it Moon Croft. It's all a piece with the Salammbo bit. Needless to say she plays the *Moonlight Sonata* — not all that well." Doris shook her head, but she looked proud.

"Tell me," said Kate, "is there a gorse bush?"

"On the moors? Masses of them. What do you want with a gorse bush?"

"Oh, I just forget what they look like. Does James stay there alone?"

"More or less. There's an old woman from the village comes in to do for him. I must say he manages awfully well, considering he was right handed."

"What do you mean?"

"Hasn't anyone told you then? James had rather a hellish time of it in the war. He lost an arm."

Chapter XI

> I have *tremor cordis* on me: my heart dances;
> But not for joy; not joy.
> —William Shakespeare, *The Winter's Tale*

"You know you can speak frankly to me, my dear. I'm just the right age. Damn." Doris had been holding a piece of bread on a long fork over the sitting room fire and it had fallen off. It was a real fire, Salammbo was asleep on the hearthrug, and a chiming clock had just gone midnight. "You've made us frightfully jolly. Mum hasn't had such a splendid time doing the sights since before the war — but I somehow catch the odd hint of sadness or pale ennui. Have you left a faithless lover behind? Or do you miss the excitement of cops and robbers?"

Kate took a sip of sweet milky coffee and answered, "Oh, rats. I'm having a wonderful time in a way. I love it here. But I have to admit that life on the ship was pretty thrilling. Why do you suppose the police are ignoring me? And none of the people I met on the ship have phoned in spite of asking for the number."

"I don't know why you should fret about the police. What could they want *you* for? I expect they're about to clamp leg irons on some felon from Chicago. As for your shipboard romance or whatever you'd best forget it. These sorts of situations are just ships that pass in the night. I had a mad affair with a bod in Gibraltar during the war. Lord, one would have thought that our bones would lie in the tomb of the Capulets. Well, he sailed at dawn and I never heard from him again. We met by chance in Charing Cross tube station two years later and hadn't a clue what to say. Here, have this piece. It's just right." She held out the toasting fork.

"Thanks. I guess you're right." Kate smiled wanly. "Your mother's going into Croydon tomorrow to get her dentures fixed. Shall I go too?"

"Much better not. You come into Town with me and see my studio. We'll have lunch and make a day of it. I want a holiday."

So it was settled. Kate went to bed deciding not to think about Tony, and before they left the house in the morning Mr. Dobbins delivered a letter for her in a heavy cream colored envelope. She studied the surprisingly thick, bold handwriting and the postmark: Inverness.

She sat down. Doris came in, shouting, "*En voiture*! We'll miss the half past train. Hallo. Invitation to the palace?"

"I'll read it on the train. I'm all ready."

While Kate scrutinized Tony's letter with an eye to possible ambiguities and ironies Doris studied her pocket diary. The letter was brief but highly satisfactory.

Braemorpeth House
nr. Inverness

That much was engraved in the upper right hand corner. Beneath it the sender had written: 17 October 1947. And then —

> My dear Kate
>
> I had hoped to be in London this week but family business prevents it. The fact is I have the management of some mining interests of my aunt's; my visit to America was in that connection.
>
> I should be very pleased to hear your plans. Do you intend leaving Kent at all? It seems that I would like to know how to find you the moment that I am free to look.
>
> I have thought best to carry the stars in my pocket so that we can have them wherever we meet.
>
> Until then,
Tony

She read it three times. When she looked up Doris was smiling at her. "That ought to cheer you up."

"Oh, it does. Not that I needed it," she added defensively.

"Of course not. So let's talk family. What do you remember about me?"

"Oh, you and James were both terribly old and superior. And I don't remember your mother being so marvelous, though she was very nice."

"Perhaps she hadn't the orange socks yet. Were you happy with Uncle Albert? Mum said he was grand."

"I think he didn't really know what to make of me. He was awfully nice, though, always. He was something like your father."

"That would be all right then. Bother. I've forgotten my list. Do carry on with your thinking, will you?"

So they lapsed into silence again and Kate found herself wondering about Fred Bell, so very unobtrusive. In the evenings he would ask whether anyone wanted to listen to "Much-Binding-in-the-Marsh" on the wireless, or perhaps have a cup of something.

But what if he was an iceberg, as Uncle Albert seemed to have been? An innocuous little white tip floating around with a deep dark sub-structure no one suspected? Kate wanted to tell Doris about Uncle Albert's unknown lady, even about Harry and Fan and the cottage on Snake Lake — but she didn't.

Doris's studio near SoHo Square was a jumble, with canvasses stacked against every inch of wall space. "I've just finished this," said Doris, displaying a congeries of angles in puce, grey, and ochre.

"What's it called?"

"Twenty-nine."

"It's very powerful."

"That's what Felix said," said Doris.

"Oh, Doris, what's this one?" Kate had pounced on a portrait of a British officer in a red coat standing upon some clearly foreign strand.

Doris snorted. "Ghastly, isn't it? Everything about it's dead wrong, including the glorification of Empire, though of course that's irrelevant. I buy these old things for the canvas and paint over them. Makes a saving. Oh, by the bye, we're meeting Felix at the Ganges. I hope you like curry."

"I've never had it. I've never seen an Indian restaurant in New York. It's all chop suey in our price range."

"You'll like it. It's good for Felix because he needn't have meat things."

"Is he a vegetarian?"

"All his family are. They get extra eggs and cheese on the ration. The first time I went to them for a meal his father said in a deep voice, 'Of course we have no flesh in this house.' Gave me quite a turn. I pictured them wandering around in their bare ectoplasm."

"Is Felix your fiancé?" asked Kate, who had been wondering.

Doris looked indignant. "Certainly not. We don't go in for middle class morality. We live together if we like and when we like. No marriage, no sham, no hypocrisy."

"But don't your parents mind? East Tinkham must be a bastion of middle class morality."

"Oh, Dad would like us to post the banns, but Mum really likes it the way it is, I think, not that she'd admit it. After all, wearing ankle socks is a pretty tame way to *épatez les bourgeois*."

"But what if you have a baby?"

"That's not part of the plan. I say, Kate, you are the innocent abroad, aren't you? I thought you were an actress. No wonder you only get to play flies and germs and things. Hasn't anybody ever recited 'Gather ye rosebuds' into your tidy ear?"

Kate was annoyed to find herself turning pink and Doris was abashed. "Sorry, pet," she said contritely. "Felix says it's a real pity that I'm such a tactless clod when I look so trustworthy. Of course accidents do happen. We ought to make a plan, Felix and I."

Kate liked curry. She pushed delectable mouthfuls onto pieces of flat bread while Felix grumbled morosely about the waiters, the other patrons of the

Ganges, and most of all about the occasional customers who visited his small antique shop. These last seemed to be unworthy vulgarians, one and all.

It was hard to guess what circumstance had caused Felix to comment on Doris's want of tact since he himself made no effort whatever to be agreeable or courteous. He was a slight young man with bad teeth, a grubby sweater, and pale eyes.

When he had polished off every grain and legume on the table and they sat waiting for the check he suddenly growled, "Where's the bloody war hero nowadays?"

Doris answered in a quiet voice, her consonants enunciated with unusual care. "If, Felix, you are alluding to my brother James, he has gone down to the family place in Yorkshire. May I ask what prompts you to inquire?"

"Hell's bloody bells!" exclaimed Felix, addressing Kate directly for the first time. "'Our family place in Yorkshire!'" His voice minced momentarily before resuming its former sullen tone. "A kitchen sink and a cow shed, that's about the size of it." He snatched the check from the waiter's tray with a savage paw. "There's no hope for the English, don't think it. You want to know why the average Englishwoman's glad the war's over? Because the men are back? *Wrong*. Because Hitler got his? *Wrong*. Because peace is wonderful? *Double* wrong. The average Englishwoman's glad the war's over because now she needn't sit next to tarts in the bomb shelters or scruffy soldiers in the trains."

"Oh, come off it, love," said Doris calmly. "I don't know why I egg you on."

"I know why," said Felix darkly.

"Well, why *do* you ask about James? He's not your super family favorite."

"A pal of a pal of mine did some work for him and he needs the money, that's all."

"What on earth sort of work could a pal of a pal of yours do for James?"

"Oh, make some jewelry or something. I wasn't to say, but damn it all, Doris, the poor blighter must eat. *He* doesn't have a place in Yorkshire where he can indulge in new-laid eggs and self-pity."

"That's not fair, Felix. However I'll mention it to James for you. Perhaps Kate and I will go to Moon Croft for a few days." Felix looked sour. "Excuse me for a moment. I'll just ring Mum to say we're off to the Tate Gallery and won't be home till evening."

Felix began counting out heavy coins onto the table. He looked at Kate and gave her a rather rueful but completely friendly smile. "Sorry to be tiresome," he said.

Inspiration struck Kate like sun hitting a mirror. "I do not find the Hanged Man," she gasped.

"'Fear death by water'," he replied promptly. "I used to play that game with my sister. Splendid poem. Eliot's a bastard, you know."

They chatted pleasantly till Doris came back, when Felix offered a surly good-bye and darted off.

"Come along, my dear," said Doris. "You'll do well to avoid the loo. The one in the Tate's ever so much nicer."

Going home on the train Doris canvassed Kate's opinion of various modern works hanging in the Tate. Then she said, "You mustn't mind Felix. He's cross as a bear because I moved out. He's awfully nice, really."

"He was very pleasant while you were out phoning."

"Exactly. He's only beastly when *I'm* around. He's in love with me, you see, so he can't help it."

Kate had a sense of widening horizons. "Does he really dislike James?" she asked.

"Well it's not so much *personal* if you know what I mean. James is rather glamorous and very idle. Felix feels James hasn't really earned the way he's allowed to live."

"But surely if he lost an arm...?"

"Lots of people lost lots of things. Felix was a foot soldier. He was evacuated from Dunkirk and back in France on D-day. He essentially lost a kidney and often has to pop into hospital. But the girls don't look at *him* with melting eyes."

"Not even you?"

"Oh, *me*," she said. "You know the country's paved with heroes but Churchill really handed the old bays to the RAF boys. Mum's gaga over James but poor old Dad was brave as a lion — out night after night with the Home Guard, all wielding garden rakes and wearing saucepans on their heads, ready to repel the invaders when they landed."

"It's hard to think what it was like. We were so safe at home. In America, I mean."

"Well, I was in Gib for a long time. I mentioned Gib."

"You're in your WREN uniform on the mantelpiece. You look ever so smashing." Kate grinned. "Were you serious about going to Moon Croft together? I'd love to go, especially with you."

"Then go we shall, in a day or two. Just let me finish my brides. Did I tell you I make oil paintings out of wedding photos? That's how I make a living. I hide them in the cupboard at the studio in case anyone calls."

"Your American friend rang up," said Sally, coming out of the kitchen to greet them. "He left a number where he'd be until seven. He sounds lovely."

"Oh he's *neat,*" said Kate, giving Sally a hug. "A proper gentleman." She sat down and dialed the number.

Sumner asked whether she could meet him next day at some famous landmark.

"Have you been to St. Paul's?" asked Kate, who had been with Sally.

"I've hardly been anywhere. I need a guide who speaks the language. Are you at liberty, ma'am, to assist a friend from the Old South?"

"I could make myself available. Were you thinking of lunch at all?"

"I insist upon lunch. Shall we go to Claridges? It's the only place I've ever heard of."

"There's a pub near St. Paul's called Dirty Dick's. I'd rather go there if you don't mind much."

"That would have been my first choice," said Sumner. Kate smiled, thinking of Sumner and Mrs. Barnaby. "But isn't St. Paul's a rather large edifice? Shall we meet outside or inside?"

"What about the whispering gallery? It goes round the inside of the dome. You can murmur my name in your southernmost accent and I'll hear you all the way at the other side. It's quite spooky."

"But what if you're not at the other side? Why not meet at the altar?"

"I won't hold you to that," said Kate, giggling. "Tell you what. We'll meet at John Donne's tomb. How's 11 o'clock?"

"Not as good as midnight in the Confederate cemetery but I'll see you there."

Dirty Dick's was crowded. People stood toe to toe and back to back — eating, drinking, and talking with no apparent difficulty despite having no more than the usual quota of hands and mouths.

Sumner, immaculately American in a grey flannel suit, guided Kate to a dim corner with as much finesse as a pub regular. Excusing himself, he made for the bar and returned with two brimming mugs of beer and a plate of sizzling hot sausages with mustard.

"I haven't asked about the voyage. St. Paul's seemed like an unsuitable place and all around here it's hard to think of anything except the blitz." He spoke soberly.

"It's awful, isn't it? Everyone seems amazed that St. Paul's survived."

"There was a fair amount in the New York papers about the transatlantic murder. Seems the customs on both sides knew the woman. And the crew of the *Queen* had been alerted to keep an eye on her if she seemed to be drumming up bridge games."

"They didn't say so!"

"Well, I don't suppose they'd announce it over the P.A. system, Katy."

"Don't call me Katy. I'm not a grasshopper."

"Sorry. Is something the matter?"

"I was the one who found her, Sumner. I reported it. It was grim."

"Good lord. The papers had the body found in a lifeboat by a crew member."

"Somebody hid it there. I found it in the corridor first."

"You're very lucky no one told the press about you."

"The police are ignoring me, too. What does it mean?"

"Perhaps they're simply protecting an innocent bystander."

"But Sumner..." She stopped and looked at him.

"Kate, I have something to tell you. It has nothing to do with the ship. We can go back to that. It's not something you had to know right now, but as I had to come to England..." Sumner stopped too.

"What is it?"

"Do you know that man over there?"

"Who? there's a cast of thousands."

"He's on his way out. Thought he was staring at you." He smiled. "And come to think of it, what's funny about that?" he added gallantly.

"Did he have a beard?" Kate surprised herself with the question.

"No. No black cloak either."

Kate made a face. "Well, what were you going to tell me, anyway?"

"The lady to whom your uncle left the cottage has disappeared."

"Disappeared?"

"Well, Partridge, Partridge, and Rand can't find her anyway. We wrote to her, of course, and more than once, but she never came in. About the cottage, of course."

Kate looked hard at Sumner and then took the plunge. "Sumner, that other woman, that Fanny Birdsill, she was interested in my uncle's cottage on Snake Lake."

"How on earth do you know?"

"I met her on the Orange Blossom Special going back to New York. Oh, Sumner, *she* wasn't my uncle's friend, was she? She had a husband. At least she said he was..." She hesitated.

"Your uncle's friend was called Rosa Szastris. She had a British passport. She kept to herself as well as she could, but that's not easy in a town like Titus. People noticed her, but not after your uncle died."

"What did she look like?"

"I happen to have a picture of her. A reporter from Jacksonville snapped her coming out of the post office. She'd apparently forgotten to put her sunglasses back on and he's the kind of guy who gets hunches."

Kate took the picture from his hand. It was the gypsy all right. If Kate Clark was being used, she hadn't been chosen at random after all.

Chapter XII

> Who doth forever to his thoughts bequeath
> The legacy of your lamented Death.
> —Henry King, "An Elegy Upon My Best Friend L.K.C."

When Kate woke up the next day it was very cold. For a while she shivered under the blankets, trying to tuck herself together like Salammbo, who was making a big fur mound at the bottom of the bed. It didn't work, so she rushed across the room in her thin cotton pajamas and closed the window. The outside world had a morning bleakness. The bottom of the little garden, where Fred Bell had his tool shed, cold frame, and tidy heap of grass cuttings, was barely visible. She jumped back under the eiderdown and waited for the situation to improve, and while she waited she studied the room once more.

Her own clutter sprawled like an imposition across the available surfaces. Basically, the place was austere. The biggest piece of furniture was an enormous dark wardrobe with a key, and some of James' clothing, including a uniform, still hung there, pushed neatly to one side to allow room for her own things. The chest of drawers had been cleared out, and one drawer of the desk had been emptied and left open so that she would have a place for her writing material. The rest of the desk was locked.

The contents of the modest bookcase seemed to present a survey of the stages of the owner's life so far. There was a row of boys' school stories and simple tales of heroism; some works by John Buchan, Negley Farson, and H. Rider Haggard; a King James Bible bound in black leather and inscribed "To my beloved grandson James Oswald Bell from William Birkie"; a group of venerable works of romance and chivalry, all in modern English translations: Malory's *Morte d'Arthur*, *Sir Gawain and the Green Knight*, the *Tristan and Isolt* of Gottfried von Strassburg, and the *Nibelungenlied*; and a heavy group of philosophical works. Of these last only a rather slim *Basic Thought of Friedrich Nietzsche* looked read.

There were two framed pictures on the wall — one a watercolor of a Spitfire emerging from a grey cloud into an improbably blue sky, the other a photo of Richard Wagner in a beret. A pre-war political map of Europe was mounted on the inside of the door with thumbtacks. Kate had studied it at close range and she knew that the red mark inside Germany was the word KAHLBERG inked in neat capitals. Kahlberg was the fortress where James Bell had been a prisoner, and from which, she had been amazed to learn, he had escaped, alone.

"Oh, didn't Mum tell you?" Doris had asked. "She thinks everyone ought to tell their own tales. One of the many nice things about old Mum, actually.

You know how most parents are forever blathering on about everything their kids ever did from the time they first quickened in the womb. And of course Dad's not one for extra chat, so that's that."

"But how did James...?" Kate had begun.

"Ask him yourself, my dear. I'll just pop off to the pub to give you the chance. Sisters are generally the last people wanted on these occasions."

Kate stretched out her toes and Salammbo gave a disgruntled yawn. Speculating about James Bell was a luxury, at this point. If she rolled her mind over she confronted the disquieting news Sumner had brought from Florida. She had told him at once of her own meeting with the woman called Rosa Szastris. He had looked at her in amazement. Lawyers, like doctors, weren't supposed to look at people with amazement. They existed to soothe.

Sumner had been very sure that her uncle's friend had never set herself up as either a clairvoyante or a restauranteur. She had lived a very quiet life in a small room with a kitchenette that one of the truck farmers on the edge of Titus had installed for his mother-in-law.

"She helped pick the bell peppers and tomatoes sometimes," Sumner had said. "She was very graceful. Always wore big skirts and straw hats. She wasn't around long. Her romance with your uncle — if that's what it was — seemed pretty sudden for people their age."

"But you don't think she opened up a teashop just so she could meet me?"

"It looks that way — but why, Kate? She didn't make your tea with deadly nightshade or anything. There'd be no point. If she's dead you get the cottage but if you die without heirs everything goes to your cousin Sally Bell. You *are* sure she didn't tell you anything?"

And now Kate was lying in bed wondering why she'd answered Sumner's question with a rigamarole about a letter, a tall man, a dog, a snowstorm. On the other hand she thought she knew, now, for whom the message was intended. Sumner had had his chance. She rolled her mind back to James Bell and found no rest there after all.

There was a tap on the door, followed by Sally's cheerful voice. "I've brought you a cup of tea, pet, so you can enjoy it with the post on this ever so English morning." Sally brought in a tray with a steaming cup, an American air letter, and a picture postcard. Kate sat up and reached for her cardigan. Salammbo stretched and went to work on the backs of her ears.

"Now you just enjoy being cosy, ducky. I've lit the fire in the back room for when you come down. I'll grill you a nice kipper. I have to fly back now, as it's time for the reading from *Beowulf* on the Third Programme. It's in Anglo-Saxon."

"I didn't know you understood Anglo-Saxon, Cousin Sally."

"No more I don't. That's the best part. Lovely old noises."

With postcards, Kate liked to look at the pictures first. She looked now at the sepia photograph on the ornamental side. Old buildings surrounded a tablecloth of courtyard with a stone basin in the center. Small white letters at the bottom said, "Tom Quad, Christ Church College, Oxford." She turned it over.

> Dear Kate
> Unfortunately these buildings (the color of crumbly biscuits) are not the only antiques in Oxford. Joe maintains his sanity by spending half his time on the other side of town, at a clinic near the motor works. Hope you are enjoying England. Best from both of us.
> Alice Collins

The air letter was well stuck. Kate opened the drawer of the bedside table to see whether there might not be something with which to slit it open. There was a letter opener. No doubt Sally brought James his mail just like this. But then, how could he manage? Perhaps she slit it open for him on the spot, like an Italian waiter peeling an orange at your table.

> Friday
> Dearest, beloved roomie
> I played the harp on a float in the Columbus Day parade. The rest of the girls sat around eating spumoni, or pretending to. It was freezing.
> Harry Feather came to see if you were coming back so I spoke to him in the parlor. He was carrying a dog in a pink sweater so at first I thought he must be part of some act — isn't that what you said? — Harry and Fan and trick dog Ruggles? He was rather pathetic. Said he just wanted to ask you something on account of you being on the ship. When are you coming home, by the way? In a month or so? I mean it's just a visit. I know you're paying for half the room (which I am using for my dirty laundry) being an heiress and all, but I miss you.
> Thank you for your marvelous letter. I'll keep mum about your role in the murder. Why is Lisa Dragonette so attracted to Sam? Something is missing in your report. He must be a Dark Horse. But you are in love with a belted earl or a laird or something. At least a gentry. Does that mean you don't want Sumner Partridge? I just ask.
> I'll write more next week. There's talk of pulling down the Third Avenue El.
> Love
MaJa

Kate put the letter opener back into the drawer, which she noticed had not been emptied. Tsk, tsk, James. There was an empty Player's box and a cigarette lighter. A tube of cough lozenges. A floor plan of the British Museum. A railway timetable for London-York. A pair of old photographs in a pasteboard folder. The woman's picture was an enlargement of the one in the locket; the man opposite her had eyes like Sally Bell's.

"Cousin Sally?" asked Kate, wiping her plate with a piece of cold toast and reaching for the marmalade.

"Yes, pet?" Sally came in from the kitchen with floury hands. "I'm just popping in a suet pudding for Fred. He does love them so."

"Would you mind telling me more about your brother Oswald? I know you said he married a German. I gave you the certificate Uncle Albert had in his box."

"Well if you really want to know, dear, of course I will. So sad it all was. Poor, poor Ilse. She sang Schubert lieder and Oswald played for her. Just let me finish the pud." She took the brown teapot with her and when she came back it was full of fresh hot tea.

"Oswald and I were just a year apart, and Albert Clark had been born the same year as myself so we three were very close as children. Your father was five years younger, and was like the baby brother for all of us. When Oswald was killed it was a terrible blow to the family — not that every family didn't lose someone, mind, but it didn't help — my Mum and Dad went old over night. They shut themselves up in one room and Ilse shut herself up in another.

Albert came home from the front and I shoved things at him in a fury — the scroll should by rights have been Ilse's but I was half crazy. I hated everybody. 'They killed Oswald the lot of them,' I said, daft like. 'I only care for Art,' I said.

"Then I quick married Fred Bell, who cares no more for art than a sausage. He liked my odd ways, and we've jogged on all right." She took the lid off the teapot and stirred the contents with a spoon.

"As you know, pet, my mother and your Grandpa Clark were sister and brother. Their father had done well in the drapery trade in Leeds. But my own father was a schoolmaster and he was full of intellectual ambitions for his children. I was trained for a teacher myself, and Oswald, being the boy — that's how people felt, and very unfair it was, I always thought so — was sent to Germany to walk about and learn the language. For some strange reason people thought that Germany was it. That was in the summer of 1913."

She poured the tea, and looked out at the grey garden. "When Oswald came back he was very brown and handsome. He told us that he had fallen in love with a German girl who had been with a walking party. She was from an aristocratic family that had seen better days but still had a lot of land — and pride! They were violently opposed to any marriage between one of them and the likes of us.

"'Pity about them, Oswald,' said I, though Mum and Dad were not at all keen on the connection. 'What is she like personally?' He smiled at me, the winning way he had. James is very like him. 'She's as fair as an angel, Sarah,' he said. He never called me Sally, Oswald didn't. 'And she sings like an angel too. And she has brains. We Birkies must have brains!' Ah, poor Oswald.

"He went back to Germany and married her in some Rathaus or other. She told her people in advance but none of them appeared. He fetched her back to England. She was lovely, but not very strong somehow, and when the war came it was horrid for her. Everybody went absolutely wild with hating the Germans. Oh, I suppose the top ones didn't. They always stay pally. But our sort, the backbone of England, they spat on Ilse. She couldn't go into the street. We were all ostracized. And then Oswald went and got killed on the Somme — just an ordinary soldier he was, sent out to be butchered like all the others. It killed my mother, too, and Father died soon after." Sally had tears in her eyes.

"Oh, Cousin Sally, I'm so sorry. Uncle Albert never told me."

"I expect you'd never asked, pet. Albert was a bit like me. Not one to offer to tell sad tales."

"Uncle Albert wasn't like you!"

Sally blew her nose and smiled. "You mean because I blather on so, I expect." Kate shook her head, but Sally held up her hand. "Family resemblances pop up in funny ways. You've not had enough family to know."

Kate put her hand on Sally's. "What happened to Ilse when the war ended?" she asked.

"She had a baby, a son, born after Oswald was killed. She named him Franz. People would stop me in the town and say, 'How's Franz the Hun then, Miss Birkie?' — even though Oswald had gone and died for them or for the king or for something.

"After the war Ilse went home to Germany. She died in 1935. We know because they sent Oswald's letters back to us, and his medals. Didn't even want those. I had written each year on Franz's birthday but no one ever answered. I hope he didn't turn out a Nazi."

"So then Franz and James would be first cousins?"

"Yes, and Doris, of course. Second cousin to you. I think I'll have a go at my Bach sonata if you don't mind."

"Oh, please do. Leave the door open. I'll do the dishes."

"There'll be a sticky pot or two."

"Not to worry."

Chapter XIII

> I believe it is customary in good society to take some slight refreshment at five o'clock.
> —Oscar Wilde, *The Importance of Being Earnest*

Kate and Sally had arranged to go into Town that afternoon and meet Doris at the National Gallery. They made three-quarters of a grand tour of the place before they agreed to collapse on a bench. Before them stretched the Piazza San Marco, depicted by the painter Canaletto through one of the arches of a colonnade. As it happened, Sally and Fred had been to Venice on their tenth wedding anniversary — their only trip abroad. James and Doris had stayed with Fred's sister in Tooting.

"Did I ever tell you," began Sally, "about that little cafe (she pronounced it caffy), just down there to the left, away from the lagoon, where your father and I had two espressos each and the Englishman at the next table was hiring someone to follow his wife?"

"Wrong again, Mum," answered Doris cheerfully. "It was down there that you finally found a *gabinetto*."

"Your vulgarity means nothing to me, my dear. I'm above all that. Kate, however, always wants to hear my experiences."

"She's damn polite, I must admit. Not like Yanks in the cinema. Must be her early English training. But after all, Mum, though these sort of pictures hardly interest me at all these days, the man was an artist. We're not looking at your snapshot album. For example, notice how skillfully he handled that expanse of pale sky, right at the heart of the composition."

"My word," said Sally in alarm. "Do you notice how quickly those dark clouds are coming up there, from behind the cathedral? It will almost certainly rain. That lot of folk out in the middle of the square had better take shelter. That sort of clothing would be inclined to spot, and I daresay cleaning methods were not so advanced as they are nowadays."

"Get on with you, you old fake," laughed Doris. She turned to Kate. "Sometimes I wonder when Mum's going to add painting to her Art Appreciation Arsenal." Sally stretched her legs and looked blandly at Doris, who continued, "By the way, Mum, do you have a clue why James would have had something made by a friend of Felix who does jewelry and things? I thought maybe it was a surprise for you. The ring of the Nibelung or a gold swan for the mustard pot. It was some time ago and it seems the chap's not been paid."

"Oh, my, I do hope it was something for a young lady. I'd like James to settle down. Not that I have ever regarded 'settling down' as the be-all and end-all of existence, mind, but James seems to need responsibilities. Always mooning about listening to the gramophone." She stifled a sigh and said, "Have a Smartie. It's the last of my sweet ration."

Kate looked at her watch. "I'm meeting my friend Sumner at Gunter's for tea, you know. He's going on to Paris for a few days and then back home. Do come with me. You'll like him. He's very southern, sort of like Ashley Wilkes."

"It's very kind of you, pet, when your own visit with him is so short. However I'm off to Covent Garden to pick up some tickets and Doris must come with me. She doesn't care for Gunter's. Too swell."

Doris laughed, and they made for the entrance together. Kate stood on the pavement and watched them streak off across Trafalgar Square, Sally's socks flashing in a late burst of sunshine.

Gunter's was crowded. When Sumner and Kate were seated at a table for two they smiled at each other like any pair of triumphant tourists.

"Are you feeling English or American?" asked Sumner. "After all, you've been here before."

"Not in Gunter's. I guess I feel more American in England than I do in New York. Isn't it funny? I remember how English I was when I first went to school in Florida, with my knee socks and jumpers."

"Did you carry a hockey stick?"

"No, but everyone made fun of my accent. I didn't mind all that much, though. I guess I like being a foreigner."

"Why?"

"Oh, if you do anything gauche or stupid you can't be expected to know any better if you're a foreigner."

"That doesn't sound like Katherine Clark of the New York stage."

"Not her, me."

The waiter appeared and Sumner ordered tea and cakes for two, then said calmly, "This time there really is a man with a beard looking at you. He's at a table by the window with an exotic lady in a black rooster feather hat. If this were Titus I'd say they were a sinister looking pair. Maybe you could see him in your discreet pocket mirror."

"I bet ladies don't," said Kate, laughing, and more interested than she meant to show.

"But since you're a foreigner, it doesn't matter."

"Exactly." She got out her compact and pretended to study her nose. "Do you know him, or is he just coveting my new Bond Street necktie? He looks carelessly dressed for a place like this."

"I know them both. They were on the Queen. She's a stage designer named Lisa Dragonette. Maybe you've heard of her."

"I think I'd remember the name. It doesn't matter, though. Nobody in Titus has heard of any stage designers. Here comes the beard."

Sam was very polite. Whatever Sumner thought of his attire, his opening manners could have consorted with a bowler hat and spats. The two men acknowledged her introduction rather formally, then Sam turned to Kate.

"Lisa Dragonette sends her compliments. I fear she is glued to her chair. You wouldn't expect chewing gum or peanut butter in a posh place like this but no matter. In precisely ten minutes she must be pried loose and sent off to another glamourous tryst. Would it be all right if I came over for a few minutes then?" He looked at Sumner and added, "Not for long."

"Please do," replied Kate graciously. As soon as he left she said to Sumner, "He's okay, I think."

"Possibly," said Sumner. "Listen, Kate, there's something new. I phoned Dad this morning."

"Ooo," gasped Kate. "It must have cost a fortune."

"It was a business call. But he did add that he'd rustled up a court order to inspect the cottage out at Snake Lake. The inside was a shambles. Somebody was looking for something." He smiled at her. "Dad was especially grieved because your old teddy bear was torn apart. He seems to think you're very young."

"But my old teddy bear is at Barnaby's. MaJa's taking care of it."

"Good for MaJa. I hope it's a mannerly bear. Maybe Rosa Szastris had a bear. Anyway the place was ransacked. Along with your uncle's death and the Szastris fade-out the whole thing's got Randy Macoon — he's the sheriff — rushing around like a polecat on moonshine. The simile is Dad's."

"But Sumner — there's nothing funny about my uncle's death. He knew he was dying. He probably told your father. He just didn't tell me, is all. I guess he didn't want me to feel I had to go down there and stay with him. But he had told my cousin Sally because of James...well, that's irrelevant, but...she told me..."

"Look, I suppose you're right. But back in Titus all they know is that he was cremated with unseemly haste. His affair, if I may call it that, with Rosa Szastris now ranks with Antony and Cleopatra in the public mind. The news about the search is the biggest thing to hit town since the kudzu vine."

"Your father told you an awful lot in a telephone call!" As far as Kate was concerned transatlantic phone calls were the prerogatives of heads of state.

"Kate, you're somewhat unworldly for an actress from the big city. It looks as though you're mixed up in something rough. I'm worried about you." Sumner spoke earnestly. She noticed that his former tone of mock gallantry had, like the Old South, gone with the wind.

"Sumner, having you here feeding me tea and crumpets and interesting news from home is wonderful. However it's plain as day that I'm just a bit player in whatever's going on. As usual." Kate had a practiced trick of producing a dimple and fluttering her lashes. She tried it, and added, "I might not even have the ingenue part."

Then she noticed Sam, standing there, looking much more like his former self.

"Oh, do sit down, Sam," she said. "Everyone's looking at you."

"On the contrary," he replied, unceremoniously grabbing an empty chair from the next table. "It's you they are looking at. They wonder whether you could possibly be Shirley Temple, all grown up." Kate stuck out her tongue, and then regretted it.

Sam turned to Sumner. "It hasn't taken our Kate long to find another landsman. Are you here on vacation?"

"Kate and I are old friends. I was not aware that your interest in her would justify the possessive pronoun." Sumner was starchy.

"Oh, it's just my way," said Sam cheerfully. "What the hell. I'm not at my best in some teashop." The way he said it made it sound as if teashops were Sumner's native habitat.

Kate jumped in. "One doesn't call Gunter's 'some teashop.' It's *the* place," she said in a rather English voice.

"Oh, doesn't one? Sorry about that. Mind if I have that last raspberry tart? I didn't have any lunch."

"I must say I didn't expect to meet you here."

"Where *did* you expect to meet me? In the Queen's Arms? A plague o' these pickled herrings."

"Desist, Sir Toby," said Kate.

Sam looked at her admiringly. "Speaking of Toby, have you heard from our friend Tony at all?"

Kate tried to sound casual. "I had a very short letter. He's with his aunt in Scotland."

"That's a helluva note." Sam smirked, then turned to Sumner. "Tony's a refined Englishman who was in our gang on the *Queen*. Excuse us for droning on. You know how friendly you can get on ships." His tone was conciliatory.

"I was in a few ships in the South Pacific," said Sumner, still irked. "These days I travel by air."

"Oh, I'd just hate not to come in a ship," said Kate. "It makes England seem so far away. I mean because it takes so long."

"You flew over just now?" asked Sam. "Stopping at Gander and Shannon?"

Sumner thawed a little. "Quite a while at Shannon, as a matter of fact. They fed us on porridge while we waited. It was a lot like lumpy grits. Have you made the flight yourself?"

"Once or twice."

"Sam's a Soldier of Fortune," said Kate.

Sam helped himself to a slice of pound cake and said, "Kate's a Dizzy Dame."

"There seem to be people waiting for tables," said Sumner. "Maybe I should order another pot of tea."

"Definitely. If you don't the waiter will stab you with a butter knife as you leave. It's very neatly done. You don't drop until you get to the sidewalk." Sam stood up. "I have to go, though. Thanks for the cake. Nice meeting you." He offered Sumner his hand. "Are you still in East Tinkham, Kate?"

"For now," said Kate. "But I expect to go to Yorkshire soon with my cousin."

"Okay then. I'll try to give you a buzz. So long."

They watched him out, then turned to face each other.

"I'll order some more tea, if you don't mind. I don't have much time left. I have to buy my Dad a Rolls razor and my mother some china doodad or other and I'm dining with a Mr. Barrington Jarndyce."

"I can guess his profession."

"I wish I could have taken you to his office. There's an old clerk there — you know, as in Kate Clark — who sits on a high stool and dips his pen into an inkwell. Jarndyce has a fountain pen, though. It leaks onto his pocket."

"How did you like Sam?"

"Very amusing."

"You don't think," said Kate.

"What does he do?"

"I don't know. He was a Yank in the RAF but I suppose he must have done something since then."

"Don't get too friendly with him, Kate."

"Oh, he's all right. Everyone liked him, especially Lisa Dragonette. I was surprised to see them together. He pretended not to care for her on the ship."

"If she knew you on the ship it was mighty rude of her to ignore you."

"She didn't ignore me. I saw her nod."

"Kate, did any of these people know the murdered woman?"

"Oh, no. At least — well, no. They didn't say so. Sumner, stop being so solicitous for Pete's sake. Don't worry so much. I'm not a poor little orphan."

"Yes you are. At least you're an orphan."

"Oh, phooey. You just take care of things in Titus and let me know what happens. And if you see MaJa give her my love."

They left soon after that, Sumner insisting on getting Kate a cab for King's Cross. He kissed her good-bye. On the cheek.

Chapter XIV

> Sounds fluttered
> Like bats in the dusk.
> —T. E. Hulme, "Images"

"Hell's teeth," said Doris, slamming a bulging string bag down onto the piano. "There are millions of them! They're falling out of the trees! It's the downfall of the Rational Order. It's the return of the Dark Ages. They're like lemmings, whatever *they* are." She threw herself onto a chair and gasped, "Tea."

Kate was painting her nails with Prince Matchiabelli's Red Red by the sitting room fire.

"Who is, pet?" asked Sally, who had been reading aloud from the secular poems of John Donne, and had just got to, "So, so breake off this last lamenting kisse..." when the door was flung open.

"Brides," said Doris grimly. "Everyone is getting married. One would think the last trump was about to sound. And then they all must have monster oil paintings made of their wedding photos — all sleazy satins and lace doilies. Oh, well. We artists have always had to prostitute ourselves. I can't let someone else have my jobs. I'll lose out next time. Isn't that the kettle I hear boiling?"

"I'm so sorry," said Kate, waving her fingers like a field of Monet poppies. "My nails are wet."

"They look a bloody fright, too," said Doris. "You'd do far better just to buff them with some pink paste. You can get it at Boots. Americans are so grotesque."

"Doris dear," said Sally, "prostitute yourself if you must. This door shall always be open to receive you. But I must ask that you treat our Yankee cousin with civility."

"She's really English anyway, come to that. A fake Yank. Besides, who was saying only yesterday that Americans always play to win?"

"What's wrong with playing to win?" asked Kate. "Don't the English play to win?"

"Bad form," said Doris. "Come on, Ma, let's have some tea. Are there any of those fatties left?"

Sally made the tea, and wheeled it in on a squeaky cart. There was a plate of Fat Rascals, plump scones stuffed with currants, and butter and jam to spread on them.

"It's better than Gunter's," said Kate, testing her right nails against her left.

"Lots of things are better than the best," said Doris more affably. "That's why there are so many fairy stories about sad kings and queens. Dad's roses are ever so much sweeter than the ones in Regent's Park, and cricket on the village green far better than what they play at Lord's."

"It doesn't hold for Art, though. There the best is always the best." Sally looked thoughtful. "I don't think kings can have been so sad when they had Bach and Mozart dashing off bits of music just for them."

Doris went to the piano and played a few improbable notes.

"What's that funny noise?" asked Kate.

"It's an augmented eighth," answered Doris. "Or possibly a diminished seventh."

"Doris," said Sally, "is it true that the Communists don't believe in private property?"

"More or less," replied Doris, who was leafing through the available music. "Where's Bartok's *Microkosmos*?"

"Well, I'd like to see the Communists try to take away my piano."

"Whatever gave you that idea, Mum?"

"Mr. Dobbins the postman says this Labour government is just the hole in the dyke. Or maybe it was the opening wedge."

"Maybe it was the foot in the door," offered Kate.

"Is that a toe on the carpet?" asked Doris. "Oh, bother. It's some mess of Salammbo's. Any letters for me, by the bye?"

"My dear, you put it right out of my head with your ranting and raving. There's a letter come for you from James. I'll fetch it."

Doris read it quickly.

"He says he's busy, but if we want to come to Yorkshire one time will do as well as another. That sounds like James. Well, I shall have to tell him to contain his eagerness for a few more days whilst I cope with these fresh jobs."

She thrust the letter into the pocket of her cardigan.

"What does he say about Felix's friend's jewelry work?"

"Nothing. That is he says he paid by check at the time and the rogue's got a damnable cheek. I'll have to soften it a bit for Felix. Come along, Kate, let's walk round the park a bit. It'll be dark directly."

But as Kate opened the hall closet to get out her new Jaeger coat the telephone rang. Being nearest, she answered.

"Is Miss Katherine Clark there please? Scotland Yard here."

"This is Katherine Clark."

"Sorry to bother you, Miss Clark. Inspector Bucket was wondering whether you might step in tomorrow morning round about half past nine."

"Yes. Sure. Is it all right if I ask what for?"

"Quite all right, miss. He feels you may be able to assist him with his inquiries into the untimely death of Mrs. Fanny Birdsill."

"But I told them everything I knew on the ship,"

"Yes, miss. But Inspector Bucket finds a second telling useful on occasion. Just give your name at the front desk. Thank you, miss."

The speaker hung up.

"What's the gen?" asked Doris, who was pulling on a tweed coat of pre-war vintage.

"The police want to talk to me about the murder."

"My hat! I thought they didn't care a bean for you. I daresay they haven't got anywhere so they're making the rounds again."

"Do you think that's it?"

"Well, there seems to have been damn all in the papers. Dad would have said. He reads it all."

The park was only a block from The Oval, and Kate and Doris were quickly inside the fence. They were striding briskly along when they heard a scuffling on the gravel behind them. A small boy in a large heavy sweater accosted them.

"Miss Bell! Miss Bell! Yer Mum says will you please get a packet of Bird's custard?" Seeing Doris's face, he added mysteriously, "She come upon a tin of plums in the glory hole."

"Oh, all *right*. Thanks, Reginald."

"What's Bird's custard?" inquired Kate.

"Powdered. Look here, I'll simply have to dash to Simpkin's as the shops will be shutting directly. You carry on toward the lake and I'll catch you up." She sped off.

Kate strolled along, musing. She was glad that the police had called her back, maybe. It would depend on what they said. Suppose they produced Madame Sosostris and then they all told her, "Not to worry."?

The park was very big, and most of it had been left in its natural state. There were deep woods, open spaces, a lake, three ponds, streams, and small wildlife in season. Some areas were laced with well-worn paths, and there were even a few benches along them, but there were also many acres where few people ever ventured.

After several years of leisurely debate it had been decided to allow small rowboats on the lake in summer. One thing led to another and a modest platform had been built at the water's edge where people could sit at tables and drink tea or orange squash. Other times, such as October, the park was mainly the preserve of earnest walkers and dutiful dog owners.

A very large black animal with paws like Fudgcicles bounded out of a thicket and knocked Kate over. She liked dogs, but was worried about her camel-colored coat. The beast's master came pelting down the path panting apologies and hurling monstrous threats at Caliban, who had decided to sit down and guard his prey. Kate was helped to her feet, and made to say that she was quite all right several times before the incident could be considered over. It was very *Jane Eyre*.

The light was fading, and she decided to hurry toward the lake in case Doris was coming by another route. They had been to the park several times. On one fine day Sally had come too and they had had a Thermos tea on a little folding table. Kate knew that there were several paths to the lake, but she wasn't sure which was the direction for Simpkin's.

The waterfront was deserted. Because of the empty platform and the shuttered refreshment kiosk it seemed more desolate here than in the wooded paths. Damp fallen leaves clung like black footprints to the weathered floor. England had turned away from the long afternoons of summer. The northern nights were devouring more and more of the season's spare share of daylight, and the shimmer of the lake seemed to cast more light than the sky.

Sound, too, had withdrawn. Away at the opposite edge of the park, across a deep zone of silence, she could hear the faint undifferentiated hum of traffic on the London road.

She stood, hands in pockets, facing the lake and shivering a little. Then she heard a noise somewhere behind her, the sort of noise made by a soft foot moving among the fallen debris of the autumn forest.

She turned, smiling, expecting to see Doris. She saw no one.

"Doris?" she said loudly, and then, thinking it might be another dog, or even Caliban come back, whistled, her lips resisting the necessary compression. The response was a still deeper silence. The still, cold air seemed thicker with the oncoming dark. She stood, her back to the glassy lake, her limbs heavy with panic.

"Doris!" It was a terrible effort, yet she hardly heard her own voice.

A rogue breeze threw the trees into a shifting confusion of greys and among them a figure in a short bulky coat seemed to stand. It was impossible to distinguish a face — just a gleam, matching the gleam of the lake, where watching eyes would be. For a long moment they faced each other, staring like statues at either end of a long-abandoned pleasure ground. Then the figure took a step forward, and Kate found that she could flee.

The silent stranger commanded the familiar path that led back to The Oval and fires, teapots, laughter, shelter. She ran away in the opposite direction along a path that followed the lake's edge and was slippery from recent rain. Her shoes were too thin. Small stones and roots were like obtrusive punctuation in a simple sentence. To her left the lake had concentrated what light remained from the dying day; to her right spread the near total darkness of the wood.

They could not be the last two people in the whole vast park. That was what she hoped. Her fear, confirmed by a narrowing of the lakeside path, was that she was plunging into less frequented territory. She knew from Doris that even in summer many of the "best spots" were seldom visited. Now she found more branches blocking her way, a ribbon of long-dead leaves glossy at her feet. The cold still air hung like a monstrous curtain.

The ground to her left began to drop away and soon some six feet of steep and pebbly bank separated her from the glimmering water. Her own rapid foot falls, her breathing, the heavy beating of her heart all effectively covered any sound of pursuit. Dismayed, she noticed the ground rising to her right. Her narrow path had become a treacherous track cut into a rocky slope. She slowed down, afraid of falling.

Here where the trees had receded there was dying light enough to make out a sign planted in the rough terrain:

MEMBERS OF THE PUBLIC
BEWARE OF FALLING STONES

Something sharp inside her shoe made an exquisitely painful thrust into the ball of her foot, forcing her to stop. She tried to reach it with her fingers, steadying herself against the metal stake of the sign. Her knees were custard. Again she heard, far and faint, the steady traffic sound. The park was still as death.

She listened. *Nothing*. All at once she was sure that she had been mistaken. Doris must be wondering what on earth had happened to her. I got lost, she would say. Young twit, Doris would say. No need to reveal what a total idiot she was. She slipped her shoe off and felt for the offending pebble.

And ahead of her some other pebble slithered down the hill from somewhere above and broke into the water with a small *plop*! Yes, that was what the sign said. Nevertheless, her heart contracted. A groping forefinger found a stone no bigger than a seed pearl inside her shoe. *A seed pearl*. Fan's body swam face up in the darkening lake below her, and vanished. Trembling, she reached inside too quickly and the shoe, already half off, tumbled to the ground and rolled down the bank, coming to rest at the edge of the water.

How to recover it without precipitating a small avalanche? She could hardly see it, stone colored among the stones. But with the loss of vision came a sharpening of those perceptions needed by creatures of darkness. Something back in the wood she had left behind could hardly be called a sound, but she knew it for the unnatural agitation of a twig. Though silent as an Iroquois, her pursuer had been betrayed by the forest.

Careless for everything but flight, fueled by panic, she ran on, hobbling half shod through the slippery stones. Her clatter woke echoes and somewhere, she couldn't tell how far away, a dog barked cheerfully.

The path veered oblique right, leaving the lake to hide itself in shadows, swinging easily upward into a thicket of tall shrubbery. Here the ground was smooth and the way wider, as if to draw breath in the dense web of slender branches. There was almost nothing to be seen, but ahead of her a lighter grey showed Kate the way. She thought of going to earth, sliding into the darkness close to the ground, but dreaded being found there and pounced on like some beast whose camouflage has failed. She ran on, casting her second shoe and moving more easily on the bare cold earth.

Soon the path broke free into a great open space. It was Lion's Heath, five hundred acres covered with wild grasses and dotted with the sleeping burrows of small animals. Out there, there was no hint of cover. She hesitated, listening. Nothing, only the broken rush of her own breath. The night's first owl cried out, back near the lake. Run away. She ran.

Somewhere she would stumble onto a broader path again, a main route leading to a gate, a gate that swung out into that ring of fortresses that surrounded the King's Park — secure castles where even now free born Englishmen were listening to the BBC news and eating Heinz beans on toast. *But what if the park were locked at dusk?*

There were two trees ahead, a stunted duo that had mistakenly abandoned the wood and struck out into the open space. As she approached, one of them seemed to step forward and block her way. She stumbled and a strong hand gripped her arm. She began screaming and screamed until she felt her face pushed against a rough tweed shoulder.

"For god's sake, what on earth is the matter? The local constabulary are just making their final rounds. I have no wish to explain myself." The voice was unfriendly but not threatening.

"Oh please. Oh thanks. Oh please. Someone is following me. Back there."

"I've been after you for at least a quarter of an hour. For some reason you've chosen to make it quite an ordeal."

"But...why? Who *are* you? I was supposed to meet my cousin."

"I know," he said dryly, releasing her.

They stood together in the dark, then he turned and shone a flashlight onto the path. "Shall we go? I dare say my mother will be keeping the meal hot. If you want to take my arm you can hold the torch yourself with your free hand."

Kate gasped. "Then you are...?"

"I'm James Bell."

Chapter XV

> Because that fellow can't sleep — that's why. Dash me if he hasn't been doing a think just now! What business has he to think in the middle of the night?
>
> —Joseph Conrad, *Victory*

"Here you are, James. I've taken the stones out for you." Sally looked apologetic.

"You needn't have bothered, you know. I eat like an American now. Americans eat with only one hand. Isn't that so, Kate?" He was very cool.

Kate nodded, eating her custard coated plums with a spoon and ignoring the dessert fork that had also been provided. She was very cozy, in pink fuzzy slippers and a twin sweater set. Her seat was closest to the gas fire.

James had said almost nothing on their way out of the park and she had been too shaken and bewildered to take the lead. But when they got home and he said laconically, "I found her," she heard herself saying that she had been frightened by a dog, and then lost her shoe in the lake. He let it pass. Her terror was their secret, and whether his silence was indifference or sympathy for her folly — or even something else — was not apparent.

"I've put a cot in with Doris for you, just while James is here," said Sally. "You don't mind, do you, pet?"

"Oh, I'd *love* it," answered Kate cheerfully. "Doris and I can talk all night. She never lets me tell her my secrets."

"Oh, bother. I expect I should just pop straight back to Felix."

Fred Bell looked pained, and James said calmly, "Don't be ridiculous, Doris. I shall only be here for two nights. You might at least pretend to have some manners."

"James, you're an ass," said Doris. "Kate and I are chums. What on earth did you come for, if one may ask? I just had your letter today."

"Doris," said Sally, "I can't think how it is you're so blunt. I never cared for that sort of question. Surely James may do as he likes? I expect he has come to hear the Berlin Philharmonic. For those who like them, they are very fine."

"Whatever that may mean. Honestly, Mum, your wits fly out of the window as soon as James surfaces."

"Doris," said Fred sharply, "you'll not speak to your mother like that again, if you please."

"Sorry, Dad," said Doris, and turning to Sally, "I'm really sorry, Mum. I'm just nervy for some reason. I daresay it's subconscious." She smiled at her brother. "It's nice to see you, James. You look jolly fit." Doris seemed to have assumed a rather superior manner, as if she had risen a notch in the social scale.

"You look all right yourself," James said. He was looking at Kate. "I met the local vet in the post office and he offered me a quick lift to Henley. I'd a thing or two to attend to in Town so here I am." Still looking at Kate he added, "I can't drive, you see. At least not legally." He was grave, but his voice was without self-pity. His hair was thick and fair, his eyes a light hard blue. Taken all in all, he was exceptionally handsome.

He's like the Prince all right, Kate thought, wondering what genetic scramble had made him so much more splendid than the others. There was no photograph of him on the mantelpiece. She had once asked what he looked like and Doris had fished out a dog-eared snapshot of a schoolboy whose face was half shadowed by a peaked cap.

"Are you going to stay at home this evening then, lad?" asked Fred. "I can light the fire in the sitting room."

Sally said nothing but looked worlds, and Doris added, "A little time in the family bosom can regenerate the tissues you know, James." Then she gasped and covered her mouth. "Oh God. I'm sorry."

"Doris, you too are an ass," said James without rancour. "I wanted to look up a game of chess, actually. There's no one to play with round Netherbeck except the vicar."

"Is that still old Broadbent? But isn't he the one with the lovely daughter? Divinely tall and most divinely fair? You'd do well to get off with her, James. A regular Brunhilde, and the only grandchild of a rich brewer on the female side."

Once more Sally jumped in. "Doris, *must* you be so ridiculous? James' relationship with Rosemary Broadbent is his own affair, surely?"

"It's not an affair at all at the moment, I'm afraid," said James with great equanimity. He seemed the only one of the family at ease. "However if you'd really like my company we could have some music I suppose. I shall be going into Town first thing in the morning." He got out a packet of Woodbines and offered them to Doris and Kate. "Sorry. All I could get." Kate saw that they looked very small. Doris took one and held the lighter for James and then for herself.

"I have to go in to Scotland Yard tomorrow," said Kate. "Perhaps we could take the train together, James. Doris wants to go in very early." It was the first remark she had addressed to him directly since their meeting in the park.

"I am at your service," he answered seriously. "May one comment on your destination? I hadn't heard of Scotland Yard booking sightseeing tours."

"Someone has been boiled in oil. The Yard wonder whether Kate could assist them in sorting the matter out." That was Doris.

"Really, my dear," said Fred kindly, "as there was a real and dreadful crime committed, I'm sure Kate will not find your remarks amusing."

"Oh that's okay, Cousin Fred. Don't mind Doris so much. It's just her way." Fred and Sally Bell looked at each other in a sudden complicity of parental interest and Kate, feeling like a fool, went on, "I mean I guess Doris knows from all our conversations that the whole thing's begun to seem like a mystery novel I left on the train. Now I'll never find out if the steward did it."

"Did what?" James looked at Sally, who scurried to get an ashtray. Doris was absently stamping her cigarette out onto her bread and butter plate. She answered first.

"Don't you get the newspapers up there on the moors, James? I should think your chum at the Vicarage might shovel along the *Times* after he's finished the crossword. There was an American woman murdered on the *Queen Victoria*."

"And how does that concern my cousin Kate?"

"It doesn't really. It's just that by some incredible coincidence I had met the woman before on a train. She seemed nosy about Uncle Albert and his house and everything. The police found out she was a regular crook though. It's funny, isn't it?"

"Rather," he said. The light hard blue eyes studied her face. He lit another Woodbine, the last of a packet of five.

"You're being very prodigal of those beastly little fags," said Doris. "Have you more hidden away somewhere? You were always keen on hidey-holes. Lord, I used to go positively mad searching for peppermints amongst your socks and underdrawers."

James ignored her and addressed Kate. "Bad show for Uncle Albert. Still, it seems to have been quick at the end, if my mother has it right. Did you see him at all much before he died?"

"I hadn't seen him for months. I had no idea he was so ill. He didn't tell me. Cousin Sally told me you had thought of emigrating to Florida. I'd have been glad to let you have the cottage, you know. He didn't leave it to me." She found herself speaking rather quickly.

"Indeed? I understood he left everything to you." He smiled at her, a smile of such considerable charm that she realized he had not smiled before. Sally beamed. "We've got Moon Croft on our side, you see. Not to mention Mother's Wedgwood jam pot and Apostle tea spoons for Doris." Doris snorted.

Kate noticed that Sally was always "Mother" to James, to Doris never.

"To whom did he leave the cottage, then? Is it a home for crocodiles?"

"It's alligators. We don't have crocodiles." Everyone smiled briefly. Crocodiles and alligators were equally exotic. "He left it to a foreign lady, a mystery woman."

"What does she look like?"

"Well, that's an odd question, surely James?" Doris seemed determined to challenge him. Kate, an only child, had a vague notion that if she'd had an older brother like James she'd have simply basked in the glow. "What, in America, constitutes a mysterious foreigner? Would I do?"

Doris, even in her black beret, always managed to look more English than the Queen and Kate laughed. She answered James' question. "Sumner Partridge says she is very handsome, dark and graceful. Not young, though. I mean not too young for Uncle Albert."

"Well I never did," said Sally. "I am so awfully pleased. Fancy Albert taking up with a lovely lady at the end. I always thought his wife must be a proper stick. There she was, living in the tropics so to speak, and yet in photographs she was always dressed in the most absurd fashion in cardigans and stockings." Sally was now wearing cotton stockings herself, but had put her ankle socks over them. "She did needlework as well, you know. 'Needlework is an invention of the devil to keep fools from applying their hearts to wisdom.'"

"Who might Sumner Partridge be?" asked James, extinguishing his cigarette and putting his arm round the back of Sally's chair.

"My dearest bro'," Doris began, "I've not heard you ask so many questions since we told you about that American captain looking you up. Whatever happened..."

"Oh, *do* let's move to the other room," said Sally. "My fingers are dreaming of a Bach sonata. The one that starts 'Um da da da dum dum...'"

"Is that Bach then?" asked Fred. "Sounds like Ivor Novello." He pushed his chair back, earning a grateful glance from Sally.

The evening passed pleasantly enough with Sally providing music while James glanced at a heavy volume on the German Expressionist painters that Doris had brought home. Kate, who was playing a frustrating game of gin rummy with Doris, glanced surreptitiously at him from time to time. When Doris asked him whether he didn't think Max Beckmann was "smashing," he shrugged and answered, "That cynical international sort of thing's too far off the great German tradition to suit my taste."

"Felix says they represent the very *best* German tradition and the sooner it reappears the better for the world."

James didn't bother to answer and Kate thought, *So much for Felix*.

About 11 o'clock Fred appeared with cups of weak frothy coffee and a plate of biscuits on a tray. When he came to Kate he said kindly, "This will help you to sleep, my dear. We none of us drink tea at bedtime. Too stimulating by half."

"Doris?"
"Um-m-m?"
"Are you awake?"
"No."
"Oh."

Kate turned over and pushed her face into her pillow. She could not sleep, not at all. Standing on the upstairs landing Sally had advised them all to "sink at once into the arms of Morpheus," and when Fred had directed a friendly glance toward her Kate had suddenly been reminded of Harry Feather jerking his head toward Fan and saying, "*Don't mind her.*"

She was frightened. She knew that she had counted on adventure and romance, and a mystery should be a bonus — imagine regaling the table at Barnaby's with her scene at Scotland Yard! Even the most jaded members of the group — Mrs. B. herself and Svengali (whose real name was Louie Callahan) — would hang gasping on every word. But after all, despite her demur, Fred had been right. A terrible crime had been committed. And she knew, somehow, more about it than she had so far revealed, even to herself. Madame Sosostris had given her a clue and then vanished. Scotland Yard wanted to know that clue. And so did someone else, someone who had looked at her beside the lake.

She turned again and stared at a bar of light that splintered and shifted across the ceiling. I don't believe that *was* James Bell there in the park, watching me. I'll ask him. She said these thoughts to herself in a methodical way, then added in a rush of feeling, *I'm not going out alone after dark.*

On the other hand, the exciting promise of her voyage seemed to have melted away. Her shipboard acquaintances were playing no major role in her life. Tony had vanished into his own world, dropping a brief letter as proof of passage. Tom Burrows might have gone up in smoke. Lisa Dragonette was more than indifferent, and clearly had no intention of providing Kate with an entree to the London theatrical scene. And Sam, who had said more than once that he would phone her, never had. So much for Sam. She had never taken him for a sincere type anyway. Not like Tony. Sigh. Sleek Lisa and shaggy Sam were birds of a feather despite appearances.

As for Sumner Partridge, he had turned into a good friend. A good friend is better than rubies, but 3000 miles away? Another sigh. Doris stirred.

"Are you asleep, Doris?"

"Yes."

"Oh."

I love Doris, though, and Sally. Sally was, for Kate, being Home. She wished Sally were her mother — ankle socks, piano, and all. She thought that if her own mother could somehow be aware of that wish she wouldn't mind, being her mother. Mothers were not jealous. Sally Bell would certainly never be jealous or possessive. That was why her children loved her so much. James loves her too, that's clear, even though he's so cool. *But not as much as she loves him.*

They all said James was rattled by the war. That's funny. They're all rattled by James. Even Doris, the great sibling rival. They should all relax.

We should *all* relax. With that she sat up and put her feet over the side of her bed, groping for her fuzzy slippers. She slipped them on and wrapped herself in her bathrobe. Once she found the door and opened it she could see by a dim light on the stairs. She descended as quietly as she could and opened the kitchen door. James Bell was sitting at the kitchen table with a glass before him; Salammbo was on his lap.

"Hello, Kate," he said.

"Hello, James."

"I shouldn't have taken you for an insomniac. Are you hungry?"

"Not really. Perhaps I'll have some warm Ovaltine."

"Doris is snoring, I suppose."

"No. Was Salammbo?"

"You've noticed what a loud motor she has. But no. I sometimes have trouble."

"It's war nerves, I guess. They said you had had a rough time." She flushed.

"Not especially. It's just my arm bothers."

"You manage beautifully. I would've thought you'd been left-handed at birth."

"Perhaps I was, secretly. The left hand is the hand of the imagination, you know. I'm afraid I find a lot of right-handed rational types hard to take these days. The ones who want to face facts."

"Oh, dear. I've just been facing facts furiously. That's why I got up."

"Not to worry. I think you must have your share of imagination, judging by the panic in the park." His hard blue eyes were disconcerting in the fierce glare of the kitchen light. Sally, who cooked, was nearsighted.

"It really *was* you, all the time?"

"Must have been. It was I, and the shadows, and the odd noises. One gets into a state sometimes. I noticed it coming out of Germany. Every fence post was an enemy."

"Oh, how ever did you escape? It's so *thrilling*. And all the Nazis after you. Were you alone? Oh, I want to know everything."

"Ah, you must come to Moon Croft, fair cousin. I shall tell you an installment every evening while the fire roars up the chimney." He smiled. That's the second time, she thought.

"I want terribly to come. To see the moors…and everything. I just must wait for Doris."

"Must you then?"

She started looking noisily for a saucepan to warm her milk. James rattles all of us, she thought.

Chapter XVI

> CABALA, however, is the word; nor let the secret escape thee even in thy dreams.
>
> —Samuel Richardson, *Clarissa*

"Now then, Miss, I hope you've been managing to enjoy your visit to England, in spite of your troubles on the way?" Inspector Bucket made a question of it. He glanced at a folder of papers on the desk before him. My *dossier*, thought Kate. "You look and sound a proper Yank if you'll pardon my saying so. My youngest daughter was very pally with a Yank during the war. Cheerful chap. Turned out to have a wife and three little ones at some place called Kalamazoo."

"Oh, I've been having a good time I guess. I love England. Besides, my whole family is here." Inspector Bucket assumed an avuncular expression. "What there is of it," she added.

"What *is* there of it, again?" he asked. "I have the very excellent reports taken down by Sergeant Kipp at Southampton, of course, but as a matter of routine I'd like to review it now that you've settled in."

"You haven't made any progress on the case, then?"

"I wouldn't say that, Miss, no, I wouldn't say that. In fact we never say that." The Inspector emptied his pipe with a brisk knock into a large tin ashtray on the desk. "However I think it would simplify procedure if you left the questions to me. Routine, you know. Routine's the thing hereabouts."

"Well, there's my cousin Sally Bell. She's a first cousin once removed. She was my father's first cousin."

"Your father left no brothers or sisters?"

"My father's only brother died last summer. He lived in America."

"And your mother's family?"

"My mother came from Australia as a sort of nursery maid when she was very young. No one from there's ever written to me. Cousin Sally told me a man in the ANZAC appeared at tea time once during the war and said he was a cousin of Hannah Raferty — that was my mother — but after eating ten scones and a whole pot of Damson jam he never wrote or came back. I could tell she didn't care much for him."

"Well, that's all right then. Plenty of those sort of scenes during the war. The far-flung seeds of Empire brought home in full flower, if you take my point. Now had your father any other close cousins, do you know, besides this Sally Bell?"

"Cousin Sally had only one brother too, and he was killed in 1917. She says there are some cousins in Yorkshire that she had a falling out with before the war. That's it. But she's married herself and has two grown children."

"Ah, yes. I was getting there. Those children are...?"

"James and Doris. James was in the RAF. He escaped from Germany, and he lost an arm. He hasn't settled on a career, but he lives in a house his grandfather bought in Yorkshire, on the moors."

"Bit lonely in the winter, it can be up in those parts. I'm a southern man myself. He's on his own, then? Hasn't settled down with a wife?"

"No, I think someone comes in from the village — it's called Netherbeck — to cook and clean for him. Doris is an artist, but she makes oil paintings out of photographs for a living. She's at home at the moment."

"Home?"

"In East Tinkham. 35, The Oval. Where I am. You've got it written down."

"So I do. And you have been staying there since you arrived just over a fortnight ago?"

"Uh-huh." Scotland Yard, as personified by Inspector Bucket, was very unintimidating.

"Any plans to see more of the country?"

"I'm going to visit James in Yorkshire in a few days."

"Alone?"

"Maybe. Doris wants to come but she's got a big glop of new work." Kate sensed an unspoken query. "I suppose you think it wouldn't be proper for me to stay there just with my cousin James."

"*Second* cousin, Miss."

"James says there's an old inn just down the road where I can stay. It doesn't get many overnight guests at this time of year. It's mainly the local pub for the farmers."

"That's all right, then. We'd just like the name before you go."

"I could phone. But I don't suppose there's much in Netherbeck."

"To be sure, Miss. All the same, we'll have the name."

"But, Inspector, the thing I don't see is why you want to know all this. I mean none of this has anything to do with Frances Birdsill. *Or* Fan Feather. I mean I want to help you if I can, but..."

"At the Yard, we are very thorough, Miss, very, very, thorough. We're known worldwide for being exceptionally thorough. You wouldn't be in a hurry at all?"

"Oh, no." Kate looked at her watch and discovered she'd forgotten to wind it.

"What would you say to a cup of coffee, Miss? I generally have one myself round about now."

Kate had learned that English morning coffee, while not the eye-opener you got at Nedick's, was not designed as a sedative. She said, "Yes, *please*." She had had very little sleep. Inspector Bucket dinged a bell, and a rosy young man soon appeared with a tray.

"Black or white?" The Inspector gripped the twin steaming jugs.

"Black, please."

"I think you'd best have some milk, though," he said, pouring from both jugs simultaneously, quite as if he hadn't asked.

While they drank their coffee and ate some of those ubiquitous biscuits that reminded Kate of fake cookies for a stage tea party, the Inspector chatted about the pleasures of sea travel. When their cups were empty he resumed his questions.

"Have you seen any of your shipmates since arriving in England? Have you heard from Christopher Anthony MacLeod-Smith for example?"

"I had a letter from someplace near Inverness. Very short."

"May I ask whether a meeting has been arranged?"

"Not exactly. But he said I should let him know if I planned to leave Kent."

"At what address?"

"He said that he was spending some time with his aunt. I think it's her shooting box." Kate produced an envelope from her handbag.

"Ah..." said the Inspector, holding out his hand. "You wouldn't object to my taking just a glance at that envelope, now? Very fine handwriting. Neat but not gaudy. Did he happen to mention where he went to school, by any chance?"

"I've forgotten if he did. He was an officer in the army though."

"Yes indeed. Would you know his aunt's name, by any chance?"

"Hesperia MacLeod. He told me. There was a friend of hers on the ship called Lady Tingley-ffinch."

Inspector Buckct seemed reluctant to part with the envelope.

"I don't suppose you have the letter to this about you, Miss?"

"No." Kate tried not to look guilty.

"Well. Thoughtful of you to save the envelope, then." He turned it over. "I'd like to keep it in this file."

"Okay."

"And what about your countryman Mr. Burrows then? If I'm not mistaken he assisted you in finding the body?"

"He assisted me in *not* finding the body, you mean. That's why no one would believe me at first."

"Right. But I thought you very wisely decided not to tell anyone, Miss Clark. No use creating a panic on a ship, you said to yourself."

"But I went to the purser's office right away. *He* didn't believe me. Well, hardly. Inspector Bucket, you must have all this in your file."

"Soft and slow, Miss. No harm in filling in the background, painting in the clouds, taking a fresh look back. We must always go back, Miss. You see a criminal investigation begins at the end of the story. Especially a murder."

He filled his pipe again, tamping down the tobacco with a broad thumb. "Meanwhile we don't want the future to catch us napping. The principals are rushing about. I would be pleased to know to what extent they make contact with one another."

"But, Inspector Bucket, why do you call the people I just happened to be friendly with on the ship 'principals'? There were hundreds of people on the ship, *hundreds*. Paulette Goddard was on the ship. *I* found the body. So what? As Chico Marx said, 'That's an elephant.'"

"A red herring, possibly. An elephant, no. We are not inclined to regard your meeting with the late Frances Birdsill on the Orange Blossom Limited as mere chance. No more are you." He looked at her shrewdly. "If you are hiding something, Miss, I think you are under a misapprehension. And you may tell me all the same. Have a chocolate?"

He had produced a half-pound box of Black Magic from his drawer. He must think she was an absolute child. She took the second biggest.

"Amongst other possibilities I am considering this possibility," he went on. "One of the several persons who sought to make your acquaintance on the ship may have done so for *the same reason as the murdered woman did*."

She gasped.

"That had not occurred to you?"

She shook her head.

"Very natural. A pleasant young woman such as yourself will be used to attracting acquaintances. It's our job to ask questions; therefore we look for questions to ask. Very natural. Now let me ask you again: What contact, if any, have you had with Thomas Burrows in England?"

"None at all. He didn't even ask to help with my bags at the boat train. I thought he might have, seeing as how the Dragon Lady had disappeared."

"That'll be Miss Lisa Dragonette, I suppose you mean. You haven't happened to just see him anywhere, Burrows I mean, just by chance?"

"Not that I know of."

"Why would you put it that way, I ask myself. Have you seen someone who resembles him, then?"

Kate thought of the trees by the lake, and the shifting shadows, and the figure that she still did not believe was James Bell. "Last night I was in the park..."

"Yes? Yes?"

"And I thought a man was watching me...it was getting dark so I couldn't tell...at least he looked tall."

"And there was something about him that suggested Thomas Burrows, then? The way he stood? Some gesture?" Inspector Bucket, a bloodhound leashed, leaned toward her.

"No."

"What then? Something you know of Burrows, some suspicion you had of him on the ship, made you feel that he could be the man?"

"I don't know. I don't know why I said it. My cousin James had come to meet me. He said he must have been the one who frightened me." Something made her add, "James wouldn't know anyone from the ship. Unless he knew Sam."

"Mr. Sam Gordon, yes. I was coming to him. But soft and slow we go hereabouts. A man may or may not have been watching you in a suspicious manner. Looking back on the incident the name of Burrows crossed your mind. Did this figure withdraw?"

"No, *I* did. I ran away along by the lake." Kate realized that she was still frightened. "I suppose I was silly."

"The lake, you say. That'll be the King's Park in East Tinkham, I persume. Quite a wilderness in places, is the King's Park. I'd be obliged if you wouldn't go off the beaten paths on your own, Miss. Not so well used this time of the year, you know. Had you some reason to be there at dusk last evening? Walking the dog, I expect?"

"It was just chance that I was alone. My cousin Doris had to go on an errand suddenly and we agreed to meet by the lake."

"And James Bell came instead."

"Yes. What do *you* think?"

"Stick to daylight, Miss, for the present."

"But I'll be okay in Yorkshire."

"No doubt. Register with the local police when you arrive, though." Kate looked alarmed. "Just a formality, you know," the Inspector added. He seemed to consult a list. "Now, then, to Mr. Gordon. You have seen him, perhaps? Had a date, as they say in the States?"

"Certainly not." The Inspector raised his eyebrows. "If you want to know about Sam Gordon you should ask Lisa Dragonette. The only time I've seen either of them they were having tea for two at Gunter's."

"I presume you were with another party?"

"I was with an American friend who flew over. His name is Sumner Partridge. He's gone back now."

"And did Mr. Gordon take note of your presence at all? Was there some conversation?"

"He came over to our table and ate some of our cakes. He was his usual self." The Inspector took note of Kate's quarter smile.

"Mr. Gordon is an amusing chap then? Gay, witty, charming, clever, attractive?"

"That sounds like something he'd put down on his resume."

"I can't help but observe, Miss, a certain unexpected caustic note in your remarks. I was under the impression—" he glanced at his list — "that Mr. Gordon was perhaps your particular friend on the voyage."

Kate was amazed. "If I understand you, Inspector Bucket, you couldn't be more mistaken. It was Sam and Lisa all the way. I suggested that you get in touch with her. Whatever gave you such a weird idea?"

"Mr. Gordon himself, Miss. He must have mistook himself." The Inspector's expression seemed meant to pacify.

"Sam Gordon was kidding, Inspector. I *would* think he'd be serious about a matter of life and death."

"Yes, yes. But it doesn't matter to us, you know. We learn just as much from a lie as from the truth. False impressions are as good as affidavits hereabouts. By indirections we find directions out, Miss, don't you know? Sam Gordon, no, nor his fancy lady friend with the *nom de guerre*" — he pronounced it 'nomdigwhere' — "neither, pulls no wool over these eyes."

"Well, okay. I suppose you know what he *does* in that case. He doesn't seem to do anything. I mean Tony's rich, or at least he helps his rich aunt, Tom's a salesman, Lisa's in the theater..."

"Same as you are, Miss."

"Well, sort of."

"Perhaps he's like your cousin, Miss. Still up in the air about the future. You say they were acquainted in the war, eh?"

"Oh, just maybe, very slightly. Anyway Sam has both arms." To her extreme chagrin, Kate blushed slightly. The Inspector appeared not to notice. She forged ahead. "Anyway I've seen Sam once by chance and Lisa once by chance but they've obviously seen each other by appointment. I had a post card from the Collinses, if you're interested."

"Yes, the Australian couple. What would you say to their being long lost relatives of yours on your Mum's side?"

"Nothing doing, Inspector. Nice try, though." She grinned.

"I suppose you asked them." She nodded.

"Well, right-o then. If anything occurs that strikes you as at all out of the way, *at all out of the way*, why I'd be obliged if you'd let me know personally, Miss. Here is the telephone number. Say who you are and ask for me. Of course in an emergency just consult the nearest constable. You'll find him anxious to be of assistance."

"Thank you." She paused. "You couldn't — well — tell me anything interesting you've found out so far?"

"Not at this point. Not just at this point. We don't circulate information without good reason, you know. We have to see the good of it, Miss. We're not the BBC."

"Oh. Well, thanks for the chocolate anyway."

"Like another?"

"No thanks. Thanks though."

"Cheerio, then, Miss."

"Bye."

The rosy cheeked young man appeared and held the door for her. The Tarot card seemed to be sending out powerful signals from her handbag but Inspector Bucket just smiled and turned away. Kate was concealing evidence in the very heart of Scotland Yard.

Chapter XVII

> Indiscretion was my bugbear fault.
> —Mrs. Gaskell, *Cranford*

Kate and James had come into town together that morning. Kate had hoped that a lunch invitation would be forthcoming — surely James would want to hear about her interview at the Yard! — but there was nothing doing. James bid her a casual good-bye at King's Cross, saying that he had an acquaintance to see in Cartwright Gardens. If she liked, he could meet her at the station buffet at four.

Thus it turned out that when Inspector Bucket had finished with her Kate found herself with the luxury of several hours to dispose of exactly as she pleased in what Fred Bell gravely called "the capital of the Empire."

A comparatively fine morning had dissolved, and the air was full of water, which seemed not so much falling as simply getting in the way and making everything damp. She had not yet been to the British Museum. Clearly, this was the day for it, and she plunged into the nearest tube station and consulted a map.

She had some notion of ticking off the most famous objects — Rosetta stone, Portland vase, and so on — but once inside the main doors she decided to simply wander. She turned right, and quickly lost herself among the manuscripts. At Lord Nelson's last letter to Emma Hamilton she found herself thinking, *he lost an arm too.*

She wandered among cabinets and cases in an aimless fashion, sometimes stopping to stare in wonder, other times pondering James' good looks, Tony's good manners, Sam's raffish charm, and Inspector Bucket's reassuring solidity. She was glad Inspector Bucket was there. When he found out about the evidence that she had withheld — as, doubtless, he *would* find out — he would smile and offer her another chocolate. She didn't suppose he got any extra ration, either. On no account would he allow her to be shipped off to Newgate in handcuffs. Meanwhile, not to worry. All she had to do was to keep an eye out for a constable and to stay out of lonely places.

This was a lonely place.

On a week day morning in autumn the British Museum, beyond the pen scratch busyness of the Reading Room, could be almost as empty as the park at twilight. Alternately gazing and musing, Kate made her way through the King's Library and ascended the northeast staircase. For some time she had been roaming among the antiquities of the upper floor in solitary reverie.

Eventually she found herself in a narrow room crammed with Grecian urns. She was just wondering which one was the still unravished bride of quietness when some quality of the silence around her gave her pause. She had heard such a silence before. The cheap white crockery of the quondam tearoom super-imposed itself on a generous one-armed krater. Why wasn't anybody watching this stuff?

Somewhere in another gallery she heard a soft footfall. What if it was her pursuer, the King's Park phantom? She ran, not waiting to find out. This time she hadn't far to go.

"'old it, Miss, 'old it," said a red haired young man who was dusting a case directly in her path. "Wot's up? One of them Hegyptians give you a bad turn?" He smirked. "There's high jinks round 'ere after closing hif I know anythink."

"Certainly not," said Kate, promptly assuming a dignified manner. "My watch seems to have stopped and I was afraid of being late for meeting my friend. Do you happen to know what time it is?"

"About 'arf past, I'd say," he answered. "I go by my digestion or lack of same. Hif your friend's an American — same as wot you are I presume — I last seen 'im in with the 'ittites."

"Oh, really? I wonder whether it *could* be my friend. What did he look like?"

"Bit dark, with a beard. Very pleasant. Knowed 'is 'ittites, 'e did. Matter of that 'e asked 'ad I seen a young lady. Which I 'adn't, things being so slow. Hif I was you I'd go back the way I came, Miss."

There were plenty of beards in England. "Oh, that's not my friend, I'm afraid," said Kate. "My friend is a tall blond man. Thanks, though."

She hurried to the front stairs, then descended nonchalantly into the main hall. By this time it was almost crowded.

"I say, Hilary, I s'll have to get a new macintosh during this reign," said a loud cheerful voice near her ear.

"Well, let's get a cup of tea. That'll put us right," was the answer.

That's it, thought Kate. There was a Tea and Coffee Room in the basement. No doubt there would be some starchy fodder. She was very hungry.

The refreshment room was busier than she had expected. She was standing with her tray looking for an empty seat when a familiar voice said, "Miss Clark...Kate...are you alone then?"

She turned and saw Felix standing at a nearby table. "Won't you join us?" She occupied an empty place gratefully. There was another young man there, eating a big sticky bun. Like Felix, he was rather shabby. He had a cheerful expression and ears that stuck out like the handles of an urn.

"Kate, may I present my friend George Holloway?"

"Like the gaol," said George through his bun.

"George, this is Kate Clark, a cousin of Doris's from America."

"Delighted," said George, looking delighted.

"Where's Doris, then?" asked Felix without preamble. "I rang the studio but the ruddy phone's disconnected."

"Oh, Doris has an awful lot of work to finish. She's got brides coming out her ears. She said she'd be sporting her oak for at least a week."

"'Sporting her oak!'" cried George. "That's Doris for you. She's a caution all right, is Doris. Lucky man, Felix, lucky man. Give me a girl like Doris is what I say, and you can keep your film stars. A girl with spirit." He looked at Kate as if to see whether she might not be such a one.

"Doris is all right," said Felix complacently, and turning to Kate, "Been having a peep at the famous Elgin marbles, I suppose? Time to ship the lot back to Greece, in my opinion. In fact there are quite a few odds and ends we could fork over to the rightful owners."

"Well, as a matter of fact I haven't seen them yet. There's so much. But I thought Lord Elgin saved them from being blown up by the Turks or something."

"That's the line. The British always act from the noblest motives. It's axiomatic. We all learn it at school."

His tone was ironic but without bitterness, and George added, "Rotten cheek," pleasantly.

"Saving art from the rapacious hordes of the East has been a high-class form of theft for a good while," said Felix. "Some marvelous things have turned up missing since the war. One doesn't know whether the Russians got hold of them — or whether somebody else 'saved' them — unless they reappear."

"And then, bob's yer uncle!" added George, who had got three more buns on a plate and was passing them round.

"Oh, do you have mysterious art objects coming into your shop?" asked Kate eagerly. "I mean things without a legitimate provenance, if that's the right word?"

Felix looked amused. "My dear girl, I'm not a fence." Kate smiled at him.

"We none of us are," said George, "come to that. Ronnie Fish — that's an old mate of mine — ex-Naval type, funny, eh? — I mean being called *Fish* — Ronnie's had one or two odd events. Making copies sort of thing. All on the old up and up, no doubt, but he wonders what it's all in aid of. Just for instance, now, a bloke brought him a book with a photo of a rare old statue, a thing half a foot high supposed to be and didn't he want it *exact*? I mean to say Ronnie was to make him a copy of the thing, all fake jewels and gold paint. Well, funnily enough..."

"He got paid, didn't he?" interrupted Felix.

"Oh, yes, that's all right. Old Ronnie put the cheque under the butter dish and then he couldn't make it out for the grease."

In the Ganges that day, Felix had been complaining about James. "What was it a little statue of?" Kate asked quickly.

"It was an odd thing. A saint. Well, of course, half these things are saints. But this one had got himself hung upside down."

"Oh," said Kate, thinking how your heart could stop but you could go on talking for quite a long time afterwards.

Felix looked annoyed. "I thought you weren't to say, George. One hasn't to bleat away all the time for no good reason. Suppose it were the Queen's Necklace or something?" He turned to Kate. "It was a surprise for someone."

"Well, damn it all, why didn't you stop me? How was I to remember who the chap was?"

"You look all in, Kate," said Felix kindly. "Museums can do that. Better to take them in small doses if you have the time. Let's have some more tea all round, then I ought to get back to the shop. The lad I left in charge can barely make change of a florin." He got up and went to the counter.

"Sorry about that, Miss Clark. I mean me blathering away and you feeling done up." George looked very contrite. "You ought to take sugar in your tea, you know. There's another bun here. We've plenty of food in England, if you like buns."

"Oh, I'm okay. Just a little tired. I wish you would call me Kate. Any American would, and Felix does."

"Oh, but Felix is part of the family, isn't he? I mean it's all up to Doris. All she has to do is say the word." He looked mischievous, and added, "Oh dammit. There I go again. Never tell Felix I said, there's a girl."

"Please don't worry, George. I'll forget I met you." She smiled at him.

"Ah, just my usual luck." He laughed. "Hey, what's the matter now? You look taken aback, as the saying is."

"Oh, someone I know came in. I wonder what on earth he's doing here."

"Same as you, I expect. Quite an attraction, is the B.M."

"I guess so." She sounded dubious. Sam had seen her, and was making for the table where she and George sat. He had his leather flight jacket on and it didn't look damp. His smile was open and friendly.

"Hi, Kate. We seem to be fated to meet where the elite eat. This place gets a more interesting crowd than Gunter's though. I met Tom Burrows here one day, if you can believe it. Maybe we should plan a reunion."

Felix came up with the tea and Kate murmured, "Sam Gordon...Felix Fox...George Holloway."

"Have a pew," said George affably. "There's bags of room here. Felix and I have to make tracks anyway in short order."

Felix put the tray down and shook hands, adding, "I'm glad Kate's found another friend. I think she's been overdoing it."

Sam looked at her intently. "Not to worry. I'll see her home safely. Just let me join you in a mug of the local brew."

He got his tea and the three men chatted amiably. Sam mentioned a new excavation in Palestine, George knew something about it, Felix was reminded of some barrows in East Anglia, and the talk washed pleasantly around Kate. Felix seemed reluctant to break away, and gave Sam his card with the address of his shop. "I happen to have one or two things that might interest you," he said, then flushed and added, "Of course I have no interest in *selling* anything."

"I'll drop in," said Sam. "I'll call first. Maybe we could go out for some bread and cheese."

"Oh, splendid, then. Let's be off, George." George told Kate that it had been a pleasure, Felix said that he would see her soon, and then she was alone with Sam.

She turned on him. "You have some explaining to do, Sam Gordon."

"Ask me anything. I have nothing to hide."

"Why are you following me?"

"Well, for one thing I'm interested in your eyes. They're a funny color. What color is it, anyway? I suppose you've made a study of the subject."

"Don't be silly. I know now why you told Inspector Bucket that you were my — oh, I don't know how to put it..."

"Boyfriend?" His expression was helpful.

"Something like that. You wanted to have an official excuse for harassing me and butting into my private conversations."

"My dear Kate, I can't tell you how flattered I am that two chance meetings in as many weeks can appear to you as a deluge of attentions. What do you do when I'm not around? Write in your diary?"

His case was plausible, but she felt that she occupied the kind of higher ground that Henry James was so fond of. "Why were you looking at the Hittites? The guard told me you were asking about a young lady."

"You seem to have forgotten that I have been in London off and on for several years. You are not the only young lady of my acquaintance, no matter what ambitions you may have."

This challenge activated a thermal cauldron in Kate. The rising steam seemed to blur her vision. She seized a solitary dry bun and took a choking mouthful.

"As for the Hittites," he added casually, "they are my particular turf. I was a graduate student in ancient history when the war broke out."

"Tell me another."

"My name is S. Pimpernel. The beard is from Harrod's. If you damage it in any way you'll have to pay for it. It's a good one."

"Can't you *ever* be serious?" Suddenly she felt miserable.

He reached across the table and covered her hand. "Kate, listen to me. I *am* serious. I've been called in to Scotland Yard and I presume you have too. I don't know what the Inspector knows or what he told you..."

"He was very nice. He gave me a chocolate."

"...but it's clear they're looking for a link between you and the Birdsill woman. I thought your finding her was a fluke. Maybe I was wrong. Kate, are you protecting someone?"

"No! Who are you to ask me questions, anyway?"

"I think I'm one of the suspects and it happens to be a hell of an inconvenience. As you and Inspector Bucket have no doubt noticed, some of my identity cards are missing. I'm not a certified gent, like Tony, or a salesman from Ohio, like Tom Burrows, or a working career woman, like Lisa..."

A switched-on hundred-watt light bulb seemed to materialize over Kate's head. Sam the lone operator. "I see. You are playing your own game and you don't want the police nosing around."

"Something like that."

"What is it?" He looked at her in amazement. "I won't tell," she added. "It's nothing awful, is it?"

"*You won't tell*. Kate, for God's sake stay close to your family until this business is cleared up." He looked stern.

"Well, I have to go and meet my cousin. He'll look after me."

"He?"

"My cousin James Bell."

"I'll come with you."

"Don't bother."

"It's no bother at all. Where are you meeting?"

"King's Cross."

"A happy coincidence. Just exactly where I wanted to go."

"What for? It's not a very interesting station."

"You're wrong about that. It's got a lot of English atmosphere."

"If you like damp smoke."

"England has something for everybody."

Chapter XVIII

> He thought for to devise
> How he might have her companye,
> That so did 'maze his eyes.
> —"King Copetua and the Beggar Maid" (anon.,1612)

"Hi, James. This is Sam Gordon. He was on the ship with me."

James offered his left hand with a distant nod. To Kate he said, "We must board directly — unless you don't mind missing the train. You're rather late."

"Okay by me," said Sam. "I was just propping Kate up temporarily. I did think you and I might be acquainted, though, Bell."

James gave Sam one of his light blue stares. "Under what circumstances?"

"I was in the 13th Fighter Wing. Kate tells me you were a hot pilot..." Sam seemed to be doing some kind of Mickey Rooney impersonation.

"I was a pilot, yes. I was downed on a reconnaissance flight in 1943." His tone did not invite inquiry.

"Ah, yes. You escaped from the famous Kahlberg. I guess you must be writing a book about it. Clean up while you can. I sure as hell would."

"I dare say you would. Kate, shall we go?" He took her arm and began moving toward the trains.

"Good-bye, Sam," said Kate. "Thanks."

"Anytime," he answered, grinning. "I'll be seeing you." He watched them climb into a smoking compartment. Kate could see him from the window, still standing there, when the train pulled away.

James and Kate had been the last to board, and they sat opposite each other, squeezed on either side by shoppers with parcels. Kate had been irritated first by Sam, then by James. It had been a day and a half. She rested her head against the back of the seat and closed her eyes to slits. Like a sleepy cat, she watched James extract and light a cigarette, shaking his head impatiently at a fluffy woman who tried to help.

Very soon she dozed off. At Friars Hopfield James touched her arm gently. They were alone.

"We are nearly there, Kate. I see why your friend was propping you up. *You are* tired. Come north with me. You'll sleep at Netherbeck. It's darker."

"Oh, James." She opened her eyes slowly against the dazzle of his hair in the last of the light. The dull day was going out in glory. "It's all gold in the north — like the Vikings and the Saxons and the Midnight Sun."—

"The sun sleeps at this time of year. The fires are all magic. The nights are getting longer."

"I'll wait for Doris."

"You'd much better not. You could come with me tomorrow on the train." He studied her face. "You'll be all right at the Brown Bull, you know. It's been there for some two hundred years." The cool note was back.

The train stopped with a grunt and a puff. James swung down easily and held out his arm for Kate. Twenty-four hours ago she had been in the King's Park.

They took a taxi to Quo Vadis, where Sally was waiting with the kettle just off the boil.

"What's it like at Scotland Yard, then, pet?" she asked. "We've none of us been." She looked at James to see whether he would contradict her, but he was watching Kate.

"The Inspector was very pleasant. It wasn't anything special. Just a roll call of the cast, I guess."

"I suppose they have their little ways. I do myself." She poured boiling water into the teapot. "Now I've been thinking, ever since you said you were a *modern* fly, that I would like to know what Existentialism is."

"Oh," said Kate. She was aware of James, attentive. "Well, there's Being and Nothingness." Sally nodded in an encouraging fashion. "Well, um, not everything can be explained, if you follow me so far..."

"I could have told him that."

"Told who, Mother?"

"Jean Paul Sartre."

"Look, Mother," said James, looking at Kate, "you and Kate can talk about it some other time. Kate's going back with me tomorrow. We'll catch the Flying Scotsman to York and I'll show her round the Minster. I expect we'll be able to get rooms at the Links Hotel. I shall ring through to them directly. On Friday we can get the bus to Netherbeck." Seeing Sally's unspoken question he added, "There's always room at the Bull this time of year. Kate will stay there."

"Oh dear, James, what a pity."

"What do you mean?"

"I asked Simon Craddock to come in tomorrow especially to have a game of chess with you."

"Well, you'll have to take him on yourself, then." Sally looked chagrined, and he added gently, "I told you I would only be stopping for two nights."

Sally sighed, and turned to Kate. "I've not done the washing, my dear. Shall you have enough clean things?"

"Oh, plenty, thanks. I'll only stay a couple of nights myself."

The telephone rang in the hall and James got up abruptly and went to answer it. Sally said quietly, "Come back and tell me how he gets on, won't you? You know it's against my principles to fuss. It makes Doris wild if I even *breathe* over James, but all the same..." She looked sad. Kate kissed her cheek.

James had closed the door. They always closed doors. The English Closed Door Policy. At least that way you never had to wonder whether they were closing the door for any particular reason. Still, they could hear James speaking.

"I can't help you, I'm afraid. The whole matter is out of my hands. Keep off my parents, will you? It's a bore for my mother if I'm not here and my sister couldn't care less."

They heard Doris' little car bustle into the driveway and a moment later the front door banged open.

"Ring off, will you, James? I must get through to one of my customers. I've just remembered I forgot to paint her rosebuds. There she stands, all dressed in white satin — a proper vintage simpering twit — holding a bunch of grimy grey rosebuds."

Sally brightened. James returned, an angry line between his eyes.

"Someone tiresome, dear?"

"Indeed. The lack of a telephone is not the least of Moon Croft's charms." He looked at Kate. "One met so many people during the war. Well, the war is over. I don't care to be looked up by every Tom, Dick, and Harry." She knew she was meant to think of the encounter with Sam.

"Was that the American captain, by any chance? I didn't mind him, dear. At least he didn't polish off the jam tarts. He left one for your father."

The precipitous entrance of Doris made an answer unnecessary.

"Well, have you greedy beggars guzzled all the tea? Lord, since Kate moved in I feel like a *petit orphelin*."

"I'll hot it up," said Sally, seizing the teapot.

"*Qu'est-ce que ça, petit orphelin?*" said Kate.

"*Petit orphelin, petit orphelin* — some dismal kid in the French O-Levels. Hadn't a bean." Doris took her shoes off and put her feet on the fender. "Felix was waiting for me when I came out of the studio." Kate, remembering the lad who couldn't make change for a florin, wondered whether the shop supported Felix. "Said he left you at the B.M. with a reasonable chap. That praise is ever so fulsome."

"It was Sam. I told you about him." She looked at James, who was reading an article about Bayreuth in the Radio Times.

"Ah, yes, the Dragon Lady's spy friend. Felix must have been off his form today. Took him for one of those Fulbright scholars."

"Spy?" asked James, looking up.

Kate flushed. "It was a joke. The Dragon Lady's a joke too. It's fun to invent romantic stories about people on a ship, even though they're all really..." She remembered Fan, a grotesque and terrible reality. "...just going to visit their cousin." She looked at the fire.

"What *does* he do?"

"I don't know."

The front door was heard again.

"It's Dad," said Doris, jumping up to greet him. From the hall she called out, "Hooray, you lot! He's brought fish and chips. Ma, you old fox, you never said. I thought we were due for pig's liver and stark naked boiled potatoes."

"Doris, my dear," Fred Bell remonstrated. "You make it sound indecent."

"Not I," said Doris. "It was D.H. Lawrence said it. Sexy chap. Hot stuff at Oxbridge, I hear."

"Come on, then," called Sally. "The table's set. Let's not let our supper get cold."

Kate was ravenous. "Okay by me."

Early in the morning Kate and James boarded the Flying Scotsman.

"This is a very famous train," said James, when they had taken their seats and watched the station platform recede.

"Everything in England is famous," said Kate, who felt excited and cheerful. "Fish and chips and common law and fog and poetry and gorse bushes."

"Gorse bushes?" James spoke rather sharply.

"Oh, don't say there aren't gorse bushes, James. There always are."

"Natural vegetation in the Yorkshire wolds," he answered. "Not so many round Netherbeck. Mostly grass and heather on the moors."

"Oh, dear. There must be *one*."

"What for?"

"Well...I just always wanted to see a gorse bush."

"You must have seen plenty of gorse as a child. It's one of the commonest plants in Europe. It's prickly, with yellow blossoms that always seem to be blooming. I daresay you have it in the States. It's called furze as well."

"Maybe," she said, but maybe was not enough.

"I can understand wanting to see a Queen Charlotte rose or a panther orchid or even the wild swampwort for that matter, but why a gorse bush?"

James was certainly unreasonable.

"You seem to know a great deal about flowers," she said admiringly.

"Doesn't every Englishman? Our infant brains are strewn with seeds." Obviously, it was not a practice of which he approved.

"It's funny, isn't it? You don't seem so *very* much like an Englishman to me. I mean not so much as your father or Felix...or Tony Smith."

"My father and Felix are certainly basic English types — the clerk and the shopkeeper —" he was cool again "— Tony Smith is not among my acquaintance."

"Tony Smith was on the Queen Victoria. He's partly a Scot, I think. He's *called* Tony Smith, but his name is C.A. MacLeod-Smith." James gave a grudging smile, so she went on. "He's more like an English lord than anything."

"Your knowledge of the species must of necessity be somewhat limited. I presume you travelled in the Tourist Class."

"Well, everyone knows what English gentlemen are like, James. There are so many of them in plays and movies." She threw him a sidelong glance. "Oh, don't be such a stick. I bet *you* could be one if you tried."

"I don't aspire to it," he said coldly.

They were quiet for a while, but Kate was anxious to be friends. She wanted everything to be just right when she gave him the message. When he asked her to light his cigarette for him she turned eagerly. The train was near its top speed now, and he held her arm to steady the flame of the lighter. His blue eyes darkened.

The compartment was not full, but there were a pair of students in earnest conversation near the door. In the silence the girl's voice suddenly filled the space in a penetrating and superior way. "Oh, Kingsley, I do think cricket's too refined and subtle a game for anybody but the English."

James smiled at Kate, a whole smile, and she felt warm. *The fires are all magic*, she thought; then she realized that the capricious sun had come out and was pouring molten gold into her lap. The landscape basked in a radiant peace. "Oh, James," she said, "is that a castle over there in those trees?"

"Complete with the servant's washing," he answered. "I wish you could see Kahlberg."

"Oh, please tell me about it!"

His expression was inscrutable. "I must save it, Kate, or how shall I enthrall you during the long evenings? It's sheer utter quiet at Moon Croft and the company at the Bull doesn't usually run to spies with beards or members of the local gentry."

She laughed merrily. His tone seemed to cast a manageable light on her circle of acquaintances. She had filled in too many blanks, applied too much greasepaint. At that moment the door to the corridor slid open. Kate stared. So did James. Even the students, who had barely given James a tumble, were halted in mid-flow.

Bracing herself with a kid-gloved hand, Lisa Dragonette took a leisurely drag on her Balkan Sobranie. The scent of Vol de Nuit mingled seductively with the smoke. She was wearing a dark mink coat and a hat of green-black feathers that clung to one cheek like a wing at rest.

"Kate, what a charming surprise," she said in her indolent French voice. "May I join you for a moment?"

It's a free country. But James was already standing, so she murmured a minimal introduction.

"Charmed," said James.

Kate looked at him. He had to be kidding. Nobody really said "charmed." He wasn't smiling, though. He was standing very straight. If he clicked his heels she would definitely go to into her Saucy Villager act. "Lisa's a friend of Sam Gordon," she explained. That should give them both something to think about.

"Won't you sit down, Miss Dragonette?" James swept a discarded Punch from the opposite seat with an air of mild distaste.

Lisa sat gracefully, her coat parting to reveal one of those basic little black frocks from Bergdorf Goodman that seem to know their way around. Her pearls glowed like the milk of paradise. "I am so very enchanted to know you — is it Major? — Bell?"

"I'm very much ex-service," said James. His tone was not encouraging.

Lisa was, however, shameless. Smiling at Kate as if they were old and dear friends, she continued. "Of course. But you wear your military honors with great distinction." James looked extremely surprised. "You will forgive me if I observe that one sees many more such *blessés* in Germany. Perhaps the German military surgeons were more ruthless."

"The Germans saved my life. In Germany, as in England, however, the subject is not usually discussed among strangers."

Stuff that in your cigarette holder and smoke it, thought Kate.

Lisa assumed a stricken expression. "Please forgive me, both of you. You will have observed that I am neither an Angle nor a Saxon." Her eyes seemed to almondize. She turned to Kate and said, "I'm glad you have found so distinguished a companion, *ma chère*. Travelling alone can be..." She shrugged.

"We're cousins," said Kate shortly.

"Ah!" Lisa wore the expression of one who has solved a puzzle. "But you have perhaps made rendezvous with some of our recent acquaintances? And the dear Inspector Bucket? So extraordinarily considerate. But perhaps he has a penchant for the ladies." She rearranged her person for display purposes.

"Of course I saw the Inspector." Kate let it go at that.

"You travel for pleasure?" Kate nodded. James' silence was courteous and attentive. "I also. I am on the holiday."

"What's doing with *Pink Gardenias?*"

"For me, *rien*. My task has accomplished itself. And you? Do you hope to find work in the theater here?"

"I didn't know you knew."

"But of course. *Bien sûr.* We are fellow professionals, no? I think you would be wise to seek work in the provinces."

"Thanks a lot."

"For myself I require to be refreshed. I crave solitude. I need it." She glanced at James. "I shall walk about the Yorkshire moors."

"Watch out you don't land in a bog. I should have thought an intimate *pique-nique* in the Bois de Boulogne was more your speed, Lisa."

"You know Paris?" Lisa asked innocently.

"Everybody knows Paris. You don't have to go there." Kate was magnificently irked. "If you're going walking you'll need some shoes."

This sally served to draw attention to Lisa's elegant little alligator pumps, not to mention the ankles that went with them. Kate looked at her own size eight loafers with contempt. James looked faintly amused.

"I have some excellent walking shoes. They are made in Zurich." Lisa stood up languidly. "Please do not bother to rise, Mr. Bell. Perhaps we shall meet on the moors."

"The chances of that are slight, Miss Dragonette. There are so many moors in Yorkshire." He stood up. "You will find as much solitude as you require."

Kate smiled in satisfaction. Maybe Sam would follow Lisa. Fine. They could wuther on the heights all they wanted to.

Lisa glided out, leaving an aura.

"You don't care for the Dragon Lady," said James.

"You remembered the name. But James, isn't she glamourous though?"

"Splendid pearls," he replied.

The excitement over, the girl by the door let her voice go again and was heard remarking, "But, Kingsley, I didn't even know what *a priori* meant until last Friday."

Chapter XIX

> And prithee when do they light the lamps?
> —Laurence Sterne, *Tristram Shandy*

It was just November; the days ended early. James suggested that they check their bags at the station and walk round the city walls in what was left of the pale sunshine.

"I've heard of the walls of York," said Kate, following James through the crowd and into a torrent of bicycles. "When Henry VIII put down the Pilgrimage of Grace they hanged some of the leaders from the walls of York."

James turned and looked at her. "You surprise me," he said.

"Oh, one simply knows these odds and ends," she said airily. "It's all *a priori* in my case." She was a good mimic and James smiled. He seemed much less intimidating away from the deferential atmosphere of Quo Vadis. "Do *you* know much, James? I can't tell."

"I'm not a bookish type, if that's what you mean. Nor am I one of your Americans with a passion for owning information." He steered her to the opposite sidewalk. "We shall mount the wall at the Micklegate Bar. That's where traitors' heads were displayed in less dreary times, as that sort of thing appeals to you. It takes about two hours to go right round. Half that should exhaust us and the daylight."

He forged ahead, not turning to see whether or not she was keeping up. A thick pedestrian flow was against them. James sped along with surprising agility, maneuvering easily through disappearing loopholes. By the time they reached the narrow steps that scaled the wall Kate felt as though she were back in Times Square.

"You'll excuse me for not offering you my arm," said James. "I sometimes have use for it in these sort of places."

"I must say you look cool as a wombat. Half the crowd was gazing at you down there. I was afraid they wouldn't be able to tell that I was with you." She was flushed with hurrying and had pushed her scarf into her pocket.

"You do look winded. And what have you done with your hair?" His voice had an indulgent note.

"This looked like a good place for the well-known gargoyle on vacation."

She fished for her pocket comb, but James said, "I shouldn't bother up here, you know."

Their section of the walkway was empty. Kate stopped to gaze across grass and roofs at the great cathedral glowing in the westering light. James was watching her, and she was uncomfortably aware of it. "It's nice," she said lamely.

"Long before that went up there was a Roman town at York. Two Caesars died here, and Constantine the Great was proclaimed emperor...but I suppose you've got it all pat?"

"Not really. I get my history out of novels and movies, if you must know. Do you like the Romans, James?"

"Not at all. Endless regiments tramping blindly across a world of gods and heroes they were incapable of understanding."

"Sounds sort of like the Germans to me. At least the tramping part."

"You oughtn't to confound the Nazi war machine with the Germans, Kate. German ideals, German culture — these are among the highest expressions of western civilization. The Nazis simply exploited the bitterness all Germans felt at the injustices of the Versailles peace. They could have gained power among any vigorous people, given the circumstances after the Great War."

"Applesauce."

"I beg your pardon?"

"Well, I don't agree." Kate looked at him and found his expression serene and a little patronizing. She went on. "They seem to have treated *you* pretty well, anyhow. Did you soften them up by singing Wagner in the shower? And then of course you look so very very Aryan." She wasn't really sure that her tone was justified. The war was over. There was a peace on, though Sally said you wouldn't know it when you went to buy the Sunday joint.

"I look rather like my Uncle Oswald, actually. Although he died fighting for England, he also admired German intellectual and cultural achievements, and was attracted by the heroic legends of the people." James spoke calmly. His blue eyes displayed no pique at her remarks. "Did my mother tell you about him? She was very fond of him."

"'He whom this scroll commemorates, at the call of King and Country, left all that was dear to him...'" Kate's voice was hushed, her eyes full of the minster that seemed to ride like a ship in bands of horizontal light.

"Yes. That would be he."

"Funny. I didn't get the impression that Cousin Oswald was a 'gods and heroes' yo-ho-te-to-to type."

Two schoolboys came hurrying along the narrow walk, jostling each other and laughing. "Pardon!" they shouted. "Pardon!" They had short grey coats and brown satchels.

"You'd do well to be rather more careful," James admonished them.

They looked at him, awestruck, then went on more soberly. "I *told* you not to be such a guy," said the bigger one sternly.

"Guy," said Kate, when they were out of earshot.

"Guy Fawkes came from York," said James. "Perhaps you want to see his grave. Americans seem to be rather keen on it for some reason."

"A penny for the old Guy."

"Yes. Did you miss him in America?"

"We had the Fourth of July."

"Let's go on." He smiled at her.

He never smiles ironically or sourly or cheerfully or sardonically or grimly or humorously, thought Kate. He just has that one smile. But it's a bobby-dazzler all right.

"James?"

"Yes, Kate?"

"What's a bobby-dazzler?"

"It's a typical English vulgarism."

"Well, it can't be all that vulgar. Your father said that Princess Elizabeth was a proper bobby-dazzler up close. You can't tell from photographs."

"My father's diction seldom adds distinction to the language."

"I don't get you, James. I'm glad I don't have to be English after all." She gave him an oblique glance but couldn't decipher his expression.

"You have no choice."

"Of course I do. I can have dual citizenship if I like."

"You'll stay here."

The "no" her mouth formed changed to an "oh!" and James followed her glance to the dancing flame of stained glass struck by the dying sun.

"*Look*," she pleaded, aware that James had turned from the cathedral to gaze at her again. She flushed, and glanced down at the crowd below. The streets were jammed, and more and more people were spilling out of doors toward the end of a working day.

Kate saw a man she knew walking along purposefully, a tartan scarf around his neck. Her heart crashed in the vicinity of her knees.

"Tony!" she shouted. "Tony!" Her voice was blown sky high before it could join the blanket of traffic sounds that made a woolly wall around him. She turned to James imploringly. "It's Tony. I know it is. I *must* speak to him. I've just got to. Oh, where can I get down?"

"Don't be absurd, Katherine."

"Katherine?" she mouthed, no voice in it.

"You're making a spectacle of yourself."

A middle-aged couple was coming toward them, needing room to pass. The man was round with several chins; his companion wore a prickly green tweed suit. He had some sort of animal under his arm; her pockets bulged dangerously.

James flattened Kate against the wall, saying, "Your friend can't possibly hear you and there are hundreds of people milling about."

"James, please. I really want to see him. I told you about him. Oh, come on." She pushed past him and rushed along the path that clung to the inside of the white wall. Looking back, she saw that he was not following her. "Okay, I'll meet you at the baggage check in the station then. No! I'll meet you at the Links Hotel. I'll find it. I'll get a cab." She waved.

Down in the street again she turned back toward the place where she had seen Tony. She looked eagerly at the passing faces — but there were so many of them. The daylight was going fast. Occasionally she thought she glimpsed him — ahead of her (then she hurried), or down a side street (she guessed at short cuts). This way, that way, she pushed on. She was in the oldest part of the town. Above her head buildings leaned toward each other.

The lights were coming on, splotches of gaiety across the pavements. It's my time of day, she thought, remembering Inspector Bucket. Well, she certainly wasn't alone. She plunged through a handkerchief sized square, then down a street festooned with shop signs hung out like flags.

Suddenly the minster appeared, looming up magically before her, a huge intricate facade with a flash of tartan whisking inside.

"*Tony!*"

The noble front portal of the cathedral had been fitted out with a small human-sized door. As she stumbled up to it an elderly little man with a spotty red nose and a massive loop of keys barred her path.

"Closed," he said.

"But my friend just went inside."

"Nobbut us as is belonging to it, Miss."

"I'm sure, though. He's a tall man with a plaid scarf."

"Open in the ack emma."

"I *saw* him."

"Mr. Sterne, props."

"Mr. *Sterne?*"

"Incumbent over Coxwold way. Says he's meeting the dean."

"Laurence Sterne is dead," said Kate.

The little man peered at her with more interest. "You'd best be getting along to your tea, Miss."

"Oh, sugar."

"I like a bit of sugar, meself." His tone was a shade conciliatory.

"I suppose it wasn't my friend, then?"

"Just wot *I* suppose."

Her disappointment was abysmal. But it *had* been Tony she had seen from the wall. Well, why wasn't he running after her? She sighed.

"Can you tell me how to get to the Links Hotel, please?"

"Go straight along there past the Royal Liver..."

"The Royal *Liver?*"

"Their office," the old man said in a hasty manner. "Pop straight along there and you'll find a street where the cabs come along. Look sharp, mind. There's plenty be wanting 'em this time o' day." He turned away.

"Is the hotel far, do you know?"

"Right away t'other edge o' the town. I'll wish you good night." He jangled his keys.

Kate wished him goodnight and proceeded in the indicated direction. She did not, however, look sharp. She hardly looked at all. Instead, she turned her attention inward.

That she was, in a manner of speaking, madly in love with C.A. MacLeod-Smith (called Tony) was not the sole reason for her frantic pursuit of the elusive plaid scarf. She wanted someone around besides James. Already she wished she hadn't come with James the minute he asked. She could have waited for Doris, why not? It was not that she didn't like James. In a way she did, despite his absurd airs. But he looked at her too much.

On the other hand, whatever else he was, James Bell was the sort of person who could look where he liked. It was up to the people he looked at to fold up if they minded.

Whatever else he was. Indeed, there was the rub. If James Bell was, as she supposed, the person for whom the gypsy's message was intended, then why hadn't she simply come out with it? She stopped and stared blankly at a little red devil squatting in the eaves above her head. Somewhat disingenuously, she answered herself. There hadn't really been a suitable time. It was not as if they had been alone, on the train or on the walls. The devil swam into focus. *Who's kidding whom?*

Well, they would be alone now. Too alone. Maybe Lisa Dragonette would re-appear. And what on the sleeping earth was Lisa Dragonette up to? Maybe she had a date with Tony. Too absurd. Why was Tony in York then? But Tony could be anywhere at all. There was no reason to suppose they were *all* characters in her story. Not until she found them all dancing around a gorse bush.

Kate had wandered along without noticing much and now she found that she had been staring into a window full of art books. Spread before her was a reproduction of a 15th century German woodcut depicting the Dance of Death. Imagination had changed the figures to those of the gypsy and Harry and Fan and Sam and Lisa and James and…But James must be at the end. He could hold on with only one hand.

She shivered. It was colder. She went on, strolling and musing.

The sounds of people and traffic were so close they had deceived her. In fact she had turned into one of those long narrow dark back streets that exist only a few steps from the illuminated bustle of old cities. A door slammed, taking away a carpet of light that had lain across her path. A cat shrieked in passion or panic. She began to hurry.

Solitary footsteps sounded behind her. Oh, Inspector Bucket, what did you tell me? She didn't dare to look back. One of these days, she tried to say to herself, someone *will* be following me and I'll have cried wolf so often I won't even notice. One of these other days.

Midway along the alley there was a dirty yellow street lamp. As she passed beyond it her lengthening shadow was covered by a large black patch that fell across it like a cloak. A hand touched her shoulder.

She whirled to face her pursuer, giving a cry like the yelp of a terrified mouse. It was a big man in a duffle coat, the toggle buttons unfastened. He seized her arm, but not roughly.

"Kate Clark! I thought it was you, for gosh sakes. How's it going, kid? Whatcha doing in York, trying to crash one of the well-known chocolate factories?" It was too dark to see his face.

"Tom Burrows, you scared me out of my wits." Tom chortled. "Of all the people in the world to come creeping after me down dark alleys. *You* know what happened to me on the ship. My nerves have never been the same."

"Gee, Kate, I'm a jerk." He put his arm around her and propelled her toward the lights at the end of the street.

"I damn near forgot the whole episode. Do you know if they got who did it?"

That was too much. Inspector Bucket surely hadn't skipped Tom Burrows.

"Anyway, I sure as hell wasn't creeping," he added defensively, "and you picked the alley yourself. Speaking of creeps, guess who I saw getting off the train? Lisa Dragonette! What do you say to that? Just like Grand Central Station!"

"It certainly seems like it. What are you doing here, Tom? Have you seen Tony Smith, by any chance?"

"I got a customer here, A, and B, no, I haven't seen Tony, thanks a lot. Too snooty for my taste. I was an officer and a gentleman after all. To tell the truth I'm not all that gung ho about the English."

"Well, to each his own. Since when is Lisa a creep in your book? It certainly didn't look that way when you were trying to pry her away from Sam."

They emerged into a bright thoroughfare thronged with people. Tom Burrows smiled at Kate in a way she didn't much care for. "Girls like you don't always get the main idea, kiddo. Anyway I made out all right with the dish in the grass skirt. One night of love was it, though. She's got a husband who plays Rugby." He eyed a pub across the road. "Say, what about a drink in the Pig and Whistle? Are you alone?"

"No thank you," she answered quickly. "I'm meeting my cousin at our hotel. I have to get a taxi." Her eyes scanned the traffic.

"I'll escort you. Least I can do, after scaring the pants off of you." He began waving and whistling, two fingers between his lips. A taxi drew up. Kate jumped in and slammed the door.

"Links Hotel, hurry!" she said to the driver. "Oh, I'll be fine, Tom," she shouted out of the window as the car accelerated noisily.

Inside the taxi Kate got out her compact and tried to organize her hair and nose. She rewarded the driver with a heavy tip and rushed into the Links Hotel feeling breathless and contrite.

James was seated at a table in the lounge. A dazzling white cloth covered the surface, and disposed upon it were a tea service patterned in violets and the appropriate silverware for two, a plate of very very thin slices of brown bread and butter, a jam pot with a gleaming lid, and a three-tiered cake stand artfully fitted out with an assortment of delicacies of surpassing loveliness.

Kate paused.

Opposite James, and just getting ready to pour the tea, sat a golden haired young woman with the kind of complexion that is sometimes thought to be the legacy of a thousand damp and misty summers. She was smiling. Seeing James look round, she turned to Kate and smiled at *her*.

James got up effortlessly and said in an offhand way, "Oh, there you are, Kate. We shall have to have another place set." He turned to his companion. "Rosemary, may I present my cousin Kate Clark? Kate, this is Rosemary Broadbent. Her father is the vicar at Netherbeck."

Chapter XX

> Beyond the town there lies the open country
> where, gathering speed, she acquires mystery...
> —Stephen Spender, "The Express"

James and Kate did the minster next morning. There was a vast amount of emptiness; it was very peaceful and very cold. Huge blocks of sunlight fell through the windows — where they rested Kate expected warmth, but the change was all to the eye. The chill in the stones had been trapped for centuries. The pale northern sun dreamed over them like some distant lover.

The cousins moved quietly. This time James made no attempt to act the cicerone, and Kate was glad of it. He knew when not to speak. Somewhere out of sight high and childish voices, sounding like a distillation of all innocence, began choir practice. James looked at his watch, and they moved softly toward the door.

Rosemary Broadbent had arranged to meet them with her father's car, bringing their bags along from the hotel. As they strolled toward the rendezvous Kate threw out a query in what she hoped was an effectively disguised form.

"It was certainly very nice of your friend to come and meet us in York, James." She glanced at him hopefully. She felt that by missing the opening ceremonies of yesterday's tea party she had been deprived of some possibly significant orientation. Rosemary, though perfectly, even notably, friendly, had been as cool as James himself.

"It was pure chance. She had some errands for her father, returning borrowed sermons or some such effort. The vicar knows how to make use of the cathedral establishment."

"And of his daughter?"

"Exactly."

"What kind of job does she have?"

"She looks after her father who's a widower — confers with the cook, visits the poor, the usual sort of thing I believe. Occasionally she gets some assistance from an impoverished relative named Watershed."

"It sounds terribly Victorian."

"I suppose one could see it that way. However, she's quite well educated and she makes herself useful. Careers aren't for everyone."

"Well, I'd certainly hate to stay home all the time. Wouldn't you?"

"I am not restless at Netherbeck."

Kate thought for a moment, then tried a new angle. "Does everyone from Netherbeck stay at the Links when they come to York?"

He looked surprised. "Rosemary wasn't stopping at the Links. She has an aunt living in York."

"Oh. Well."

"Well what?"

"She certainly is terribly pretty."

"So they say."

"Oh, James, what's the matter with you anyway? She certainly looks at you as if you were the bee's knees."

"You know nothing whatever about it, Kate." His manner was polar, but she persevered.

"Have you thought about what your children would be like if you married her? I mean you're such a gorgeous beast and she has those eyes like wet violets..."

He took her arm and stopped her in the street, looking at her face. "What color are *your* eyes, Kate? I think wet violets are a bit obvious by comparison."

She flushed and looked at her feet. "Okay, James, let's forget the whole thing. I deserve to be squelched. That gorgeous beast stuff is out of some show or other." He still stood, holding her arm. "Shouldn't we go?" she asked weakly. "That policeman looks suspicious."

They went on, Kate feeling as if they were approaching a precipice. It was only a curb, though, and beside it was standing a very large and handsome car. James opened the rear door for Kate and then climbed in next to Rosemary.

"Oh my oh my," sighed Kate, between relief and pleasure. "I wonder whether this sort of car *starts* easily."

"Like a Jaguar," said Rosemary. "If you'll be a very good Toad I'll give you a turn at the wheel." She turned on the motor and engaged the gears; the automobile moved down the street with a rich purr.

"I couldn't drive on the wrong side of the road the way everyone does here," answered Kate.

"Oh, that's all right out on the moors. You'll see. But perhaps you should leave it to me. I'll open it up. It goes rather fast."

"It doesn't seem like a very clerical car, if you'll pardon my saying so," said Kate politely.

"Indeed it doesn't. Father finds it embarrassing, dispensing spiritual comfort to the cottagers from such a luxurious machine. It won't pass for a celestial car."

"But if your father doesn't like it..." began Kate.

"Oh, he likes the motor car. He just doesn't like the impression it makes. He's afraid it makes him look rather caddish." She glanced back at Kate with a smile. "I bought it for him, you see. Father has damn all of his own, and one of the poorest livings in the West Riding. It's not very genteel my telling you but as nothing is at all sacred to the supposedly taciturn inhabitants of Netherbeck it hardly matters."

Rosemary reached for her handbag, which was tucked between the seats. "I say, James," she said, "can you manage to extract that packet of Licorice Allsorts from my bag? That was all I could manage. I used up my other sweet coupons at Mrs. Jellyby's shop on Monday last."

James could manage as he managed most things, but Kate liked the easy way in which the request was made. It sounded intimate. No matter what difficult attitude James was taking at the moment it was plain that he and Rosemary knew each other well.

As if in response to the thought Rosemary addressed Kate again, this time catching her eye in the mirror. "Had I known about you, Kate, I should have asked you to stay at the vicarage whilst you're in Netherbeck. James didn't say he had a young American cousin. Perhaps you would like to come anyway? You can always cancel at the Bull."

Kate opened her mouth to accept but James was ahead of her. "Kate wants to stay at a country inn, Rosemary. Besides, she'll be within walking distance of Moon Croft."

"It must be three miles, James. Well, the invitation stands."

The Jaguar advanced effortlessly with the comforting murmur of superior and pampered machinery. Kate sank back and watched the world go by. The fringes of the urban scene turned to domestic pastoral, and that in turn to the great windy vistas of the high country. James and Rosemary conversed occasionally; their words had become inaudible. The sky had clouded over and the car sped along inside a vast inverted basin of mottled grey. The landscape seemed to match the sky. The travellers rose and fell like sailors riding out some deep disturbance.

Rosemary's ghillie shod foot on the accelerator hardly acknowledged the occasional village whose few buildings clung close to the road like cats at a fender. Kate, with this bleak scene spread all before her like a feast, abandoned herself to a reverie compounded of memory and dream. The moors! And she herself the "little heiress with the gorse bush." Surely it would all turn out all right.

In time the car swung round and stopped gently but firmly.

"What say you to a morsel of bread and cheese?" asked Rosemary, turning round to Kate. "I always stop at The Old Fleece if I can. Splendid ale, and the publican's wife makes her own butter."

They climbed out of the car and were buffeted by fresh air. A swaying signboard attached to a substantial stone building advertised the premises. It's emblem was severely weathered, but appeared to represent a particularly passive sheep, very wooly and tied up with a broad ribbon.

A dim hallway led into a large cheerful room made merry by a wood fire that hissed, crackled, and sent reflections to dance on the glasses, knobs, and gleaming surface of the bar. It was late for a midday meal in the country and the place was empty except for a few regulars nursing pint mugs. The host came forward wiping his hands on a clean rag.

"It be Miss Broadbent then," he said.

"How do you do, Mr. Howcroft? I expect you remember Mr. Bell. And this is Miss Clark. I wonder whether we might have your very superior lunch all round. With Mrs. Howcroft's butter, of course. And three pints of ale."

"Sit ye down, then. I'll see the missus abaht the grub. Young Tom'll fetch the ale."

"Just a half pint for me, please." Kate was apologetic, but it didn't spare her Mr. Howcroft's plain contempt.

"We might have one of them small glasses, happen," he muttered.

"You mustn't be offended by his manner," said Rosemary softly, as soon as they were seated at a table in the corner farthest from the bar. A hound-sized dog of ill-assorted parts got up from the hearth and came over to greet them, his tail crashing against the empty tables. "It's partly the custom of the country and partly the Howcrofts' own trouble. They lost two sons in the war, both fine young men. They've Tom still — he's the youngest — but I'm afraid he's a bit wet."

As if to confirm this diagnosis, young Tom appeared with the ale, a fair amount of which was sloshing onto his apron. His father came after him bearing a wooden trencher with a loaf of fresh bread and a plate with a golden wedge of cheese.

"Now then, Tom, plates, and fetch them pickled onions. Look slippy. Yon Jack Mason's glass be nigh empty." He turned to Rosemary. Kate was surprised at his seeming indifference to James. Perhaps the sight of James, a visible survivor, touched a sore place in him. "Butter be nigh ready."

"Oh, wow!" said Kate. "I've never had fresh butter."

A very slight softening was perceptible in Mr. Howcroft. "Another American here this morning liked the ale all right," he volunteered.

"Oh, really?" said Kate, and James looked at her sharply. "Was it a tall man with a big booming voice, wearing a duffel coat?" James stamped his cigarette out. Kate didn't wait for an answer but asked quickly, "Or a slim dark man with a beard?" A flicker of interest surfaced in Rosemary's violet eyes.

"Nobbut o' that. Small fox-faced man. *Walking*, he says. Walking? say I to meself, looking at his mites o' shoes. Be making for Netherbeck, he do say. Had one o' them little maps like. Jack Mason's been here since opening. Showed him where he be. Athwart Sheep's Head Moor." Mr. Howcroft turned away, his oration finished.

"Fill me ruddy glass, any road!" It was Jack Mason at the bar, despairing of securing the attention of Tom.

James turned to the bar and spoke politely as the host rushed to man the taps. "How far did this traveller mean to go today, Mr. Mason? If we overtake him perhaps Miss Broadbent can give him a lift."

Jack Mason wiped his mouth with his sleeve preparatory to starting afresh with his brimming mug. He found a pair of wire rimmed glasses in his pocket and put them on to peer at James appraisingly. "Dunno," he replied.

Kate was disappointed and showed it.

"Do you think it's an acquaintance of yours?" asked James, giving her one of his hard blue looks.

"No."

"You seem rather interested."

"Just ordinary curiosity."

"Perhaps another of your admirers from the ship has come into Yorkshire to seek you out."

"Don't be silly." This wasn't like James. She glanced at his face, and what she saw there dismayed her.

"My dear James," said Rosemary, her voice noncommittal as a blancmange. "Anyone can see that Kate knows nothing about the person."

"Sorry," said James, turning away.

The butter had come, a lovely pale lump on a small brown dish. The trio fell to serious eating. Without asking or being asked Rosemary cut bread and cheese for James. He accepted it without acknowledgement. They were quiet until a low grunting whirr suddenly provided a counterpoint to the melodic murmurings at the bar.

"The Art of Fugue," said James, who loved music. Kate and Rosemary grinned happily. Suddenly they were three outsiders having an adventure.

The sound had come from a little red-nosed man who had been silently absorbing fluid at the far end of the counter. Tuned up, he spoke in a small but penetrating sing-song. "Be a foreign lady at t'Bobby Shaftoe in Weatherhead. Came in a hired car last night."

"A foreign lady?" asked Rosemary courteously. "Was she an American too, do you know?"

"Nay. French, they do say. Or mebbe Chinese. Summat o' that." He wound an enormous scarf round his throat. "I'm off then, mates."

"Cheerio then, Billy!" shouted the chorus at the bar. As glasses were drained the group was thinning out.

"Lisa Dragonette?" said Kate to James.

"So it would seem."

"Lisa Dragonette?" asked Rosemary. "But what an absurd name. Surely not?"

"Well, she's in the theater," said Kate. "My best friend's name is MaJa."

"Shall we be off too, Rosemary?" James was adroitly extracting silver coins from his pocket. "I'd rather like to get home."

The wind slammed against them as they struggled to open the heavy doors of the Jaguar. Once they were snug inside Rosemary turned to Kate again. "My grandfather was a brewer — my mother's father. He made a jolly little packet. I like pubs, but I'm asked not to frequent the two in Netherbeck. My father likes us to sit at home decorously swigging sherry. I do hope you'll join us. James can come. I try to keep some decent hock on hand for him."

"Oh, what's hock please? High class people in novels are always drinking hock."

"Rhine wine," said James.

"James likes these German sorts of things," said Rosemary lightly. "Have you noticed? I expect he'll be swept away straight to Valhalla when he dies, in the arms of some glorious Valkyrie."

"For that to happen I should have to die in battle," said James equably.

"Who knows? Perhaps there'll be another war. Gods versus giants or something of that sort. All very grand and uplifting." Her voice had a bright edge in it but her eyes on James were soft.

She started the engine and backed into the road. The car soared off like a kite. Kate gasped and clung to the seat.

"Is this flying?" she shouted.

James turned to her. "Not quite," he answered. He should know.

When they got to Netherbeck Rosemary pulled up in front of the Brown Bull. "I'll see whether there's anyone about to take Kate's bag up."

"We'll just leave it here and go on," said James, getting out. "Please don't fuss, Rosemary. I *had* hoped to arrive at Moon Croft in the daylight."

"How will she get back? You can't mean her to walk all the way in the dark, surely? Shall I come for her this evening?"

"Mrs. Stonehouse is coming in to do us a simple meal. Ernie will be coming for her later. He can drop Kate at the Bull."

"What if the scheme falls through? You're not on the telephone, James."

"Not to worry, please."

Rosemary shrugged.

In the north at this time of year there was not enough daylight to last the day. The new fallen sun seemed to have dragged the wind behind it. The stillness of the world outside settled on the occupants of the car during the brief remainder of the journey.

The old farmhouse that Sally Bell had re-christened Moon Croft crouched darkly on the side of a steep slope, a stone wall extending from either side at the back. The main building was not large but there were sheds and a barn clinging to it. The upper windows commanded a sweep of valley floor, vast and mysterious.

"It's all so bare and wild," breathed Kate. A great tree, ragged with clinging leaves, dominated the dooryard. Some few shrubs against the wall showed ghostly black in the afternoon moonlight. "What things can grow here?"

"The tree's a very old oak," said James. "I suppose it must have been planted by the person who first settled here."

"Those scruffy chaps over there are gorse bushes," added Rosemary.

Chapter XXI

> This is short, though not so sweet. Surely the better part of the solemnitie Here will be dauncing.
>
> —Ben Jonson, *Pans Anniversarie*

"Damn," said James. "Mrs. Stonehouse said she would have the fire laid on for us." He fitted a key to the front door lock.

At that moment they heard a chuffing in the road and an ancient many-cornered vehicle pulled up behind the Jaguar, emitting a raucous greeting from a Klaxon affixed near the driver's window.

"Out you go then, Mum. Bombs away," said a deep voice from the interior, made audible by the opening of the car door. "I'll be along to fetch you at nine sharp so mind you've finished the washing up. I'll be wanting me bite of supper."

A portly old woman stepped down. "Get along with you and your impudence," she retorted briskly. "'Finished the washing up' indeed! I'll give you washing up, you young tyke." The car turned round and hurtled off with another rude signal as Mrs. Stonehouse approached the group on the doorstep.

James had gone inside and switched on a hall light. Kate saw that Mrs. Stonehouse was wearing a good-natured expression that fitted her with the ease of habit. She carried a bulging shopping bag of disreputable appearance from which was wafted the aroma of something warm and savory.

"Now then, laddie," she shouted, ignoring the young women who made way for her at the entrance, "I'll have your tea on the table before you can say Jack Robinson." She addressed James without ceremony as the others followed her inside. Kate, thinking of the diffident respect Sally Bell showed her son, watched to see how he took it. His expression was neutral, but he said with a rather formal air, "Thank you, Mrs. Stonehouse. This is my cousin, Miss Clark. Miss Broadbent I believe you know."

"You believe I know, indeed, Mr. Bell," said Mrs. Stonehouse with exaggerated amazement, opening her eyes very wide. "You're a proper caution, you are. Haven't I known her all her blessed life, the pretty dear?" As James failed to rise to this challenge she took stronger measures. "Wasn't I the nurse that gave her suck?"

Rosemary laughed merrily. "Well, you weren't really, you know, Mrs. Stonehouse. But I appreciate it quite as much as if you had been, I assure you."

"Just you put a match to them coals in the room, will you then, pet? I'll be off to the kitchen." Rosemary proceeded into the living room, and Mrs. Stonehouse turned to James again. "She'll have to be fanning the flames, I expect. I'd get one of them gas pokers if I had your means, Mr. Bell."

"I dare say, Mrs. Stonehouse. However, my means do not extend to introducing gas lines where they have not yet been made available."

"Pooh." Mrs. Stonehouse departed and could soon be heard filling a kettle and opening cupboards. Kate and James followed Rosemary to the fireplace, where she was trying to encourage a small flame with the aid of a venerable bellows.

The room, now seen by the soft light of a floor lamp flicked on by James, was beautiful. The ratio of length to width was almost daring; the ceiling was unexpectedly high, and yet not high at all; an inch more or less here or there might have spoiled everything. It was very cold, but the fire had begun to dance. *The fires are all magic.*

There were small windows on two sides and James was closing the curtains, shutting out the pale moon. The furniture was old and massive, all polished to a somber glow except for two easy chairs by the fire. These were upholstered in a pattern of faded red roses intricately entangled. It was not a small room, but it seemed to be a room for two. Kate shivered.

"May I offer you a glass of sherry, Rosemary?"

"No thank you, James. Father will be expecting me." She looked from James to Kate with an expression difficult to fathom. "I daresay I shall see you round the village."

"Of course. I do thank you for the lift. It was an enormous help." He moved with her toward the door. "I'll see you to your car."

"Not to bother please, James. I expect you'll want a drink before Mrs. Stonehouse wheels in your tea."

"Oh, Rosemary," said Kate eagerly, following her into the hall, "can we plan to get together tomorrow? You could call me at the Brown Bull."

"I'm afraid I shall be rather busy tomorrow, now that I've remembered which day it is. But don't forget — you're to come to us at the vicarage if you're not best pleased where you are." She opened the door onto the vast heath. "The moon gives a splendid light, doesn't it?"

Mrs. Stonehouse had set up a small folding table before the fire and Kate and James had feasted on rabbit pie and a salad, followed by wedges of heavy plum cake.

Kate stretched, James watching her. "Oh my," she said. "Oh my oh my oh my oh my."

"So you said earlier on," he remarked. "Is it your own signature tune, or did you borrow it from somewhere?"

"It's from *Wind in the Willows*, dummy. One of the latter day glories of English lit." The warmth of the fire and the rich food had put her at ease. Away in the kitchen she could hear the comforting smack of a well-wielded dish mop. They had eaten slowly and quietly, and Mrs. Stonehouse had filled the teapot, which was snug in a hand-knitted blue cozy, twice.

"I never cared much for all that jolly English whimsy, actually. Talking animals bore me."

"What about Salammbo? She's obviously your ownest own cat."

"Nonsense. Salammbo is completely indifferent to everyone, even my mother who commands the pantry door. As for that notorious purring of hers, one starts it off a damn sight more easily than the average motor car." He smiled, and Kate remembered Salammbo on his lap under the bright kitchen light. "Only a nation that preferred animals to people could be so overpopulated with anthropomorphized livestock."

"But didn't you *ever* like talking animals? What about the White Rabbit? What about Mrs. Tittlemouse? What in the world *did* you like?" Of course. His shelves. "Surely not those deadly school stories where someone is always 'playing the game'?"

She searched his face and was struck anew by his heroic good looks. The prince in the fairy tale. But you got used to it.

"I liked the heroes," said James, looking at the fire. "Those who were pure and noble and brave. Those whose deeds spoke for them, who were bigger and better than ordinary men. That's the stuff for dreams — not teddy bears whom someone has chosen to pretend are garrulous and greedy." His voice was serious.

"Christopher Robin was in the RAF."

"Hardly to the point."

"Didn't Siegfried hang around with some kind of a jolly bear? I suppose you go for Siegfried?"

James jabbed at the fire with the poker, then added a scoop of coals from the scuttle on the hearth. "Kate, it does not become you to join the braying mob. Siegfried will not long be out of fashion in England. At least not among music lovers. Or among men of my sort."

"What sort is that? Your family certainly treats you as if you were a one-man band." She still felt almost carefree, as if they had agreed on a program of cousinly banter.

"Men of honor, who like to take risks. Who believe that there are values worth saving that are not of necessity important to everyone."

"If I knew what you were talking about I'm sure I wouldn't agree, James." She looked to see whether or not he was angry. He wasn't. The hard blue look was nowhere. "What is it?"

"Perhaps you should have stayed in England during the war."

He stood up and went to the phonograph and opened the cabinet beneath it. He got out a record with a red label and set it on the machine. Then he rolled the rug away from the center of the room. He did everything slowly but easily; Kate made no move to help him. He turned a knob, and as the turntable began to revolve he set the needle in its groove. "The Blue Danube" began to flow sweetly into the room — seductive, full of deceptive languor. He came back to Kate and bowed gravely.

She stood up and he put his arm around her waist. She put a hand on each of his shoulders; he was not much taller than she. They waltzed.

They did not speak. The music, the warmth and dazzle of the fire, the strangeness of the scene — above all the excitement of clinging to each other as the room whirled past — all spoke for them. For a moment she remembered the last time she had danced. *Tony*. It was like a cry for help.

When the record finished they stood silent, as if waiting for the spell to be broken. Mrs. Stonehouse broke it with a loud knock.

"Excuse me, please," she shouted, as if the music were still going on. "Excuse me, Mr. Bell. I wouldn't be bothering you in the ordinary way, not if it was ever so. But my Ernie be as punctual as the wireless now. Isn't that so?"

James answered that it was, in his experience, certainly so.

"Then where is he? He said nine o'clock and now it's gone half past — long since." She looked fiercely at the tall clock in the corner of the room.

"I shouldn't worry, Mrs. Stonehouse," answered James in his most offhand way. "I expect that motor of his gave out en route. I remember seeing it round the village when I used to visit my grandfather years ago. He'll turn up presently. Why not have another cup of tea?"

Mrs. Stonehouse put her hands on her hips. "If you would get on the telephone yourself, sir," — she was becoming more formal as her anxiety rose — "*as* I've said many's the time — we wouldn't have these hoccurences." James looked at her with indifference but she blazed out as if he had demurred. "It's not a particle of use you telling me you can't get on the telephone because Mabel Creaser at the post office says you can. There now!"

James shrugged, causing Mrs. Stonehouse to squeak with wrath. Kate attended to the phonograph, hoping to get out of the line of fire. Then the chuff of Ernie's motor made itself heard.

Mrs. Stonehouse broke into a benign smile and moved toward the door, but before she could reach the knob the outer door banged open. A second later Ernie Stonehouse came in without knocking. He was a massive man with red cheeks and fair bushy eyebrows.

"Oh, Ernie, whatever's happened?" asked his mother, seeing his face.

"It's all right, Mum. Don't fret yourself. I knew you'd be worried right enough. Naught I could do, though. Herbert Spencer found a body in the beck and asked me to give him a hand." He looked important.

"A *body*, Stonehouse?" James spoke sharply. "What on earth do you mean? Whose body?"

"I and Herbert don't know. No more do Constable Dogberry. They be sending to fetch Colonel Fletcher from Greystone."

"Is it a man or a woman?"

"A right proper big man." Ernie's glance sloped toward James in a self-satisfied way. "There ben't many clothes on him but the hundergarments don't look English somehow." He became aware of Kate's pale face. "Begging your pardon, miss, for mentioning the corpse's hundergarments."

"Do you mean to tell us that someone was wandering about the moors without warm clothing at this time of year?" James had resumed his accustomed manner with no visible effort. Before Ernie could reply he went on. "Must be some poor lunatic escaped from the asylum at Ilkingthorpe and managed to drown himself in the beck. It's been a bit fuller lately."

"Aye, they don't be calling the beck Gypsy Water for nothing, Mr. James. Folks around here knows it flows fuller when there's a tragedy brewing," Mrs. Stonehouse piped up.

"That's as may be, Mum. I've heard that many's the time, ever since I was a little lad splashing about there. Mr. Broadbent, he don't hold with it. Howsoever that may be it don't seem the beck has much to do with the demise of this person in his hunderwear."

"Why not?" asked James.

"Because he seems to have been hexecuted." Mrs. Stonehouse clapped her hands to her face. "Now then, Mum. Praps you'd best be sitting down."

"Executed? What on earth do you mean? Do you mean hanged? Speak out for once, man." James' eyes had gone back to hard blue. His voice had the cool ring of command.

Ernie Stonehouse was not impressed. His mouth clamped shut.

James turned to Ernie's mother. "Perhaps you can tell me, Mrs. Stonehouse, why the inhabitants of Netherbeck can never answer a simple question in a straightforward manner. You've lived here all your life."

"It's only our way, lad. I mind your granddad asking me own mum the same question once. Drew herself up she did, like a proper chimley, smoke pouring out the ears — she was wearing a hat, mind — 'Mr. Birkie,' says she, 'you be a furriner in these parts, but nobody said now't about your ways o' doing things, queer though they may be.' I never forgot it, and no more did he. She was grand, was me mum." Mrs. Stonehouse's tone was conciliatory, as if to make her meaning more palatable.

James smiled, his wonderful smile. Kate felt her heart beating too fast.

"Shot through the heart at point blank range," said Ernie, promptly and cheerfully.

"Good God!" exclaimed James.

"Were there any clues?" It was Kate's voice, sounding small and far away.

"Just the one, miss, pending a police hexamination. I took charge of it, thinking as how I'd best give it Colonel Fletcher meself. Constable Dogberry's a terrible donkey."

Ernie produced a playing card from his pocket and held it out for them to see. "It's a clue, right enough," he said. "'Twas in his hand."

Kate looked at the card. The room seemed to be whirling round again, and the irresistible rhythms of "The Blue Danube" filled her ears like rushing water.

Look to the lady, somebody said, but she was only remembering it. She fainted.

Chapter XXII

> Sympathies, I believe, exist: (for instance, between far-distant, long-absent, wholly estranged relatives; asserting, notwithstanding their alienation, the unity of the source to which each traces his origin) whose workings baffle mortal comprehension.
> —Charlotte Bronte, *Jane Eyre*

"Drink this." James was holding a glass to her lips, a glass like a small bubble in the firelight.

"What is it?"

"Brandy."

"The young lady's come round then. I'll be away and get Ernie a bite of supper, Mr. Bell." It was Mrs. Stonehouse, speaking softly.

"I want to go with them," Kate said, trying to rise. She was sitting in one of the big chairs; she seemed to be entangled in the twisted roses.

"Ernie Stonehouse will come back for you, Kate. Please allow me to see that you are all right before you go." James set the glass down.

"If you're worried I could go and stay with Rosemary, James. She said I could."

She heard the outside door close behind Mrs. Stonehouse. James was sitting opposite her and he took her hand. "Kate, what has frightened you so much?"

She didn't answer.

"What happened in the park that afternoon?"

"You were there."

"Yes...yes, I was there."

"Had you forgotten?"

"I have forgotten nothing since that day."

She looked at the fire.

James spoke again. "You think me insensitive to your experience on board ship. On the contrary, it has troubled me a good deal. But surely that's all over?" His voice was kind. "This new tragedy — a local affair I'm sure. Passions run high in the North."

She still looked at the fire.

"Kate," he said.

"I do not find the Hanged Man," she answered finally, her voice low and careful.

He got up and walked down the room. When he came back his face was puzzled. "What on earth do you mean?"

"Nothing. It's just a line from a poem. The card made me think of it. Didn't you see the card Ernie held out? It was a Tarot card — the Hanged Man. The woman who was murdered on the ship..."

"What about her?"

Kate looked up at him. "Oh, James. Having people really murdered does rather take the gilt off the gingerbread as you English chaps say." She tried to smile but it felt all wrong.

He sat down again. "It's a bad business. I don't understand it myself."

"But why should you understand it any more than anyone else? Except, of course, that you live in this romantic house garnished with gorse bushes."

His mouth tensed. "Oblige me by telling me what you mean, since you choose to introduce the subject again."

"James, sometimes I wonder whether I made you up." She felt relieved. "You just walked right out of one of my favorite novels. Next thing you'll be 'begging to intimate' or 'entreating permission.' Okay, then." She glanced at him in what she hoped was a matter-of-fact manner. "I like romantic novels about little heiresses in lonely English houses. You will admit this is a lonely English house?"

"Not lonely enough." James' answer should have had a wry smile to go with it, but of course it didn't.

"Well, in romantic novels houses like this always have certain props — for atmosphere, you know. There are usually rooks and fells and lych-gates and stiles and *gorse* bushes. Next to the moon, gorse bushes are often the biggest thing in sight. Of course the moon is always big, even when it's new."

"Is that all?"

"Naturally that isn't *all*. There has to be a plot. There's usually a handsome villain and a lurking imbecile and a dubious vicar. There aren't any parents, only uncles — usually deceased —"

"Kate."

"Well, James, I don't think it's any sillier than knights barging around being pure and brave. Than heroes travelling on pet swans and lovers only being happy when they're dead. I think Wagner must have been a total fruitcake."

"You are young, Kate. You don't have any feeling for the music yet, and you don't understand the dramas — the emotions and the ideals that underlie them. If you did you couldn't compare them to...works of popular fiction."

"Well, I know the Nazis liked them. They certainly had some pretty bizarre ideas. My novels are pretty innocent. I'd think someone like you, who was in the war, actually *in* it..."

"Oh, Kate, there's so much you simply haven't had time or opportunity to learn. You know nothing about the war except what you've seen in films."

"At least I know the difference between right and wrong."

"The less people know about anything else the more they become convinced of their moral insight."

"Same to you, you, you...pompous ass."

Her eyes were suddenly full of tears, tears that caught the firelight and dazzled her. James was kneeling at her feet amid all that radiance, like a knight in a stained glass window. He took her hand again; this time he kissed it. She pulled it away and sat on it.

"Don't pretend you're the Polish ambassador," she said desperately.

"Don't pretend to misunderstand me," he replied. "I love you. I loved you the moment I saw you." Her tears fell faster. "I am no longer my own man. I can no more stop loving you than I can stop the wind." His handsome face was grave.

She found a handkerchief in her pocket. "Oh, James, they didn't give the love potion to me. You know why? Because I'm not that type at all. It wouldn't work on me. It's just a silly idea you got. Oh, I should never have come. Besides, you're my *cousin. Please* get up."

He got up and sat in the other chair. "Second cousin," he said. Inspector Bucket had pointed that out, among other things.

Kate wanted very much to run away. She thought she could find her way to Netherbeck and then, things being what they apparently were, she need never come back. She could tell Sally that she had read of a play in New York she wanted to audition for.

But James would never let her go out into the dark. It wasn't even ordinary dark. It was dark full of dead men, and murderers. They sat in a silence full of her fears, and her anger at James for aggravating them. At last James spoke quietly.

"I had intended to tell you my adventures before I declared myself."

"That I might pity them?" She was shivering.

"I don't need pity. I was lucky, in more ways than one. It was just that I wanted you to know — whatever there was to know. I would not ask you to love a stranger."

"I suppose you did something desperate and brave and it's part of your code not to boast about it. I don't care to be the special person you tell, James. When are the others coming back?"

"Oh, Ernie will come in time to get back before the pubs close, I suppose. Though his mother will certainly delay him with a thousand questions."

"Of course she will. How can anyone talk about anything else? But the strange body, I mean?"

"I tell you it's nothing to do with us."

"Are you sure?"

"No." He spoke abruptly. "No, I'm not sure. But we must await events. The

Chief Constable is doubtless on the way. Someone will be found to identify the corpse."

"You and I should have gone at once." Feeling sick and cold, she jabbed at the fire with the poker.

"We shall be among the first to be asked, unless I misjudge." He went upstairs and came back with a faded eiderdown that he placed over her knees. "It belonged to my Birkie grandparents," he said. "My grandmother brought it in her wedding chest."

"It's still very warm. Oh James, she was my own great aunt!"

"Hannah Birkie had only two children, a very small family in those days. My mother worshipped her only brother, my Uncle Oswald Birkie. Like so many other brave men — English, German, French — he was killed in the Great War."

"So you didn't know him?"

"Of course not. I'm twenty-eight. But I was brought up on his story. You know we mentioned him yesterday. I had forgotten that you yourself had brought some mementoes of him from America." He reached out his hand, then withdrew it. "You perhaps know he married a lovely German woman from a fine old family."

"I guess her fine old family didn't go for the Birkies — anyway that's what cousin Sally told me."

"They should have known Oswald. They refused to meet him. Ilse von Elfenstein would never have married beneath her."

"Your mother told me that she was very nice."

"Nice! How like my mother. Ilse was superb, a lady in every sense of the word."

"Well, your mother told me the neighbors weren't very nice to her."

"Nice, nice, and more nice. It was outrageous, Kate."

"You certainly take it very personally, considering you weren't even born. It's like one of those Scotch stories where the young laird must never forget the insult done to his ancestors."

"It was not 'one of those Scotch stories' or any of your other stories, Kate." The irritation in his voice soothed her. "To me Oswald Birkie was a hero — and Ilse von Elfenstein was the mother I should have had — cultured, aristocratic, beautiful, brave. Can you understand that?"

She shook her head.

"Try," he said. "I know you really can. I know you really do. You are afraid of your real feelings."

"Well, I can't, so forget it. Your real mother is terrific. Surely you loved her? Surely you *do* love her? She's cultured, James."

"Kate, you can't be so naive as to take my mother's smattering of tunes and reviews from *John O'London's Weekly* for culture? Even Doris knows better."

"What do you mean *even* Doris?"

"My sister Doris is one of those sub-artistic types who grub up a living round London. As for her friend Felix, he's the worst sort of arrogant little auto-didact."

"I don't agree. I like Felix. I love Doris. And I adore your mother. You don't deserve her."

"Oh, I love her, Kate. Of course I do. Just as, I'm sure, you do. I even like my father, in a way."

"That's big of you."

"She was the person closest to me when I was a child."

"I get it. She was like the dear old English nanny who mans the treacle tin while your beautiful mum goes off to the ball, leaving the scent of attar of roses all over the nursery. But I'm forgetting. You don't want to be an English gent. You want to be a Teutonic knight. Poor James."

"You're tongue is afraid of your heart, Kate. Mock me if you must — only hear me out." He reached for a cigarette, and she held the match for him. "There's not really all that much to choose. The English and Germans are natural allies. That was confirmed for me at Kahlberg."

"Well, that'll be something for me to tell the folks back home. Especially the ones who always complain about having to bail the English out." But the mention of Kahlberg had wiped out her impatience for Ernie's return. Suddenly she realized that Oswald and Ilse were prologue for James' story, and that she very much wanted to hear it after all.

"I don't know how much you know about Kahlberg, Kate." She shook her head. "It was a prison for officers. There were some very important people there, and there were quite a lot of English, some from very distinguished families."

"That must have been nice for you — I mean pleasant." She smiled a little to take the edge off her voice, but when he said, "Kate", again, she said, "Go on, please."

"The prison was staffed by officers and men of the Wehrmacht. Regular army. No SS ruffians or anything of that sort. On the whole the officers were excellent types. The sub-commandant was Franz von Elfenstein." Kate gasped. "I recognized the name at once."

"But — you mean it was Ilse's son?"

"My cousin. My mother's brother's son."

"How come his name wasn't Birkie? That's how it's usually done."

"Oh, Ilse would have called him Birkie. She was proud of Oswald. She persuaded the family to send him back to England to school when he was eight — not the sort of school my grandfather Birkie spent his life in, you may be sure." James' voice was tinged with envy.

"I'm surprised she could part with him."

"Oh, people of that class don't expect to see much of their children. The family had shrunk for one reason and another. Franz was the sole heir to a considerable estate east of Berlin. Ilse was willing to call him Birkie-von Elfenstein, but he dropped the Birkie when she died in 1935."

"What did she die of?"

"I haven't a clue." He sounded surprised.

"Who's the heir when Franz dies?"

"That's far enough off, surely? I daresay he will have sons of his own by that time. Why on earth should you wonder?"

This time her smile was waiting, and had to be suppressed. "My roommate MaJa — oh, James, you should meet *her*. I mean she's so elegant and she plays the harp..."

"It's too late," said James somberly.

"Well, anyway, MaJa suggested that I might be the heiress to the von Elfenstein estates in Prussia. It was because of the locket. With Ilse's picture. In Uncle Albert's box..."

"Kate."

Oh. That she was so terribly silly was part of her charm — James' eyes said so. She shrank back. "I suppose you got all this dope from the horse's mouth," she said coldly. "I mean your beloved cousin Franz gave you his version of how it all turned out."

"Yes, Franz told me."

"Tell me more. How did you make yourself known to him with everyone being either a guard or a prisoner? I really can't believe things were all that chummy. I mean there must have been guys there who had actually taken a *dislike* to the Germans."

One thing about James. Heavy sarcasm didn't faze him as a rule. Teutonic knights were probably like that.

"Naturally Franz spoke perfect English. His manner too is absolutely correct. He is an officer and a gentleman in everything."

"Oh, naturally. But surely he didn't know who you were?"

"Of course not. He'd never had any contact with the family. His German grandfather had made that a condition of his going to England as a child, and Ilse had no say in the matter. She had no private fortune."

"So what happened? Hurry up. Ernie might come."

"There's always tomorrow. I could save some. I want you to understand."

"I understand. I do. Family means a lot to me."

"I forgot that Franz was your cousin too. Though not so near, of course. At Kahlberg we were short of many things which it is not absolutely necessary to have. But we were treated rather decently on the whole.

"There was always an unacknowledged rendezvous for secret trade with the Germans, but Franz was never part of that. He simply recognized the solidarity of military caste. He treated all officers as equals."

Kate looked at James, and saw how it must have been for him. Sally and Fred ate bread and Marmite by the kitchen fire, but to Franz James had been the equal of men like — well, like C.A. MacLeod-Smith for a modern instance. For the first time she looked boldly at the empty sleeve folded against his jacket. "You must have had both arms, I suppose," she said.

"Oh, that. I was damn lucky. My arm got smashed when I came down and was pretty rotten by the time the Germans found me. There was a medical team at Kahlberg. They amputated at once."

"A German medical team?"

"Of course."

"I guess a lot of them liked that stuff."

"Kate, you really don't understand. It wasn't a Nazi horror show. It was a very civilized place, for the most part."

"What else did they do that was so civilized?" Light broke in. "I suppose Franz helped you to escape? No wonder you don't talk about it." This time there was contempt in her voice, and James responded to it.

"My reasons for keeping silent are completely honorable." His eyes were ice blue, but he couldn't let it go, not now. He was too vulnerable. "It was not entirely without risk, coming out of Germany alone in my condition."

She sat silent — curious, but frightened and cold too. Finally he spoke again. "I shall continue until Ernie comes, unless you prefer not." He poured himself some brandy and looked at her. She shook her head.

"I'm listening."

"By 1944 things were hard for almost everyone. There was very little to eat. We subsisted on a tasteless root called kohl-rabi; none of us had ever heard of it. The weather turned bitter cold; ice would form inside the walls at night. As Christmas approached it developed that some of us in our block had hidden away odd treasures — things from Red Cross parcels and black market deals. We planned to have a party of sorts. Some of us were to sing carols, and one clever chap was organizing a pantomime. Humpty-Dumpty. He was to flash a swastika as he collapsed."

"Did you have anything to contribute?"

"Three cigarettes — Capstans — and a packet of peppermints. Franz came to us, very formal and correct. He wished us a pleasant holiday and offered us two bottles of hock. There was a secret ballot to see whether it would be accepted. It was refused. Later that night I was called out."

"Called out?"

"One of the guards came for me, and I was led away. It was assumed that I had been caught out in some illegal activity — possession of contraband material perhaps. That sort of thing happened. The commandant did not have as much faith in the honor system as Franz did, the more so as escape attempts were not infrequent. Some of them had even been successful. Do you mind helping me with a cigarette?"

He put his hand to steady her own and she felt that it was he who was unsteady, somewhere deep inside.

He went on, in a voice without emotion. "At all events, when I did escape later, my fellow prisoners suspected me of nothing more devious than not sharing my plan with them. Most escapes were group efforts.

"I was taken to Franz's room. The guard saluted and Franz dismissed him. He was alone. 'Good evening Captain Bell,' he said. '*Gut Jul.*' I waited. 'I sense a certain sympathy between us. Perhaps it is the season. Or perhaps it is because one of your Christian names is Oswald. It is a German name, but, more to the point, it was the name of my English father.' Of course I knew that, but for a few moments more I remained silent.

"'You will of course correct me if I have made a mistake,' he said. 'I simply thought that I might prevail upon you to drink a toast with me to the end of this war, an end that I assure you is not far off. The Russians will take Kahlberg, and they will be in no hurry to return it.' He indicated a table in the corner spread with iced champagne and Rhine wines, tins of French pate, biscuits, preserved fruit.

"It seems incredible when I remember how famished we were, but I didn't move. He poured a glass of champagne for me, and asked me to sit down. 'I am your cousin,' I said, still standing. 'Your father's sister is my mother.' He displayed the greatest warmth and surprise. We shook hands, his right to my left. He is a splendid man, Kate."

"If you say so."

"Ah, Kate, you like to be perverse. But it was an unbelievably moving moment for me — for both of us. You must remember the context of the war, of the feelings I had always had about his parents."

"So there you were, blood relations at a private party. So much for your packet of peppermints. You asked Franz to help you escape. How was it done?"

"I didn't ask him. It would never have occurred to me. It was Franz who suggested it."

"Why? Surely it was dangerous for both of you. If the war was nearly over why not just wait and be rescued? You couldn't go back to flying anyway." James' mouth tensed. "I mean, James, why should Franz be a traitor to his country for a cousin he never saw before? I don't get it."

"Franz said that an armed SS unit was on the way to Kahlberg. The death's head gang. With surrender in the air they had been cutting up rough. He was worried that they intended taking charge of the prisoners. There was danger."

Kate looked dubious, and he added, "They did not always adhere to the rules of civilized warfare."

"Oh, right. Everyone was so refined at Kahlberg it slipped my mind."

"He arranged for me to leave the castle disguised as one of the farmers who delivered milk and eggs to the staff officers."

"Just like Toad."

"Who?"

"Skip it. Didn't they notice you had an arm missing?"

"That was part of the plot. The man whose place I took had lost an arm at Verdun in 1916."

"What was supposed to happen to him? Surely you weren't supposed to bind and gag him — single handed as you were?"

"I suppose Franz made some arrangements for him. I didn't ask. He was just a local peasant."

"That must be Franz talking. I think the English peasantry graduated while you were out looking for the Holy Grail."

"Kate." She retreated into the tangled roses.

They heard a car door slam.

"What happened to Franz?"

Ernie strode in without knocking. "Everything all right, then?" he asked.

"A-1 at Lloyd's," answered Kate, jumping up.

"There's tomorrow," said James.

"Good-bye," said Kate. "Thanks."

Chapter XXIII

> And wherever affection can spring, it is like the green leaf and the blossom — pure, and breathing purity, whatever soil it may grow in.
> —George Eliot, *Romola*

The moon was down.

News of the murder on the moors had caused the regular crowd at the Brown Bull to double in number and swell in importance. Kate's room faced the street, and through the half open window she was being treated to a generous sample of local opinion offered by departing patrons of the public bar.

Jenny Ricks, the proprietor's saucer eyed daughter, was folding down the bedspread.

"There's running water down the hall," said Jenny, looking longingly at Kate's American suitcase. "I could unpack for you if you like."

"Oh, no thanks," said Kate, managing a smile. "Thanks though."

"It's an old place, is the Bull," said Jenny. "I could fetch hot water for your jug." Kate looked toward a massive white earthenware bowl and pitcher on a stand in a corner.

"Oh, I'll just brush my teeth down the hall for tonight."

"I know as it's cold. I put a hot pig in your bed."

"A hot *pig*?"

"You'll see." Jenny giggled. "Good night then, miss. Me Dad'll be wanting me to do the glasses."

"Good night."

She heard Jenny go down the stairs. There was a key in the door and she turned it. The keyhole was disproportionately large. It took some effort to engage the bolt.

Then she went to the dressing table and looked at herself in the mirror. Its reflective powers had faded and dimmed with age. Her own youth lay on the surface like a shimmer of sunlight. Her eyes, searching themselves, were puzzled.

As she slowly undressed and tossed her clothes piece by piece onto the floor she heard rough country voices coming from the dim world below.

"Colonel Fletcher being gone to the assizes is a rum go. Dogberry ull do nowt without him."

"If the dead un warn't strange Ernie ud know. And if he didn't know he could ask his mum." A laugh followed.

"Aye. Betty Stonehouse do see all and know all right enough."

"*And* tell all."

Kate found her pyjamas at the bottom of her suitcase, stepped into them, turned out the light, and walked barefoot toward the window.

"I be of opinion deceased be a escaped felon, shot for revenge by a former mate. Nowt to do wi' folk in Netherbeck."

"You said that afore, Edgar Thompson."

A door opened. "Aye, many a time and oft," said a cheerful voice. "I be shutting off the light now. You'll be keeping the young lady what is stopping upstairs awake with yer blather. Get along home to yer women."

Another round of good nights followed, then deeper darkness. Kate heard Jenny's voice. "Oh Dad, you'll never leave the cat out with murderers running about?"

Kate closed the window softly, fastened its bolt, and got into bed. She stretched her legs out slowly, enjoying a spreading sensation of warmth. Her feet touched a scalding hot stone water bottle and sprang back. The pig, no doubt. She stretched again, more slowly.

Tony will come, she thought. He said he would. Resting on that hope, she slept.

Sometime before dawn she heard a noise. That would be Jenny, letting in the cat.

When she woke again it was full daylight. Oh lord, what shall I do? She wondered. Someone was knocking.

"Miss, are you awake then?" It was Jenny's voice again, and the knob was being turned.

"Okay," shouted Kate. "Just a sec. It's locked." At that moment the door opened and Jenny stood rather breathlessly on the threshold.

"But I locked it last night," said Kate, looking for her bathrobe.

"I expect it didn't catch," said Jenny. "Country folk ben't much for locking up." She smiled reassuringly, then the saucer eyes widened. "Oooo. You be worried about the murder. But we have lock-ups front and back. It's like a proper castle, me mum used to say."

"Oh, well, since I hardly got murdered at all..." Kate slid her feet into slippers.

Jenny laughed with delight. Then she said apologetically, "I didn't want to knock you up, miss, though it be close on nine. But there's a person been asking for you."

"What kind of person?" Her heart achieved a precarious equilibrium.

"A man. I put him in the back parlor. I could fetch your breakfast there. Ginger's just this minute laid an egg." Jenny looked at her in a pleading way. "Oh, I do like your slippers. I never seen ones like that. I've brought some hot water, in case you wanted to have a wash in your room."

"Oh, thanks Jenny. What kind of man though? Tall? Fair? Is it my cousin James Bell?"

"Oh, nowt like that. American." Jenny was seen to make a significant distinction. "I must say, miss, that the person is not a gentleman."

"Oh, dear," said Kate solemnly. "Does he have a beard?"

"No. Though he could do with a razor all right." She thought again. "He looks a bit like a ferret."

"Oh. Well, tell him I'll be down in a flash, okay?" She picked up a blue plaid skirt from the floor and inspected it to see whether it could be worn again.

"I could hot up the iron in a..." began Jenny helpfully.

"It'll do, thanks. Why don't you just go and fix the breakfast?" She smiled. "Thank Ginger for the egg. You wouldn't have any orange juice by any chance?"

"No, but there's ever so much marmalade. It's made with oranges, you know. From Seville." She pronounced it to rhyme with "revel."

"Swell. See you soon."

Harry Feather sat in a dark little back room smoking a Camel, a cup of milky coffee cooling before him. He stood up when Kate entered.

"Remember me?" he asked.

"Hello, Mr. Feather. My roommate in New York said you were looking for me."

"Don't get me wrong, toots. I don't give a merry goddamn where your uncle hid the loot. Small stuff is all I ever wanted. No ambition, that's what my wife said. Look where it got *her*."

Kate sat down and stared at him.

"*What* loot?"

There was a knock and Jenny came in with a breakfast tray. Ginger's egg, gently boiled, was keeping warm under a small woolen hat that matched the tea cozy. Kate looked at girl and tray with eyes blank as marbles. When the door closed again she turned back to Harry.

"I don't know what you mean."

It was Harry's turn to stare. "Jeez, you're a dumb kid. That's what I said to Fan after you gave us the air at Penn Station. 'Jeez,' I said, 'that is one dumb kid. Don't mess with her. She'll screw up the works.'" He sat down again and lit a new cigarette from the stub of the old one. "See, I didn't want Fan going back to England. Especially without me. Want an American fag?"

Kate shook her head. "I knew there was something wrong about you. Your wife had a gun. Do you mean that my uncle had something you wanted to *steal*?"

"Forget that part. Like I say, that don't matter now. I just want to find out who killed Fan." He fished a rumpled handkerchief from his pocket and blew his nose. "You found her. I found out that much. You and that bastard Burrows. I wanna know could Burrows of killed her. That's the first thing I wanna know."

Kate looked at him, at his red nose and watery eyes and brown stained fingers. He wore a new, cheap, and very dirty short coat and a checked cap with a peak that shaded his thin face. He had unbuttoned the top button of his coat but no more, though there was a gas fire in the room.

"Pardon me for living, toots. Just answer my question and I'll be shoving off."

"I'm sorry, Mr. Feather. I'm just shaken up, that's all. I don't know who killed Mrs. Birdsill. Or Feather. I don't know anything at all."

"You gotta know something I don't know. You was there."

"She was dead when I found her. I saw you on the pier before we sailed. You and Ruggles. But not your wife. I was just the person who found her. You said yourself I wasn't too good at figuring things out."

"Look, sister, at least tell me who was there, how it was. Come down off your high horse. Quit playing the fine English lady."

Kate was stung. "Leave me alone please, Mr. Feather. I have nothing to tell you and...and I would like to eat my breakfast." She seized a napkin from the tray.

"Sure, eat your breakfast. What's it to you? I couldn't expect a babe in the woods like you to unnerstand," he said contemptuously, "but I was in love with her. Yeah, me, a skinny little crook, and her, a fat broad with more angles than Chinese Checkers. That's life, kiddo. If you're lucky you may find out."

Kate's eyes filled with tears and she blotted them with the napkin. "I don't see how Tom Burrows could have killed her, Mr. Feather," she said gently. "It was very confusing in the corridors but he seemed to be coming from the opposite direction when I met him. I was alone when I found her, and I thought about it a lot afterwards."

Harry pounced. "You suspected him. Didn't you?"

"Yes. I suspected him. In a way, I always suspected him. But I don't suspect him any more."

"Why the hell not?"

"Because there's a dead man in Netherbeck nobody knows. The wheels don't seem to spin very fast around here but pretty soon they'll ask *me* to look at him. And I think it's Tom Burrows." She raised a hand as if to muffle the sound of her heart. "I saw him in York. I think you came here to kill him and you did kill him and now you want me to tell you that you did the right thing."

One look at Harry's face was enough to show her how wrong she was.

"Holy jeez," he said.

"You mean you didn't know? Everyone's talking about it. Where were you last night? We heard of you yesterday, pretending to be hiking on the moors."

"We?"

"My cousin and a friend of his."

"Would that be James Bell, ex-R.A.F.?"

"How do you know?"

"I gotta blow. Look, toots, I'll see you around. I don't usually hit it off with the cops. I'm clean. I slept next to a pigsty last night. Look, do me a favor for old times' sake. Say I wasn't here, okay?"

"They'll think that's funny."

"Why?"

"Why should I say you weren't here if you *weren't* here?"

"If they *ask* ya, I mean."

"I can't promise."

"Take my advice, kid. Don't trust nobody and don't hang around."

"Are the stakes very high, then?"

"Fan thought so. I told her small stakes Rubber Bridge was her game." He looked sad again. "You ain't all bad, toots."

Harry Feather pulled his cap down, raised the window behind him, and climbed out.

Kate poured milk into her cup and added tea. The tea was still warm. She uncovered the egg and sliced the top off with a small firm whack. The toast was in a rack with capital letters on top of each separator: T/O/A/S/T. She buttered a piece and spread it with marmalade. There was a plateful of local ham. She ate slowly and steadily until Jenny knocked on the door.

"Come in."

"Oh, you *have* done well. I was afraid that man would put you off. Was the egg all right?"

"Perfect."

"I think it's a waste to fry a new egg."

"I didn't know new eggs were so good."

"Fancy that. I don't know whether I'd be wanting to live in New York."

"It's a great place to visit, though." She smiled at Jenny. "Listen, Jenny. I want to make a very private phone call. Can I use a telephone here?"

"It's not exactly what you'd call private. It's in the public bar. Makes it handy for the wives to ring up."

"Don't you have a phone in your own quarters?"

"Me Dad says there's no need. Sid Porson — he's a friend of mine over Witherton way —" Jenny tittered. " — Sid Porson says he'd ring up regular if we had a private telephone, but there you are. 'A fat lot of good that ud be,' says me Dad."

"Well, is there a private public phone in Netherbeck?"

"There's a kiosk outside the post office but I can't say how private you'd be finding it. There's usually heaps of people waiting round and somebody's gone and smashed the glass." Jenny looked interested. "There's not a great heap private in a village, miss."

"Listen, Jenny, I'm going out. If my cousin James Bell..." Jenny looked more interested still. "...or Miss Broadbent from the vicarage should come looking for me say I'll be back at tea time. Otherwise say nothing. Just say you don't know. Okay?" She opened her handbag.

"Oh, miss, I'll be happy to oblige you. I don't want no money. Where are you going to, then?"

"I'll tell you later. I promise."

"Where's the ferrety man gone to?"

"I think he's on his way back to America."

She smiled and rushed upstairs. Jenny had done her room and put some yellow-flowered gorse into a green jar. A waiting bus thrumbled outside. She grabbed her coat and flew down into the street, signalling the driver just as he was closing the door. He waited for her. She climbed in and asked breathlessly, "Where does this bus go?"

"Witherton."

"Is that where the Brontës lived?"

"It's not."
"Never mind. How much?"
"Return?"
"Round trip, please."
"All the way to Witherton?"
"How far is it?"
"Seventeen mile."
"Yes please."
She bought her ticket and looked around for a seat. The bus was nearly full.

Chapter XXIV

> He had spent the afternoon in a motion picture palace, and the fascination of the film had caused him to lose all sense of time...
> —P. G. Wodehouse, *Leave it to Psmith*

The old bus dipped through the village water splash with the aplomb of an Olympic diver. Drops spattered the windows. Kate had found a seat next to an imposing woman in a puce hat who was doing the *Times* crossword puzzle. Kate needed some anti-social camouflage herself. Her handbag furnished forth a green and white paperback: *Death Times Three* by Marvella Krispie. Under the circumstances the title was inauspicious. She wished she had something escapist, maybe one of those heartwarming English narratives about a family holiday in Patagonia. She opened to page one and began to read:

> Lettice Bagshot stifled a scream. Her uncle, Clarence Overpart, the noted big game hunter, lay sprawled across his mahogany desk, the intricately carved handle of a Malay dagger...

Someone was in my room last night, thought Kate. That was it. She opened her handbag again and within its expanded hollow tried to examine her passport case. Inside one of its many superfluous pockets lurked the Hanged Man — the Tarot card she had taken from Fan's body. She slid it out, just far enough to confirm her memory of it: the blue legs, the strawberry colored coat, the black hair and little beard, the easy way the man hung upside down from the yellow gallows, half smiling, hands behind his back.

Madame Sosostris, the wisest woman in Europe, had a *wicked* pack of cards.

Kate had just abandoned Madame Sosostris. Let the Partridges find her, and let them ask her what she meant by setting traps for innocent young heiresses. She was going to tell Inspector Bucket everything. To that end, she continued to search her case surreptitiously until she found a small scrap of paper with a number written on it. This she tucked carefully inside her shoe, under the sole of her left foot, between her stocking and her angora sock — just in case.

When she straightened up, she saw that the eyes beneath the puce hat were watching her curiously.

"It's a pad for bunions," she said rather loudly, into one of those silences public transport is susceptible to. Everyone laughed except Puce Hat, who sent a contemptuous glance around the bus before addressing her courteously.

"Are you going to visit Witherton? It has a very fine old church, St. Sidwella's. I could tell you something of its past."

Kate looked at her and met a hint of mockery submerged in her somewhat magnified eyes. "What about its future?" she asked, wriggling her foot.

"Odd your asking, as there is to be a new curate next week. A young man from Lancashire of mysterious antecedents." She was calm and pale and wore red stones in her ears.

"That was a silly thing to say. I'm sorry. I was embarrassed about my bunion." She smiled sheepishly.

"So I observed. Being rattled, you perhaps took me for a gypsy. I fear I'm pure Saxon, ruby eardrops notwithstanding. There were some gypsies about Dimmock last week. I can't think you'll have any saucepans that want mending so I suppose you wish to have your fortune told."

"No. I had my fortune told last summer."

"Were you told to beware of an eccentric spinster of a certain age whom you would encounter on a motor bus?" The woman offered a tube of hard candies. "Each one is wrapped at the works, you see. Nothing like the Poisoned Plum Pudding."

"What poisoned plum pudding?"

"Have you never read *Lavengro*? It's full of gypsy lore. But, as I say, I am a Gorgio."

Kate smiled and sighed. "You should meet my cousin Sally Bell."

"Yes, I would like to meet her."

Kate looked at her in surprise. "How do you know?"

"I'm afraid I've been rather a bore. I know who you are, you see, though I've forgotten your name. Rosemary described you. My name is Cecily Maud Watershed. I'm by way of being some sort of remote but tenacious cousin of the vicar of Netherbeck."

"My name is Kate Clark."

"And you are a cousin of James Bell."

"Yes. And of Sally Bell, his mother."

"Of course. I am also the cousin of Rosemary Broadbent, which is very much to the point as it is her largesse which provides me with winter quarters. In the summer I was generally engaged as a paid travelling companion — it is slim pickings now with so little sterling allowed out of the country." Her tone was matter-of-fact.

"But can't you do something else? Work in a store or an office?"

"Decayed gentlewomen never work in stores or offices, Miss Clark. We run errands, walk the dog, take a hand at Bridge. It's not such a bad life. When Rosemary marries I daresay the vicar will keep me on full time. I shall drive the Jaguar to Witherton on market days and give the sheep a fright."

The bus was barely creeping and Kate saw that the road was clogged with large wooly bundles on spindly legs. The sky had turned very dark.

"Is Rosemary going to be married?"

"I had hopes," said Miss Watershed dryly. "I find I'm a bit jaded with the *Promenade des Anglais* after all."

"Oh, Miss Watershed, don't plan on my cousin James!" Kate blurted out, turning very red.

The older woman took off her glasses in an apparent effort to see Kate more clearly. Her eyebrows were the same pale shade as her complexion. She appeared to elevate them slightly. "Perhaps you are aware of something which is not common knowledge in Netherbeck," she said. "I assure you that your cousin's friendship with Rosemary has been sufficiently marked to raise rather general expectations. They make a very striking couple. Of course in a village everyone takes an interest. I suppose that in Tooting or Croydon or wherever it is his people live the proprieties are not so important." Her tone verged on the malicious.

Kate was annoyed. She would have liked to change her seat but the only empty one seemed to be occupied by a piglet asleep on a coiled green muffler. "My cousin in Kent is a *real* gentlewoman, Miss Watershed. Not decayed at all," she said in a hostile tone.

It had begun to rain, and as they watched the drops fell with accelerating density, blotting out everything but the narrow road that clung to the dales. The bus crept along like a rickety submarine. Miss Watershed made a three-letter entry in her puzzle and then said blandly, "I was sure that it would bucket the moment I saw Cecil pinch my umbrella."

"Who's Cecil? Not that I care. I'm sure he's genteel as a tea tray, no matter what he pinches."

"Cecil's the vicar. We are Cecil and Cecily Maud. Our parents thought we might marry on the strength of it but old Cecil pitched on a raving beauty with plenty of tin in the background. Pity she couldn't have left a bit more to Cecil but no matter — Rosemary won't let him fall victim to the austerity program."

"How nice."

Miss Watershed acknowledged Kate's visible grievance with a smile of superior affability. "Look here, Miss Clark, I do hope you haven't taken offence at my somewhat careless remark about Tooting. If you plan to spend any time in England it simply won't do to be thin skinned. You must play the game yourself. Placing people socially is by way of being the national pastime. We don't ask *what* you are, but *who* you are."

"Well, it's both rude and stupid, if you ask me. I'm glad I had a chance to emigrate."

"I dare say you are right," said Miss Watershed unconvincingly. "In any case I had no objection to your distinguished looking cousin marrying into the family. Thomas Birkie was a very gentleman-like man *in his way*, and of course Rosemary's maternal grandfather was an *arriviste* of the first water. Or perhaps I should say beer. It never entered our heads to suspect a mercenary motive on your cousin's part but we did rather ask ourselves what he meant to live on. But, you see, I use the past tense. I take your word for it that a match will not be made. Rosemary implied as much."

"I don't really know James Bell very well. I shouldn't have said anything. I don't know why I did anyway." Miss Watershed looked skeptical. "Does Rosemary...care for James?"

"Possibly. Rosemary would consider a heart on the sleeve in dubious taste. She is young and very beautiful. I don't expect her to trick herself out in rue and pine away." Miss Watershed shifted her ground. "Had she known that you were to be left on your own I'm sure she would have offered to drive you to Witherton in the Jaguar."

It was clearly meant as a question but Kate assumed an inquisitive expression of her own. Miss Watershed continued. "Oh, I make a point of going across on the bus on market days. I get some blood sausage and a piece of Wensleydale cheese for Cecil, then have a modest luncheon at The Grey Cockatoo with an old friend of mine. I often go to the cinema afterward, but I don't care for the look of the film today. I expect I shall return to Netherbeck on the early bus — that is unless you would like me to show you round St. Sidwella's. There are quoin stones in the tower which are undoubtedly Roman."

"No thanks."

"As you like. Try to avoid 'the smyler with the knife beneath the cloak.' Another English type."

"What do you mean?" The slip of paper beneath her foot suddenly felt like a lump of gravel and she saw herself running along the edge of a lake with darkness coming on.

"Well, we have had a murder, have we not? The last one was in 1872, I believe. A *crime passionel* involving some artless rustics. The current affair should offer a few more thrills."

"The rain has let up some," said Kate.

"Let up some what?"

"It's too subtle an expression for a foreigner," said Kate. "If you'll excuse me I have a murder of my own." She threw herself back into *Death Times Three* with avid and unseeing eyes.

By the time they reached Witherton the rain had thinned to a drizzle. The bus made room for itself at the edge of the main square and Kate beheld an encampment of booths and stalls under dripping canvas. Bodies encased in Burberrys and MacIntoshes struggled past each other carrying damp bags and baskets. Kate said "So long" to Miss Watershed and plunged into the crowd. Everything seemed to be primordially moist and cold except for the braziers where chestnuts and potatoes were being roasted. She bought a hot potato and, standing under the edge of a dripping umbrella, ate it with salt and a lump of butter.

Her first objective was to find a telephone. What she had in mind was a kiosk surrounded by a large empty space, like a hilltop observation post. Not, of course, that she thought she was being followed. On the contrary, this was one time when she certainly did *not* think she was being followed.

But.

But?

Yes, but on that afternoon in York, the day before yesterday, when Tom Burrows had given her such a scare — and maybe Tom Burrows would never scare anyone again — she had hit upon an instant hypothesis: Panic is the hallmark of safety.

Obviously if she thought no one was following her she had something to worry about, under the circumstances. This would be the time, at last. She glanced around nervously. A sallow young man with forgettable features was watching her.

"May I help you with anything, miss?" he asked politely.

"No, thank you. I mean yes, please. Is there a telephone box near here?"

"There's one at the other side of the square and there's one right away along the High Street."

"Which is more private?"

"Well, if it's peace and quiet you're after you'd best go along down the High Street. The one across there —" he pointed through the congealed caravanserai "— is a bit popular on market days."

Kate set off down the indicated thoroughfare, the slip of paper burning her foot. She wished she had left it where it so discreetly was. It was going to look odd fishing it out of her sock. What if she'd lost the number? So what? She could easily find out the number of Scotland Yard. On the other hand she might have been in a hurry. What with pushing Button A and/or Button B things could get confusing.

The kiosk formed a cheerful and self-sufficient oasis on the pavement ahead. She ran to it, closed herself in, and thought of James, his hair gold in the firelight. Maybe Inspector Bucket meant trouble for James; maybe Tom Burrows was the American captain who called him up. James was all right, in his own awful way. Anyway, he wasn't even on the ship.

Sam Gordon was on the ship.

She managed to get out the number, and to hear the phone ringing far away in London. "New Scotland Yard here." She pushed the button.

"May I please speak to Inspector Bucket?"

Inspector Bucket was not available. If it was a police matter she could speak to someone else. Would Inspector Bucket return soon? Inspector Bucket was not available. Who was calling please? Had Inspector Bucket gone to Yorkshire? She was calling about the Birdsill case. One moment please.

And the operator wanted another four pence. She put in two heavy coppers and scrambled in her bag for more. The connection went dead.

An anxious queue had formed outside the phone booth. As she continued to fish for coins a distraught face pasted itself against the glass and a damp woman banged on the door with a knobby umbrella handle.

Kate went back outside and looked at the three halfpence and one farthing in her hand. Scotland Yard would trace the call, put Yorkshire and Birdsill together — they were famous for putting things together — and hop a fast express. Inspector Bucket might already be in Netherbeck. They might have identified the corpse from its hunderwear.

In any case, she would have to get more change. Phoning Inspector Bucket was only half her reason for coming to Witherton. The other half was James, who would not be able to scour the countryside for her unless he had someone to drive him. She would not return to Netherbeck until late afternoon, anyway. Meanwhile, not to worry.

She went back to the market place and wandered among the sad corpses of fowl and hare. They still wore their fur and feathers. Suspended head downward they were like so many Hanged Men.

She lunched in a bright and bleak cafe with Bakelite tabletops and a menu that ran to chips: Spam and chips, eggs and chips, Heinz beans and chips, spaghetti and chips, sausage and chips. She sat in a corner away from the window. The Grey Cockatoo was on the opposite side of the street.

When she telephoned Scotland Yard again, and asked for Inspector Bucket, an authoritative voice suggested that she report to the police station, said, in fact, that Inspector Bucket wished her to do so.

"Okay, I'll go back to Netherbeck," she said, and went to the movies. She bought a ticket for the stalls. Whoever was not following her would sit in the smoking section upstairs. The lights went thrillingly dim and the credits came onto the screen: *Nightmare Alley* with Tyrone Power.

Afterward, cold and shaken, she returned to the Town Square. It was nearly empty. Tents, stalls, odors, tables, voices had all vanished like the trappings of some magic bazaar, and a disconsolate workman was sweeping up the debris that might have served as proof of its reality.

A bus marked Witherton was parked at the spot where she had alighted that morning. It was more than half full. As she stepped in to speak to the driver she saw that the piglet was asleep on the same green muffler. It had survived the market. The driver was reading a colored comic paper.

"Does this bus go to Netherbeck?"

"It does."

"Will it be leaving soon?"

He produced a pocket watch and studied it. "In three minutes."

This time she found a window seat.

The bus pulled out noisily and was soon rising and falling with the rolling countryside. The rain had stopped but the late daylight was thickened with clouds. A scarlet strip was pasted along the horizon to the west.

Several passengers required to be disembarked en route and the going was slow. It was quite dark before they reached Netherbeck and Kate discovered that she was wiping the window with the side of her fist in an effort to see the lights of the village.

But it was not the pale twinkle that she expected that welcomed the travellers. It was a great blaze, surging billows of flame leaping and dancing up into the black sky.

"Oh, what is it? What's happened?" she cried, turning to anyone within earshot.

"Why, don't you know the date then?" answered a friendly voice. "It's the fifth of November. Gunpowder, treason, and plot."

Guy Fawkes Day.

Chapter XXV

> Lady, sweetly encountered, I come from court,
> I must be bold with you.
> —Cyril Tourneur, *The Revenger's Tragedy*

The ceremonial bonfire was in a field at the edge of the village, a parcel of land normally consecrated to the athletic contests of man and boy. For some days past a great heap of lumber, broken furniture, logs, and tinder had been rising on the traditional spot and fifteen minutes before the Witherton bus pulled up in front of the Brown Bull it had been ignited on all sides to the accompaniment of raucous cheers.

More often than not, the mighty elements of fire and water, meeting in hundreds of damp English corners, had done battle on this anniversary. It fell in a gloomy season. Far more often than not, fire, aided by its minions and myrmidons in sweaters and stout boots, was victorious. So it was in Netherbeck in 1947. Indeed the fact that it was no longer actually raining had assured an early triumph, though the cold air still lay heavy on the moist earth.

The merry blaze roared back at the admiring crowd, and as Kate came running to the scene she saw a group of dark figures preparing to hurl what looked like a human body atop the burning pile. Bits of flame were breaking away to leap higher and higher into the black sky.

She touched the arm nearest her, feeling its tweedy roughness through her glove. "Oh, what is it?" she asked. At the fringe of the crowd, where she stood, the darkness was intense.

"It's the Guy. He's burned in effigy. Is it new to you?" Out of all the voices in the world it was the one she most wished to hear.

"No, no, it's not," she answered, her heart dancing with happiness and relief. "I just forgot and it frightened me. Oh, Tony, a terrible thing has happened here."

They moved forward and Tony searched for her face. "You knew my voice," he said softly.

"I've been playing it on the Victrola of my memory," she said, glad of the burning dark. "Why didn't you know mine?"

"Ah, there are so many American girls about." He laughed, then said seriously, "One murder should have been enough for you, Kate. I wish I had come yesterday and taken you away with me." He was tall. He put his arm around her shoulders.

"But I only came myself yesterday. I saw you in York. I knew it was you, but I couldn't catch you."

A great cry went up as the straw man landed atop the pyre. Enthusiasts were rushing up with new fuel from attics and barns: barrel staves, ax handles, table legs. As Kate stood on tiptoe for a better view three men appeared dragging a large and incongruous rowboat. A passage was made for them through the crowd and they cast their burden awkwardly onto the fire.

"Ah," said Tony. "The funeral barge."

She loved his voice. It polished his words as they slipped out, giving them the rich patina of some treasured object that poor people have rubbed for luck. And underneath the ease lurked a hint of tension seductive as a hidden tide. Of all people, *he* should have understood Mme. Sosostris' message.

On the other hand, so long gypsy. It was better to have him outside the whole sordid mystery.

"Tony?" She had forgotten all about James.

"Kate?" Here, closer to the fire, she could see him watching her. Something in his expression made her want to go up like a rocket.

"Why are you here?"

"I told you I would come to find you. I telephoned to your people in The Oval and was told that you had come here." There was a slight hesitation before he said "The Oval" that displeased Kate. Her encounter with Miss Watershed was too recent. Oh well. The whole thing was probably too beautiful to last anyway.

Amateur refreshment stands had been established around the periphery of the charmed circle, the empty space the crowd left between itself and the fire. Kate noticed a hand-lettered placard, which read: Proceeds to the Belfry Repair Fund. A thin man in a clerical collar was dispensing hot sausage rolls while several eager ladies made change and washed tea mugs. The Vicar and his female satellites. Miss Watershed was serving tea with airy condescension. There was no sign of Rosemary.

Rival establishments offered more potent libations for the ritual occasion — cider, beer, ale. There were plenty of customers to go round, all queueing up in the estimable British fashion.

"May I offer you something? Have you had tea? We can dine later."

"Oh, no thanks. I ate a lot of starch in Witherton and I had a lemon squash at the movies. Tell me when you came and who you saw. What do you know about the murder? The reason I went to Witherton was to phone Scotland Yard. Are there many police here? Do you know that Lisa Dragonette is around here somewhere? Can you feature it?" She turned solemn. "I met Tom Burrows in York. I liked him less than ever. But I think they killed him, Tony."

"Why do you say 'they,' Kate?" he dropped his arm and took her hand, pulling off her glove and putting it in her pocket.

"There are some crooks after something." He looked a question. "That's all I know." She felt the inadequacy of it and wondered at herself. The loyalty she had been feeling toward Mme. Sosostris seemed to have settled inexplicably on Harry Feather.

There was a wild cheer as the fire caught and devoured some new flashy kindling and sent up bright scarlet flags to meet a new scattering of dim stars. And on my cousin James too, she thought with a sudden pang, very conscious of Tony's arm against her own. *The fires are all magic.*

"I only arrived in Netherbeck round four o'clock," said Tony. "I had some trouble with my motor car, not for the first time. It's a jolly little beast but wants to be put out to pasture, I'm afraid. At all events there was a police officer from London at the Brown Bull, and he pounced on me with more zeal than courtesy. Rather a poor show. The corpse had already been identified but I was able to provide confirmation. You were right, of course."

"I think my cousin knew him." Her voice was so low that he had to bend to hear her.

"Was that it? I had intended looking you up at your cousin's house as soon as I got transport. Moon Croft."

"What's the matter with calling a house 'Moon Croft' if you want to?"

"Nothing whatever." Tony laughed. "A very beautiful young woman named Rosemary Broadbent was waiting for you at the Bull. We had tea together."

"Oh?"

"She was called away to help her father paper over a schism in the Ladies' Committee."

The light of the swaying flames played randomly among the faces on the other side of the bonfire, lifting now one, now another, out of the busy dark. Impossible to be sure of anyone, but Kate thought she saw a man they both knew.

"Tony! Doesn't that look like Sam Gordon over there? Do you see the man I mean? I *knew* he'd follow Lisa Dragonette."

Tony drew her back from the fire, into outer darkness. A shed for sporting equipment stood at the edge of the field; its shadow was private as the back of the moon. They stopped there.

"Not this time," he said, pushing her hair away from her mouth. This time the thrumming noise was not the ship's engines. It was somewhere inside her. This time he kissed her, and light years passed before he stopped. When she opened her eyes at last she saw the stars full out, a giant's handful of sequins hurled spinning across the sky. The air was drunk with the smell of heath and burning peat.

He did not release her at once. His lips were in her hair; her cheek was against his rough jacket. "Tony?" she whispered.

"Kate?"

"This is the most exciting thing that ever happened to me."

"You mean so far, I think."

"Is there more?" The world was standing still.

"Much more. Look, we must get out of all this. If the police want us, we can come back. I've left my car with a person who does repairs in the village. I must recover it first, and if it's not ready I shall have to wait. I suggest that you slip back to your room for a warmer coat and I'll pick you up there. If you go the back way I don't think you'll be noticed."

"What if I am?"

"I don't want anyone else to carry you off. Sure to occur if you're seen."

They moved out of the shadows and he touched her cheek.

"Doesn't it say 'TONY' all over my face?" she asked. "No one would dare."

He kissed her again. "*Auf wiedersehen*," he said. "English lacks that phrase."

"*Au revoir*," she answered. She felt as if she were carrying her heart high on a string, like a balloon.

The back door of the Brown Bull was not locked, and the big kitchen was empty. Kate stood still for a minute, listening to the noise from the bar.

"God save the King!" shouted a beery voice.

"Death to the traitors!" was the reply and there was a good-natured clink of mugs.

She crossed to the hall and floated up the stairs.

There was a light on in her room and the door was ajar. She hesitated, dismayed. Before she could decide what to do she heard light brisk steps and Rosemary stood before her wearing the expression of someone who would prefer not to be annoyed. She stood aside to let Kate enter.

"I hope you'll excuse my somewhat officious behavior, Kate. I do feel that you are quite old enough to take care of yourself, but James has been frantic with worry all day."

Rosemary's even gaze was disconcerting, and Kate crossed to the mirror and combed her hair. Rosemary probably found her flushed cheeks and lack of lipstick indecorous. She turned back.

"But didn't Miss Watershed tell you I went to Witherton? I sat with her on the bus."

"Cecily Maud has been here patronizing the local populace for hours." Rosemary half smiled and Kate threw her a look of gratitude. "Well, no matter. One wouldn't have fussed about you at all in the ordinary way. The Murder on the Moors — yes, the press has arrived — has put us all on edge. James is unusually nervy. It seems the police have asked him to remain in the vicinity." To Kate's surprise, Rosemary lit a cigarette.

"Oh, how awful. Where is he now?"

"He's back at Moon Croft. I'll run you out so that he can see you're safe and well."

Kate flushed. "I can't go, Rosemary. Can you possibly tell James that I'm okay and I'll see him tomorrow." Rosemary's eyebrows rose slightly. "*Please*."

"Sorry, but I'd really rather not. It's you he wants to see, as I'm sure you know. Leave a message for your friend. I can't think *he'll* panic."

"I forgot you had tea with him."

"Yes. He takes lemon. Jenny Ricks found that rather exotic. Between James and Mr. — C. A. MacLeod-Smith? — she's in transports. Her young man from Witherton will have to change his spots." Rosemary managed another minimal smile. Her eyes were sad.

"Does he have many spots?" asked Kate, sorry.

"I'm afraid so. Come along, Kate. I must get back to the Vicarage. My father will want me to pour the sherry after all his labours at the revels. He's full of Christian forbearance as a rule but Cecily Maud can be a bit much undiluted."

"Will you bring me right back? Tony asked me to stay here."

"I hope you'll excuse me if I say that you're being rather a bore. James is your cousin, after all, and he's in trouble, however short-lived it may prove to be. I can't imagine for a moment that your friend wouldn't go to Moon Croft for you. If Barker hasn't been able to repair his motor, young Barker runs a kind of village taxi."

Kate felt all the justice of the rebuke.

"I'm sorry, Rosemary. I lost my head. Hold it a second and I'll leave a note for him with Jenny."

Rosemary took a note pad out of her handbag and tore off a ruled slip of paper. Kate took out her fountain pen and wrote:

> Dear Tony
> I just *had* to go see my cousin at Moon Croft. Could you possibly pick me up there? I have no way of getting back to Netherbeck unless I walk and I think my cousin wouldn't agree to that. Jenny Ricks can tell you which road to take.
> "Not to worry."

There was an envelope in her bedside drawer and she enclosed the note in it and licked the flap quickly. "Let's hurry, then," she said to Rosemary, flattening the gummed edge with her fist.

She and Rosemary said little on the way to Moon Croft. Kate was not looking forward to an interview with James. She wanted to be safe with Tony again.

The curtains had not been drawn and the windows of the long living room shed a pale glow into the still, cold darkness that was wrapped around the house.

"Will Mrs. Stonehouse be here?" asked Kate hopefully.

"I shouldn't think so. Everyone goes to the bonfire, or nearly everyone. I'll just see you safe inside. Then I must really fly." Rosemary had swung the car round so that Kate could get out close to the front door. "Tell James I shall be at home should he need anything. You could ring me after your friend picks you up." Her face was hidden in the shadow of the car.

"Thanks for everything, Rosemary." Kate ran to the door and pulled the old-fashioned bell. She heard the clang of it inside, but no one came. Through the window she could see the empty living room. The fire was business-like, well tended. She turned the handle and found that the door was open.

"James, it's me," she called.

She waved to Rosemary, stepped inside, and closed the door behind her.

Chapter XXVI

> Yet I devour'd the Bait was layd for me.
> —Michael Drayton, *The Epistle of Rosamund*

James must be upstairs or out at the back. His chair by the fire had an aura of recent occupancy; an open book lay face down beside his ashtray. Maybe the plumbing conked out. Kate's idea of rural plumbing had been formed at Snake Lake, where the pipes periodically fell victims to the strangling clutch of tropic root systems.

"James?" she called again. He should have had a dog. Or brought Sal-ammbo. An animal can always do the honors.

She went through into the kitchen, not bothering to flick on the light. The lamp in the living room threw an illuminated path to the sink. She turned the tap, and the water fell cold and sparkling into the iron basin. James' few dishes had been washed and set neatly to dry; she extracted the cup, filled it, and drank. An inverted bowl on the counter proved to conceal the remains of a pork pie. She decided to take it into the living room and eat it by the fire. Her hand was on the plate when she heard the front door open.

A man was speaking. It was a voice she knew, cultured and easy, with a hint of tension underneath. Relief and happiness suffused her. He must have come after her right away.

"Sorry to hear you've run into trouble over this American, old man," Tony said. Kate stood still, bewildered. Why hadn't he told her that he knew James? James' answer turned her heart to ice.

"I don't understand all the mystery, Franz. You've been a long time." He paused. "And you're frightfully pukka in those British tweeds. Surely that's hardly necessary now."

"You forget I'm half English, my dear cousin. I was educated at Harchester. An English public school marks a man for life. I suppose your enthusiasm for the defunct German aristocracy rather carried you away — and a certain notable family heirloom with you." He laughed easily.

A small passage with a pantry opening off it separated the kitchen from the living room and assured a deeper darkness where Kate stood. James moved into her line of vision. He was wearing his fleece-lined flying jacket, the empty sleeve hanging slack like one of those wind direction funnels at airports. There's no weather tonight, she thought numbly. That's what the airmen say, no weather. James was not smiling.

"You're right, Franz. Your request appealed to my sense of honor and family pride. I was quite prepared to consider myself a near connection of the von Elfensteins, and to save an object of cultural and historic value from the approaching Red Army." He extracted a cigarette from his pocket and Tony flashed out his lighter. Kate remembered the German crest on it. "'A family treasure that once belonged to Herman von Salza, Hochmeister of the Teutonic Order, who had in turn got it from Conrad of Mazovia in 1226.' You see how well I remember your very educational lecture." This was the cool James Kate had met first, the one who rattled them all. Tony was not rattled.

"Yes, the provenance of the piece is a fascinating one. Its recent history is what interests me this evening, however. Uncle Albert's death complicated our plans in an unforeseen way, of course, but my old friend Rosa Szastris obtained the object from you, apparently carried it to Florida, and disappeared. May I ask what happened?" Tony's voice was still easy, as if he didn't notice the hardness in James.

But it wasn't Tony. There was no Tony. Kate had not moved, and she already felt the ache and dizziness of a sentry. In silent horror she took a step backward.

"In a minute, Franz. There are a few things I'd like to be clear about." There was a knife-edge in James' voice. "What do you propose to do with this valuable object? It had been taken to Kahlberg for safekeeping during the war but we agreed that it was to return to the von Elfenstein estate where it could continue to inspire future generations in the family chapel. Your idea of using Uncle Albert as a repository was something I never quite understood. I worked on it as I hid in the frozen ruins of Europe. I am working on it still. Of course it did not occur to me not to trust you."

"And now it does occur to you? I assure you, my dear James, my heart is quite as pure as that of the average Teutonic Knight of the old order. How *can* I return it to the von Elfenstein estate? Whatever the ancestral spread may consist of is now in East Germany, safely under the all-seeing protection of Father Bear. Neither of us foresaw that in 1945. Let us be thankful that we saved something from those vulgar paws."

The two men shifted position, James moving away and Tony coming into view, his hands in the pockets of his Harris Tweed jacket. *There was never any Tony.* Kate was suddenly struck by a family resemblance between them. She thought of them together at Kahlberg, clasping hands in the twilight of the gods. German mythology always seemed to involve worlds collapsing.

James spoke again. "You will agree that I have gone to a good deal of trouble, Franz, one way and another. Your little statue is very valuable — perhaps even more valuable than I was led to believe. When I realized that that American was after it I was reluctant to let it go out of my possession, especially without consulting you further. I did not choose to discuss it with that rather theatrical woman you sent."

"Then you still have it?" The tension lurking beneath his easy speech was wound tighter now. So that was why, thought Kate. It was just for...that.

"I had a rather handsome replica made," said James coldly. "I found a photograph in the British Museum. Your courier took the copy. As to subsequent developments I haven't a clue. I don't think Uncle Albert was best pleased at what looked to be a very fishy scheme. I had hoped to get over and offer some reasonable explanation." Franz looked a question and James said shortly, "It was too late. He indicated that he had done what he could for me."

Franz smiled. "Well it was a good show on your part in any event. Sorry about the problems you've had to deal with. I'd have been here sooner but it's hell's own work getting things sorted out in the Fatherland since the war. As you still have the venerable object in your possession so much the better. I can take charge of it now." There was no hint of menace in the smile.

"I said just a moment, Franz. If the venerable object — as you are pleased to call it — cannot be restored to the von Elfenstein estate it can hardly be said to belong to you personally. I suggest that we find a legal way to turn it over to the West German government to be placed in a museum. I daresay we can stipulate that it be returned to the family when the country is put together again. Germany will hardly remain divided indefinitely." Kate could not see James but his tone had not changed. He was cool, and he was in no hurry — no hurry at all.

"I think we have to adapt ourselves to the post-war world, James, bleak and ugly as it is. There's nothing inherently wrong with our standards of honor. They simply won't wash." Franz smiled again, the smile of a sensible man. "I have always liked that English metaphor — 'it won't wash.' It's no one's fault that things haven't worked out as we planned, but I'm rather sure that we shan't be seen as heroes if we attempt to return our treasure to Germany. I shall have betrayed my sacred trust — I was, after all, a professional soldier — not some party hack risen from the local beer hall. It will be observed that I arranged the escape of an enemy officer."

"You exaggerate. My word, and the object itself, will speak in your defence."

"*Your* word, James? Who will believe your story after all this time? You'll not only lose all the credit you have as one of the happy few who escaped from the famous fortress at Kahlberg — without even a hand from MI9 — you'll be seen as a thief into the bargain. Your gesture will suffer the usual fate of the quixotic."

There was a harsh sound from James.

Then a car was heard rattling along the rough road outside. Kate felt a thrill of hope, even as she saw Franz's hand move toward his pocket. *His name was Franz.* She had not taken her coat off but the cold was inside her heart, her bones, her nerves.

"Who is that?" asked Franz.

"There are farms out on the moors. Sheep, mostly." James sounded preoccupied. Then the question registered. "Why did you park round at the back, Franz? Had I not happened to go to the shed just then I might have taken a pot shot at you. We're a bit jumpy in these parts after last night."

"You are armed, then?"

"Of course. One does not look after something so many people seem to want without protection. You haven't answered my question."

Franz shrugged. "A rather *verliebt* young woman I haven't time for at the moment may come looking for me. She is eager and resourceful."

Kate felt warm rage. Under the circumstances, it was a good feeling. The thought of rushing out with a lethal frying pan made her feel almost cheerful for a second.

Franz continued. "I should have supposed that the police would have cleared out your firearms, considering your status as a murder suspect."

James had come back into the center of the room and stood facing Franz. The lamplight was on his face and Kate could see his contemptuous expression. "Be careful of misjudging me, Franz. Something or somebody set that fool Burrows after me long after the escape. I was forced to act. I sent a copy to Florida to throw him off the scent but he was back by return post. He was terrifying our cousin Kate Clark — Uncle Albert's ward — all thanks to your ingenious Florida scheme."

"So you had to kill him?"

"For me, the stakes have not yet reached that level. However, I'm finding it increasingly hard to swallow the programme you sketched out for me in Kahlberg. There's no reason on earth why a family heirloom should be safer in America than here, as the event has proved all too well."

"On the contrary, James. I suspect that I know considerably less about the late Captain Burrows than you do, but one thing is clear. His link to Florida was through you. Obviously, something went wrong, but the original plan had much to recommend it. Suppose someone were looking for a stolen German object. *You* could spring to mind. You were in Kahlberg, after all. But a retired haberdasher in the Florida swamps? It would be safe with him until we saw the German picture clearly." Franz offered James a cigarette and lit it for him. James was silent, hard-faced.

Franz went on. "As for our cousin Kate, your concern shows the proper family feeling. However, with Burrows out of the way, she should be safe enough." Something in James' expression seemed to strike him. "Your face is as a book, my dear James, wherein men may read strange matters. You don't tell me that there are deeper feelings at issue? What were you hoping to play at, Siegmund and Sieglinde? I should have thought that the vicar's lovely daughter would be more your style — a superb Nordic type."

James did not answer immediately but Kate saw the gleam of his eyes and knew that they had gone ice blue and dangerous. Crazily, she felt that she should warn Franz: You go too far. Franz, who was leading a treacherous double life, who was the taller of the two. Franz, who had two hands and a gun in one of them, in his pocket.

When James spoke, his voice was controlled. "I suggested that you not underestimate me, Franz. It is I who have possession of the Hanged Man and it is I, as you have surmised, who have some knowledge of Burrows."

"The Hanged Man? I am curious."

"Burrows' nearly unaccommodated corpse had been provided with the Tarot card of that name. The connection is obvious."

Kate tried to swallow.

"All right, James, we may as well come to an arrangement. Time is getting short for me. I have an engagement. There is no hope of ever restoring the von Elfensteins to their former grandeur, I do assure you. Characteristically, we do not cry. But I had grown used to a certain standard. There is no possible career for me save the military and that, alas, is out of fashion in modern Germany."

"Go on. I'm waiting."

"Your situation is similar, though you are perhaps in a worse case." James' face betrayed nothing; his empty sleeve was like a banner. "I have been at some trouble to find a suitable buyer for our little statue. He will keep it safe — sacred, if you like, since it is also a reliquary. He fully appreciates its special value as a historical souvenir and as a sometime object of religious veneration. It is supposed to contain the wristbone of St. Ernulphus."

"So you told me," said James dryly.

"Did you try to open it?"

He spoke too quickly. James was there at once. "It didn't occur to me. Perhaps I should do so before we — what was it you said? — come to an arrangement."

"Better not to," answered Franz in an indifferent tone. "I was worried about your doing some damage. As I told you, my buyer wants the object intact. He also wants no publicity. I should not like to lose him."

"And the arrangement? I presume you have something to propose, Franz."

"I intend, of course, to share the proceeds with you. But since it is I who have taken the trouble to find a discreet customer you'll have to let me manage the details."

"What security do I have? Surely I am not your only accomplice, Franz? What about the woman courier, for example?"

"You have the word of a gentleman, James." Kate, watching him, thought of Tony. "I am interested in protecting the 'Hanged Man' from the kind of criminal class that seems to be milling around *you*. As for Rosa Szastris, her family owes mine many favors. Her mother's people were gypsies who had been allowed to occupy our lands unmolested for over a century. A necklace will satisfy her. She is fond of jewels. They need not be diamonds."

"Where are her people now?"

"Hitler didn't care for gypsies. I suppose they were shipped off somewhere or other. Too bad. We always found them useful."

"Like poor but deferential English relations? Sorry, Franz, but I don't intend to part with the goods for a string of beads — or a season ticket to Bayreuth." James moved out of sight again, toward the fire.

"The goods, James? Where on earth do you pick up such expressions? The comedy is finished. I want the object I entrusted to you at Kahlberg."

Kate saw something in Franz' hand glint in the firelight, but James' voice betrayed no alarm, revealed nothing.

"It's not here, Franz. I thought it prudent to conceal it away from the house."

"Then lead the way, James, I'm anxious to get out of England. If you cooperate I'll get in touch with you."

"I'll need my torch. It's upstairs."

"Be quick, then."

With a grim acceleration of her heart, Kate listened to James' steps on the stairs. The mysterious cousin in the lonely house on the moors. What else? And then she knew. She knew where James had hidden the Hanged Man. And it was up to her to save it, for the sake of all the people Franz had betrayed.

Silent as a leaf on running water she moved toward the back door, seizing a long-handled spoon with a pointed bowl from a hook on the wall. The door did not squeak.

The air was damp and bitter cold; clouds had come back to obscure the stars. There was barely enough light from the house to show the shed beside which the gorse leaned against the wind. She knelt before it and began digging with the spoon, striking roots first, then something more resistant. She scrabbled in the earth around it with frantic fingers. With her hands she could feel a parcel, about the size of a pint milk bottle, but, as she worked it up, heavier.

The front door opened with a portentous creak. She heard male voices, and for the first time she wondered whether she ought to have tried to help James. He was so cool; he had his own plan.

James and Franz were moving round the house. She could see the beam of James' flashlight.

"Hold the torch, will you Franz?"

"Don't be absurd, James." Franz laughed. "It was a risk if you were going to escape but I guessed right. Just as I guessed who you were from your papers. Herr Doktor Schwartzwald thought he might save your arm but I urged him to amputate."

There was a cry from James, passionate and grieved. "You god damn bloody swine," he said.

Kate stood up, a darker figure against the darkness, holding a bundle. There was a shot, then James called desperately, "For God's sake, Kate, *drop it*. He'll kill you."

Then two more shots. A sound of stumbling. Footsteps coming toward her.

Kate ran, a wild creature fleeing the hunters' guns, up into the black emptiness of the moor. The Hanged Man was clutched against her heart.

Chapter XXVII

> For when things are once come to the execution, there
> is no secret comparable to celerity; like the motion
> of a bullet in the air, which flieth so swift as it outruns the eye.
> —Francis Bacon, "Of Delay"

The ground sloped upward in back of Moon Croft. The house had been built to take advantage of such shelter as the rolling land would provide and Kate had seen the high ridge stretched out above the roof. The darkness was intense and the wind had risen, shrieking like a whole bag of demented witches. She ran straight up. She was not afraid, but her fingers, clutching the parcel, were very cold.

Rocks and tussocks of earth, the impedimenta of the moors, were a menace — even more after she crested the hill and felt her toes pushing against her shoes. She stopped to listen then. Someone was coming; there were footfalls on the hill behind her. Something in the sound of them suggested an uncertainty, an imperfect ballasting. *James*.

"James!" she called, the wind an ache in her throat.

"Kate, my darling girl!" It was Tony's voice in the dark. "Wait. You don't understand about James. I didn't want to tell you."

She plunged on, downhill now. No matter what, he shouldn't have said *my darling girl,* she thought contemptuously. She felt very old. She turned slightly to take the hill on the bias, breathing deeply like a swimmer. It seemed a long time before the ground felt level. After that she ran more easily, but with no sense of direction and not daring to stop.

Then the cool wet kisses began, on her face and bare hands. Snow. In the morning there would be footprints. In the morning! Morning was hours away. She could never last until morning, running.

Somewhere across the rampaging void a cheerful glimmer of light appeared. Kate guessed at a farmhouse and turned that way, knowing it could be miles but having no other lodestar. She splashed through water — not much, but enough to fill her shoes and soak her feet. It would be the beck, the beck in which Tom Burrows had lain, dead.

She wanted to take her shoes off to empty them. She had emptied her shoe one day and it had fallen into the water. That was a long time ago. That was Tom Burrows after her in Kings Park, Tom Burrows who was found dead in the beck. He had been after the Hanged Man too. Now there was a reason for running. Now she had what they all wanted.

The light she had been making for went out, extinguished by an indifferent hand. What if there were people lost on the moors? That was *always* happening. But not in real life.

She kept on, every sloshy step like a new crossing of the bone-chilling little stream, until suddenly she ran against something blacker than the black air. Blacker, and decidedly more solid. With one hand she explored a wall, stone-built like the walls of Moon Croft. Searching for an opening, she found a corner. Beyond the corner she found a wooden door. It gave way to her hand and she passed through, closed it behind her, and searched for a way to make it fast.

Whatever it was, it wasn't a place anyone bothered to lock. Standing with her back against the door she could register sensations that she had ignored outside; the over-hasty respiration, the heart's heavy beat, the prickling skin, the slack and trembling wrists and knees.

She listened, and heard the night whisperings of agitated straw. Mice. Voles. Nothing, at this point, to fear. Of course it was black as Halloween in a coal mine. So much the better.

Moving cautiously across to the opposite wall she judged her first surmise to have been correct: it was some kind of hut. It must serve some purpose connected with the care of livestock. She would stay until someone from the farm came, but first she must secure the door. Up here on the moors there was little to lock out except the wind, which even now was noisily probing some chink near her ear.

The door had a handle — nothing so sophisticated as a knob, but an efficient curved protuberance that seemed made to have a chair braced under it.

A chair! Well, why not a chair after all? Suppose a shepherd were caught in a storm on the moors. He could come in here and sit down.

Kate felt along the wall cautiously. Her shin made contact with an object in its path. She took her free hand from the wall, reached down and grasped a rung, slid her palm and fingers down the rung until she came to a flat surface. She had guessed right.

Carefully putting the parcel onto the seat she dragged the chair back, guiding herself along the wall until she found the door again. There was no floor except the one the earth provided. It felt smooth but resistant to pressure. When the back of the chair was pushed under the door handle the rear legs dug in. If anyone tried to open the door they would dig in deeper.

The best, the cosiest, thing would be to find the straw and sit on it, or in it. But Kate had never been able to really *enjoy* mice. Especially invisible mice. Picking up her package, she crossed the empty black space again and sat down with her back to the wall and her knees bent. She rested the parcel underneath the tent her skirt made. Then she begun rubbing her hands together. After a while her fingers were sufficiently flexible to undo the laces of her shoes.

The place was very cold, but at least the assaulting wind was shut out. The wind and the restless straw were all she could hear. She took off her shoes and emptied them, then wrung out her socks. She tried to dry her stocking feet with a corner of her skirt. Maybe she was near a house. She crammed her hands into her coat pockets and found one glove, a handkerchief, and a half-full bag of toffees. Corn in Egypt.

Continuing to bellow in a lusty and impartial way outside the wind resumed its insinuating whistle somewhere at her back. A small but bitter draught made a Vampire lunge at her neck.

There must be a hole she could stop up somehow. There was a pencil light in her handbag. Luckily she didn't have it. It would be insane to show a light — even a thread, a pin prick. She put her socks back on, surprised at the warmth of the damp wool. Her shoes seemed to have shrunk.

Putting the parcel against the wall she got onto her knees and groped. In less than a minute she found an unexpected aperture. There was a window, no less. No windowpane, though — just heavy wooden shutters with great metal hasps. The fit was not perfectly snug; the searching air had found a crack. She was trying to plug it with her handkerchief when she heard a voice out of the tormented dark.

"Kate, thank god I've found you." It sounded like Tony. She stopped, still as death. "I had no idea it was you I was following until you cried out back there." She tried to swallow.

She could hear that he was pushing against the door. She seized her handkerchief from the opening and the wind rushed in, squealing. How could he know she was inside?

"I was afraid that you were that Eurasian woman of Gordon's. It's imperative that those people not get that parcel. I couldn't explain to James." It was Tony's voice all right, conjuring up tea in the ancestral hall, peacocks on the green green lawn, dinner jackets at Government House somewhere where the sun never set. But it was Franz outside, and her mouth curled when he said, after a pause, "I can explain everything." Maybe he would try *I just had to come* next. He was desperate. How desperate remained to be told. "I've been injured, Kate. It was James, an accident."

He might be lying, but even so her momentary panic ebbed away. He couldn't know for sure that she was inside. She wouldn't wait for daylight, but try to escape quickly. She heard a grating noise at the door that puzzled her for a minute, until she realized what it must be. The door bolted on the outside to keep the hut dry and snug! It was a prison.

But why lock her in? Because at dawn he would find a way to reach her. Meanwhile she was safe, trapped. Or so he thought.

She found the parcel and held it awkwardly under her arm while she unfastened the shutters. It was a bad moment. The wailing wind might not mask the sound of a banging shutter. She opened the left side and with her free hand threw the parcel outside. The right shutter, though no longer secured, seemed to fit tight against the stone. Still holding the opened shutter she put one leg out, feeling the wet snow through her stocking. The window was small but it was just the right height. Stepping out was like stepping over a low wall. Sideways, she could manage. Her second foot came down on top of the parcel and she picked it up. Only then did she see the danger.

The wind had once more pushed the clouds aside and a thin coat of wet snow shone all around her. Tony had seen her footprints at the door. She set off like an arrow shot straight from the window. It was the only way she could go and she hoped that it would not be uphill.

The rest in the hut, sweetened with toffee, had done wonders for Kate. She ran easily for a long time, but whether toward safety or away from it she had no idea at all. There had been no outcry as she sprinted away from the hut but she did not dare to hope that she had lost Franz. The sound of her own footfalls seemed like the echo of his heavier ones. But if she did not have to stop she might yet escape — if he were wounded.

Another mile or two and time ran out. Fatigue flowed so heavy down her legs that they simply buckled. Beneath her knees she felt hard, cold, bare ground — nothing growing to provide a cushion. Trembling, she set the parcel down as if it were an infant in a basket of eggs.

The capricious wind had dropped.

Into the frightening silence came two sounds, far apart but seeming to converge. The first, back in the darkness she had already traversed, was made by the unsteady but unremitting progress of some living creature. The second, further away but coming on more rapidly, was the hum of a motor. Then there were lights, growing brighter fast. The smooth ground was a country road.

The car must find her first.

And then she realized what would happen. The lights of the car would be like spotlights, revealing herself but not her desperate pursuer. Kate Clark, center stage at last. But the show would never leave the provinces. Franz would shoot her, take the parcel, and disappear into the wild moors. Even if he didn't escape it would be curtains for her.

Before the idea was half thought she was up and running again, but it was too late. The lights of the automobile caught the skirt of her coat, and a shot rocked the world. Her shoulder stung like fire.

The car screamed and stopped. She turned toward the lights. They were dancing. Rough arms seized her and forced her to the ground. There was another shot, then returning fire and a cry of anguish.

"Don't move at all," said an American voice. "I'm going after him."

"Don't," Kate said. "Please, Sam. Please don't. He'll kill you."

"I think he's had it," said Sam. "James winged him. Only fair I guess. But don't you move at all."

He went off, slow and crouching like a commando, and after a while she heard his footsteps coming back. He helped her up, holding her steady and not trying to take the parcel from her. "Tell me," she said.

"He's in bad shape. We'll have to get him in to Inspector Bucket at Netherbeck. He's past hurting anybody, but I'll tie his hands anyway."

He half lifted her into the car.

"What about James?"

"I'm sorry, Kate. He's not going to live." It was better to have it flat out like that. "Tony shot him. But maybe you know who Tony is."

"My cousin Franz."

He closed the car door and looked anxiously at her through the window. His gaze dropped to her shoulder. She looked too, seeing in the light from the dashboard the small burned tear in her coat. "It can be invisibly mended," she said.

"You're hurt." He sounded matter-of-fact.

"Just a scratch."

"You're okay, kid," he said.

He went off with a flashlight and came back with Franz in his arms. Tony was taller than that, thought Kate, puzzled and numb. Sam put him into the back seat, tied his wrists together, and covered his knees with a blanket. He looked ghastly in the dim light.

Sam got into the driver's seat and turned on the ignition. "I'll drop you at the vicarage first," he said. "Rosemary Broadbent can dress your shoulder."

"Rosemary?"

"She drove an ambulance during the war. She's very competent. She'll get a doctor if she has to."

"Oh."

"There's someone else there you may be pleased to see."

"I want Sally and Doris," she said, feeling the tears at last.

Sam covered her hand with his own. "I'm sorry, Kate."

In a while she said, "Sam?"

"Look, we'll talk about everything later. I have to watch the road."

"I do not find the Hanged Man." She spoke slowly and gravely.

"What was that?"

"I do not find the Hanged Man."

"Then what the hell's in that package you're so attached to?"

Chapter XXVIII

> People never give your message to anybody.
> —J. D. Salinger, *The Catcher in the Rye*

"Take care of her wound first, will you, Rosemary? I have to see a policeman. We'll hang on to the package for now, though. See if you can find a safe place." Sam turned back to Kate, who was sitting numb and frozen in a chair by the door. He was smiling at her. "That's if Kate will let go of it, of course. I think you'd better lock this door — and any others you may have."

Then he was gone, and she heard the car engine catch, roar, and fade away. Kate looked up at Rosemary and saw her violet eyes full of tears. She was holding a glass full of amber. "It's super brandy," she said. "Father keeps it for distraught ladies."

"I think James is dead," Kate said.

"He is. I telephoned," answered Rosemary. "Sam said he was very brave."

"I think he must have always been very brave. Has someone notified his parents?"

"I shouldn't think so. The police like family to do it if they can, or a friend. But you must let me look at your shoulder first. Can you come to the kitchen now? I shall need hot water in any case, and my kit is there."

Kate stood up and reached for the wall as a telephone table, hat tree, framed mirror, and elephant's foot umbrella stand rose and fell. There was a woman standing in the door to the sitting room. It did not look like Miss Watershed.

"My dear child." The voice was warm, sober, strange. It belonged somewhere else. "You have been splendid. You have trusted me, and you shall know all."

"Madame Sosostris!"

"I am Rosa Szastris. Franz von Elfenstein was my enemy. Your Uncle Albert became my friend. But we will talk later. Now, first, we help you to the kitchen."

So Rosemary the fair and Rosa the dark each took an arm and started to move Kate away from the chair. "Oh, please," she said. "It's okay." She eased her coat off, dropping it without giving up the parcel. A dark stain had spread on the sleeve of her pullover. She looked at it curiously. "Nothing much," she added.

Sitting in the kitchen under the bright overhead light she watched Rosemary cut away the torn sleeve of her sweater and the blouse underneath, then bathe and bandage the raw gash where the bullet had grazed.

No one spoke until the job was finished. Then Rosemary brought Kate a pale cashmere cardigan to cover her bare arm, and Rosa fitted a cigarette into a long black holder studded with glittering stones.

"Father and Cecily Maud have gone to bed," said Rosemary. "I told them that you were all right and not to bother. They were both done in what with one thing and another." Kate looked at the clock on the mantelpiece. "It stopped short never to run again at some point or other. It's past three. You can ring through to London from Father's study." Rosemary sounded sad again.

"Now?" asked Kate. "Shouldn't I wait until morning? The call will frighten them so."

"Afterward, they will not want you to have waited." Rosemary spoke with conviction. She was not the Vicar's daughter for nothing. "Can you manage? Would you like me to come?"

"Yes. No." She followed Rosemary to the door of the study, then went in and closed it behind her.

She had to wait a long time for the operator but as soon as she gave the number she seemed to hear the phone ringing in the little hall at Quo Vadis.

"Tinkham 8520." It was Doris.

Kate sat down, putting the parcel on the desk beside the telephone. "Doris?"

"Kate, what is it?"

Doris was afraid. They had all been afraid, puzzled.

"Doris, James was...is..."

"He's had an accident?"

"Doris, Doris, James is dead."

Kate heard Doris cry out, then there was a sound of voices behind her.

"Mother! Dad, can you help her? Kate, what happened? How much will they have to bear? Was he...?"

"Oh, Doris, your poor mother. It was awful. But James was fine, truly he was. He saved my life. But Oswald Birkie's son killed him."

"How can such a thing be?"

"He didn't tell you they met in Kahlberg?"

"Never." Doris' voice was dry with pain. "I must go to my parents."

"Will you be coming?"

"Of course. Where are you?"

"I'm at the vicarage." She gave the number.

"Goodbye, then."

"Goodbye, Doris. Oh Doris, I love your mother very much."

"I know, my dear."

Kate sat by the telephone with hot eyes until there was a knock at the door. Rosemary came in, bearing a tray with three cups of cocoa and a plate piled with slices of thick buttered toast. Rosa followed her, conservatively dressed but managing an inaudible swish.

Rosemary set the tray down and added coal to the fire. She said to Kate, "After this cocoa you must go straight upstairs. Cecily Maud put a hot pig in your bed."

Kate smiled weakly, thinking of the stone bottle with the porcine snout.

Rosa drew three comfortable chairs closer to the fire. "Gypsies are at home everywhere," she said matter-of-factly.

For a few moments they sat quietly, watching the fire. The parcel was tucked into Kate's chair. A clock pinged the half-hour.

"I hope Franz von Elfenstein is now dead," said Rosa. It was clearly an opening statement but Rosemary jumped in before she could elaborate.

"Oh, you mustn't say that, Mrs. Szastris! God has reserved vengeance for Himself."

Rosa looked surprised. It was clearly not an idea with which she was familiar but she assimilated it quickly. "I have tried to help Him," she said solemnly. "The offering would have smelled sweeter had I personally found von Elfenstein myself in Brazil. That I admit."

"*Brazil?*" Kate and Rosemary spoke in unison.

"What you think? Franz is going to leave the Hanged Man in Florida for the good Uncle Albert? Pah. You know nothing."

"I can't speak for Kate," said Rosemary, "but I know nothing whatever. I knew Sam Gordon in London during the blitz so when he brought you here I didn't question him."

So Rosemary knew Sam Gordon. Everybody knew Sam Gordon. Or if they didn't he introduced himself.

"But the Hanged Man wasn't *in* Florida," said Kate, looking at Rosa. "It was a fake. That was what you wanted me to tell Sam. That you did not find the Hanged Man."

"Yes. You have been a very good girl but you did not deliver the message." Rosa smiled at Kate. "I do not know why I was so sure you would know to give the message to Gordon. Right away you meet him, because he knows who you are. And he is a very attractive man, is he not?"

"I didn't notice," answered Kate, looking at the fire. "I gave the message to Franz, though."

"Ah, that would give him to think, *nein*? He is smelling a rat and wondering where it is." Her eyes gleamed gold in the firelight. "Of course he is following you too, that distinguished gentleman from hell. You are the little heiress, and he does not know what Albert has done with the Hanged Man. Perhaps you have it in your possession. That is what all thieves think."

Kate finished her toast and licked the butter off her fingers. "But what *had* Uncle Albert done with it — the false one, I mean?"

"He has the idea to give it to an alligator."

Kate grinned. It felt strange and wonderful. "Madame Sosostris, I think you must be mixed up with a crocodile and a clock."

"Ah, the alligator doesn't swallow it. He is an intelligent alligator, a friend of Albert. Each evening Albert gives him odds and ends from the dinner and so he is always waiting around the little dock. It is a place where some people might not want to look for something."

"But what had James to do with this bizarre plot?" asked Rosemary, looking vulnerable.

"Everything and nothing," answered Rosa succinctly. "Forget about James Bell. He was the tool of von Elfenstein. Or should I say fool? I saw at once how it stood." She looked disgusted. "Naturally, seeing what a fool he is, it does not occur to me that Bell would pass me the ersatz goods." She fitted another cigarette into her holder.

Kate looked at Rosemary and saw that all the warmth that gave charm to her beauty had drained away. "My cousin James was a Romantic Idealist," she said firmly. "It would never have occurred to *him* that Franz could be so... so...cynical."

"Cynical?" Rosa's eyes and voice were full of hate. She looked from one to the other of them. Then she shrugged. "My English is not well," she said hollowly.

"But, Madame Sosostris..." began Kate.

"You must both call me Rosa." The gypsy made a large gesture.

"Okay, Rosa..."

"It is my real name."

"How did you happen to know my Uncle Albert so well?" A vision of Mr. Partridge hovered, looking kindly upon her perplexity. She smiled ruefully.

"I tell it my way."

Kate nodded.

"Albert Clark knew that he was going to die before I arrive with the parcel from his nephew James Bell. James asks for him to keep it safe until he comes for it himself, that's all. Then would everything be satisfactory explained. What would *you* think? Albert does not like it. However he would like to do something for his cousin Sally while he can. They have been children together." She looked at Kate and said simply, "You are too young to understand."

"I'm not as young as I was before."

"I have had a part in that, Kate." It was the first time she had used the name. "At any rate there is much family feeling with your people. It is like with us gypsies."

"Yes," said Kate. "Lots of family feeling. James Bell and Franz were first cousins."

"Franz used everyone. He cared only for the person living in the skin of Franz. I should have seen that. I should have seen that." The rage was back, but there was much grief in it.

"What about you and Uncle Albert, though?"

Rosa looked at her intently, then she reached out and touched her cheek. She smiled. "You will like the story. Me, I have not opened the parcel I carry, and no more do the customs. The young man in New York, he is fresh from the *Oberland*, you know. He is very very solemn. 'Madam,' he asks, but not smiling, 'Is that your teddy bear?' 'It is magnificent, yes?' say I, very grand. 'It is a pre-war German bear,' I say, looking at him boldly. I hold out the bear. 'Please to hold it,' I say, 'while I find the key to my jewel box.'

"There is a very pretty girl next in the line and she laughs. Meanwhile his partner has opened my jewel box, which is not locked. Such a treasure trove of nothing, what the French call the *fantaisie*. The young man is flustered. I pass through, the bear in my arms."

"A teddy bear? You mean James hid the Hanged Man in a teddy bear?"

"Ah, no, that was not James Bell. I bring with me the bear from Germany. Germans make the splendid bears. I have made an empty place in the heart of this great big bear, and there I put the parcel James gives me when I get to my hotel. We have met on a bench on the Thames Embankment. The parcel was taped like a mummy, and his face says only that he does not care to make my acquaintance. Why should I suspect such a man? He is indifferent to what I think."

Rosemary was sitting very still, her hands folded.

"Then what?" asked Kate.

"I go to Titus and I establish a beachhead. For me the war is not over. I do not attract attention." Kate smiled. "I live very quiet and I make friends with Albert because of an interest in animals. Gypsies know animals."

"Well, I've heard that they like horse trading," said Kate imprudently.

"That is not all by any means," said Rosa with an offended air.

"That was swell, you both liking animals. So you didn't fork over the parcel right away."

"Not right away. I need to know what he is, what he knows, this uncle who lends himself to the affair. I am very strange in Florida. I want an ally."

"And you found one?"

"More. I found some happiness — not much, but I have not asked for anything at all for a long time. Except revenge."

"Oh, *Rosa.*"

"Albert and I, we open the parcel together. We are laughing and drinking gin with orange juice. But then I see at once the thing is false as Franz. The stones are all paste. It all sparkles, but it is all glass, just glass. Then I am frightened. My blood goes cold from my heart. I do not understand. I do not know what to do. The next day Albert goes to hospital and I must wait then. But after, I am desperate to get a message to Sam Gordon.

"I am afraid to trust any means but one. Someone must tell him. I will send a message with you. You are the heiress. I think Sam will find you. He is not stupid."

"So the whole teashop was for me? So that I would give the message to Sam Gordon?" Kate knew the answer.

"Forgive me, Kate. I do not know that Franz is come to America himself. Perhaps I should have guessed that he would want to keep his eye everywhere without taking the risks! But I did not, I did not. Of the others, the American gangsters, I don't know nothing. Anything."

"They weren't gangsters, I don't think. They were just...free enterprise."

"As you like."

Kate yawned.

"Kate must go to bed at once," said Rosemary firmly. "Her people will be coming tomorrow."

"Oh, please," said Kate. "I couldn't sleep. I know I couldn't."

Rosemary poked at the fire, then went out with the tray.

"Of course Franz is in agony. That is what I should have known. He has waited so long because he has the smelly connections and the German authorities know it and he doesn't know what conversations they may now be having with the Allies. He would have liked to snatch the Hanged Man away from Bell and fly away in a silver plane — but he is afraid. No, the Florida scheme is good, he thinks. But then — what if? He trusts me, faithful old Rosa..." Rosa's was the smile of the shark. "...but what if I fail? He goes to America incognito."

"But how did he manage it? Rosa, he *was* Tony Smith."

"Ah, poor Kate. But come now. You never really cared for Tony. He was just part of a make-believe."

"How do you know so much?"

"You forget. I am a gypsy."

This time they smiled at each other like conspirators.

Rosa continued. "For Franz to become Tony is easy as falling off a stick. Remember he is a student at a famous English school for some years. He only takes a chance he meets someone in the old school tie. He is careful not to hobnob where that may happen, I guess. As for the necessary support — he has, as I say, friends. He hears that I contact Bell. Then, the rest is silence."

"The rest is silence," repeated Kate. It sounded familiar.

"The day after you — the little heiress with one is not sure what — leave Titus here comes the beautiful Englishman, Mr. C.A. MacLeod-Smith, touring what is called the bushes. I hear this in the post office." Kate thought of the suave Partridges. "I am more afraid than ever," Rosa went on in a cheerful voice. "There was other strangers in the town too, a couple with a dog who ask questions about Albert..."

"Harry and Fan."

"I have done what I could to get a message to Sam. I back out. I too have another identity and Franz does not know it. He thinks his friends see all around me but I have another life I can live. My new friends have provided me with the passport of a Jewish woman who disappeared in Budapest in 1944 and whom I much resemble in the face. I become a refugee with a sister in Chicago. Of course, I am not afraid to die. Only Franz must pay for it."

"I know he's a terrible rat, Rosa, but why do you hate him so much? What's the story on Brazil? Who is Sam?"

Rosemary came back with the tray and Kate could see steam rising from the cups. "I do cocoa," she said, "and in the afternoon, cream teas." She tried to smile. "My father has a safe for some of the church plate. Please let us put the object away at once. The more I hear the less pleased I am to have it in the house."

"Franz is finished," said Rosa. "If he weren't I would know it."

"So are Fan and Tom Burrows," added Kate. "Harry doesn't want it."

Rosa's eyebrows went up. "Tell that to a sailor on a horse," she said. "Besides there may be friends of Franz here around for all I know. Rosemary is right. We will lock it up."

Rosa picked up the parcel and looked at it. "But first! If you please..."

Slowly she undid the parcel, worrying the knots with her teeth. The others made no move to help. At last she set the figurine on the table beside the cocoa tray. It was a statuette fashioned in a medieval manner, formal but not austere, representing a man hanging upside down from a tree which served as his scaffold. Man and tree formed a single piece of gold and the tree was burdened with a melange of jewels.

"Not bad, eh?" asked Rosa.

"I don't like it," said Kate. "Let's put it away."

"It is Saint Ernulphus," said Rosa. "It is said to contain a relic. I am curious to see this relic. There must be a way to open it."

"Oh, no, please don't," said Rosemary, but Rosa had clapped on a pair of glasses and was poring over the surface of the statue.

She emitted a sound that was part purr and part hiss. "I like the clever things," she said. "Here is the crack, just here where the bark of the tree pretends to fold upon the roots. Fetch a thin knife."

"We should not do it, Rosa," said Rosemary. "It is a sacred object."

"You would not see the crack, yes? It is as if the monks wished to hide the good saint's little bone. Not at all like the glass boxes in the great churches of Middle Europa. Yes, I confess I am curious."

She turned the statue upside down and her strong hands twisted as if she were opening a recalcitrant jam jar. The bottom came away and she peered into the cavity made by the upper tree and the hanging figure. Then she looked up. "It is not bones," she said.

"What is it?" Kate and Rosemary spoke at once.

Rosa brought a cigar box from the desk and removed two cigars. She emptied the contents of the statue into it. There was a brilliance like the moon in winter, like Ali Baba's cave, like many diamonds. "It is many diamonds," said Rosa.

"Maybe they're paste," said Kate.

"Paste! Don't I tell you I know paste? Does the cat take chalk for cream? As you ask, now I am asking — who is Sam?"

"We must put everything into the safe immediately," said Rosemary in a determined voice.

"Maybe you know the big something," said Rosa, a sudden glimmer in her eyes. She was fitting the bottom of the statue back into place.

"As I told you, I know nothing except that several people are dead." It was Rosemary's very best voice, the voice of an Englishwoman coping. "The safe is in the den upstairs. Bring the valuables and come with me."

Her instructions came too late.

The study door opened and a fourth woman stood there. She was wearing an Eisenhower jacket of dark mink, black wool pants, and running shoes. She was small, but she had a gun.

"Back against the bookcase and turn around," she said very softly. "I am in a hurry."

"Lisa Dragonette," said Kate.

"Young Kate, the so-delightful ingenue," said Lisa, looking at Kate. "I abandon the theater for the present, *chérie*. Now, please, *vite*."

As Kate backed away from the fire she knocked against the cigar box and the lid fell shut.

"It is convenient that the English are so fond of locking doors. This room is provided with a key, and I shall lock you in as I leave. The pantry window is open, however."

As they heard the key in the lock they turned. Rosa sprang for the door. The Hanged Man was gone.

"Goddam," said Rosa. "Who is that?"

"She's another friend of Sam Gordon," said Kate in a small voice.

Chapter XXIX

> What griefe can be, but Time doth make it lesse?
> —Michael Drayton, "The Epistle to Rosamund"

James Bell was buried in Netherbeck churchyard. Almost every adult in the village came to the service in the little greystone church, and heard Cecil Broadbent deliver a simple eulogy in a deep voice that shimmered like old glass. The inhabitants of Netherbeck hadn't much liked James, but they had respected him. Word had got round that he had been the victim of a foreign plot, involving some Germans and an American, which he had tried to foil. They didn't like Germans at all. They didn't like Americans much. For that matter they weren't fond of the Scots or the Welsh. The south of England was almost a foreign country. But William Birkie, who had come of a Northumberland family, was remembered with tolerance. These things Kate had learned from Rosemary.

"But what about your father?" she had asked.

"Well, he's a Yorkshireman, you know. They don't hold his accent against him. Rather the reverse. The vicar's supposed to sound different."

The day of the funeral was bleak but dry. Rooks clung like black leaves to the bold bare trees that would give shelter to the graves in summer.

When the ritual was over seed cake and coffee were offered at the Vicarage. The Bells were staying at the Brown Bull and when Rosemary had asked whether she might be allowed to provide some refreshments Sally had agreed numbly. It was assumed that Rosemary and James had planned to marry. No tactless voice was heard to inquire.

Rosemary looked exquisitely sad.

"Rosemary looks exquisitely sad, does she not?" murmured Cecily Maud Watershed in Kate's ear. "She has the very pallor of white roses and then those glorious violet eyes."

"There is a garden in her face," quoted Kate gravely.

"Not to worry, however. An old flame is motoring down from London tomorrow, it seems. A Harley Street specialist from the ambulance days. Quite the catch."

When the visitors had gone Sally came to Kate and reaching up, kissed her on the cheek. "You'll be coming tomorrow, pet?"

"I think so. Or maybe the day after. But I'll just come to get ready for home. I can get a berth on the *America* next week."

"You'll come to England again now you know us, I expect." She tried to smile. "We could go and have a look round Hampton Court one day. You'll like the Maze."

"Oh, *yes*. I do want to see the Maze."

Fred kissed her too, and then he and Sally went to the Brown Bull to pack. They had come in Doris' little car and were ready to go back home. Kate had said she would take the bus.

Doris lingered briefly. "So now do you understand everything?"

"Not really."

"Did Franz do those murders?"

"It seems so. Inspector Bucket said Franz had confessed to them both, and that I was not to worry any more."

"You mean those Americans?"

"Well, of course, he killed James too. That's three. He didn't want to kill people. They just got in his way. That's what Inspector Bucket said."

"Fancy his being our cousin. James *was* a bloody fool. But we were afraid it might be something worse only we daren't talk about it. It would have seemed disloyal. James' behavior seemed odder than necessary, you know, even accounting for the arm, and the escape. One doesn't know, of course, what terrible thing may have happened in a war. Mum will bear this, the way it is. She'll put James back on the piano and life will go on. Just like the other bereaved mothers. She won't be like her own mother."

Kate said nothing.

Doris went on. "So what happened to the *objet d'art*?"

"It's gone. Stolen again."

"I wish I could have had a peep at it. What does the Inspector say?"

"He says no one has reported a missing valuable of that type."

"Will you tell me everything some day? I'll stay awake."

"If I can." Kate smiled.

"Well then, my turn first. My dear, Felix and I are getting married."

"How come?" Kate was amazed.

"I'm going to have a baby. I'm keeping it under my hat."

Doris was wearing a dun-colored beret with a little stalk. Kate looked at it curiously. They embraced and laughed and wiped their eyes, then Doris rushed away to help her parents.

Rosemary had washed the dishes herself, Kate wiping everything dry with a thin soft towel. Kate loved the Broadbents' china and silver: pink cake plates with fluted edges, translucent cups full of liquid light, gleaming little tea spoons, enchanting sugar tongs. When everything had been put away she said, "I'll be going now. Please say good-bye to your father and Miss Watershed for me."

"Won't you dine with us this evening?"

"Oh, no thanks. I'll just have something at the Bull. I'll probably be off early in the morning."

"As you prefer. Do write to me from America if you can bear to."

"Rosemary, of course I will. And thanks so much for everything. It was kind of you to make things easier for my cousin Sally."

Rosemary looked out of the window. "One does these sorts of things in my position."

As Kate was buttoning her coat in the front hall Rosemary said suddenly, "Kate?"

"Yes?"

"What did Sam do with those diamonds?"

"Search me. I thought maybe you knew."

"I?"

"Well, isn't he an old friend of yours? You met in the blitz." Kate had discovered that her ability to manufacture mental movie posters was unimpaired despite the sobering discoveries she had made. At the moment she envisioned a golden English girl in an immaculate uniform being admired by a dark and dashing Yank. Explosions, flares, and flames provided dramatic lighting.

Rosemary looked surprised. "We were acquainted."

"Oh, well," said Kate. "If I find out I'll let you know. Maybe I can get

Inspector Bucket to spill the beans now he's got my cousin Franz. I just can't believe he knows nothing about it."

"Your cousin Franz. How very strange."

"They'll never believe me at Barnaby's. So long, Rosemary."

"Good-bye, Kate,"

Kate had not told Rosemary that she intended to return to Moon Croft. She had managed to pry the key from Mrs. Stonehouse, not without some difficulty. When she explained that she wanted to make the place tidy against whatever time the family should want to return Mrs. Stonehouse declared roundly that she herself would make everything neat as a new pin. In fact Mrs. Bell had particularly asked her to do it.

Okay, agreed Kate. Only her cousin would want *her* to pack up Mr. Bell's things. She simply hadn't thought to make that clear. If Mrs. Stonehouse had hoped to do a little sleuthing she gave in with good grace, and even urged Kate to "pop a jam tart into her mouth" while pocketing the key.

Kate headed out into the moors on a bicycle borrowed from Jenny Ricks. Moon Croft lay against the hillside like some natural feature of the landscape, as indifferent to the seeping mist as a moorland crag. The still air was aching cold. A brown hare slipped across Kate's path like a shadow. She leaned the bike under a window and went inside.

Wandering around downstairs she was struck with how lightly James' occupancy seemed to have touched the place. The police had taken her handbag from the kitchen and returned it to her. The partial pork pie was gone from under the basin. The little group of clean dishes had not been put away, however. In the long living room she emptied the ashtrays and smoothed the rose print chairs. "The Blue Danube" was still on the phonograph. She put it away carefully.

Upstairs, where James had slept, everything was in order, the room nearly bare. James had had a taste for grandeur, but not for luxury. She opened drawers and found things so minimal, so neat, she realized she had nothing to do there. In the single drawer of the deal table James had used as a desk she found a photograph of herself. It was a snapshot she had sent to Sally at Christmas, and it had been put into a leather frame. She had seen it on the mantelpiece at Quo Vadis.

Holding it in her hand, she closed the drawer and went back down the stairs. That, at least, she could take away. Perhaps she could return it unnoticed.

The old doorbell suddenly rang, a clanging peal that made her nerves lurch. When she opened the door she found Sam Gordon standing there.

"Hello, Kate," he said, rather formally. "May I come in?"

Chapter XXX

> Let us go in; And charge us there upon inter'gatories,
> And we will answer all things faithfully.
> —William Shakespeare, *The Merchant of Venice*

Kate held the door open wider and said, "Hello, Sam." He came in. "It's a bit parky outside," he said pleasantly, but without the old insouciance. Kate missed it.

"What's *parky*?" she asked.

"That's what they say around here when they catch you going outside without your woollies."

"How do they know whether or not you've got your woollies on?"

"Obviously, the designation 'woollies' includes more than you suppose." He glanced at the object in her hand and said, "Taking away a photograph of your cousin?" His voice was kind.

"No," answered Kate, turning to look for her handbag. "Did you come for something?"

"Sorry. That friendly girl in the Brown Bull told me you'd come out here, and as I'm in a hurry I thought I might be able to speak to you privately."

"Oh."

"I think that you are entitled to know the whole story, but I must ask you to say nothing to anyone else. Can you agree to that?"

"Sam, I haven't told anybody about the diamonds. I don't suppose Rosemary has either. It didn't sound that way. You probably know. Rosa Szastris seems to have disappeared again, and your friend Lisa Dragonette came and went like a firefly."

Sam smiled. "Rosemary's a friend. So's your formidable gypsy. Lisa Dragonette's one of the bad guys. I should have thought *you* could tell. She's right out of the funny papers."

"I don't read the funny papers any more."

"Look, Kate, what if we sat down? Could we have something to drink?"

"I think there's some Rhine wine. Hock."

"There must be tea. Put the kettle on, will you?"

She went to the kitchen, filled the kettle, found the cups, and set out some sweet biscuits on a chipped plate. The tea tray was in the little pantry. By the time she came back Sam had managed to start a fire in the living room and she took her coat off.

"Okay, Sam," she said. "Tell. Who are you, for instance?"

"Well, we can start there. I'm really Sam Gordon, a guy from Brooklyn. As

I revealed on the ship, you may recall. I had been industriously going to college on the subway for several years before I noticed that Hitler meant to do us all in. I got into the RAF in 1940, thanks to being some kind of amateur pilot, so by the time the US came into the war I'd been there over a year."

"Why rush off? Did *you* want to be a hero too?"

His glance was so cool that she was rocked back. One thing about Sam, he didn't go in for cool glances as a rule. "I'm a Jew," he answered. "I like to think I'd have gone anyway."

"Oh. Well, it never occurred to me. That you had any special reason, I mean."

"The Nazis provided enough special reasons to go around." He lit a cigarette. "After the war I was going back to my study of the Hittites — no doubt you remember the Hittites — when I was looked up by a cousin in the Jewish Intelligence Service."

"A cousin! And what's the Jewish Intelligence Service?"

"It's this outfit my cousin is in." The wolf's grin was back, and Kate felt relieved. "They needed pilots badly. I started flying refugees and arms to Palestine from Central Europe."

"Is that legal?"

"With whom would that be?" She felt stupid. "The service has a double function just now. One, to prepare for war with the Arabs — no, there's no way it can be avoided. And two, to find Nazi war criminals who slipped through the net. It was a loose weave. I was supposedly recruited in the interests of the former, but late last year Dov — that's my cousin — arranged to meet me in a dismal café on the smoky fringes of Budapest. The goulash was a minefield, but that's the Intelligence business for you. Because I am who I am — a clean cut vet from the USA, free to go anywhere without attracting undue attention — he had a different job for me."

"Clean cut!"

"Is that all you can say?"

"Go on, Sam." She heard a softness in her voice and hoped he wouldn't think it was phoney.

"Do you know who Dieter Wenzel is?"

"No."

"One of the bigger Nazis who disappeared. Dov's bunch had an idea that he found a hideout in Brazil. I think your kettle's boiling."

Kate came back with the tray and set it down between them. "Is that why Rosa mentioned Brazil?"

"Precisely. Among the Dachau survivors who managed to wriggle into Palestine was a woman named Hannah Stein. She came to Intelligence with a bizarre and fascinating story. In the camp she had made friends with a gypsy girl named Diamondy Szastris."

"Oh." There lay the rage and grief of Rosa.

"Yes. Rosa's only child died in Dachau, but not before she told Hannah Stein how she came to be there. She had been betrayed to the SS by her lover, the son of an old Junker family. The man was not a Nazi, and he had promised to protect the gypsies who had been living on and around his ancestral property for some hundred or so years. Gypsies are very proud — they had paid their rent in many useful services. This fellow had used them. Even after everything went smash he counted on using Rosa Szastris, who had fled west ahead of the Russians believing she had a better chance of finding her daughter that way. After all, how would she guess the truth? The tears of the crocodile are nothing to what your German cousin could shed."

"Sam, did *you* know it was Tony?"

"No. Let's call him Franz von Elfenstein. A man who had in his possession a rather wonderful old statuette, unusual and very valuable, which he was anxious to convert to cash. Of course, he had no right to do such a thing. It was an heirloom if there ever was one. But even before the war wiped them out, the von Elfensteins were going broke and young Franz had no desire to scrimp and save to maintain the family position. Pour out, will you?"

Kate filled the cups. "But why...?"

"Patience. As you know, Franz was an officer in the regular army, the Wehrmacht. Home on a brief leave he was enjoying the company of his gypsy sweetheart in the intimacy of one of those hunting lodges that add such romantic charm to your average forest. Who should break into this idyll but Dieter Wenzel? Diamondy was horrified to find that they were well acquainted. She did what her mother would have done — she eavesdropped. What she found out put iron in her soul. Wenzel had managed to confiscate a fortune in diamonds, the property of Jews who had been sent to the camps and had no further use for them. He and Franz agreed to amalgamate their treasures."

"So the Hanged Man was worth a double fortune?"

"Yes. It was valuable enough in itself to interest any professional thief who got wind of it — witness Fanny Birdsill — but with the diamonds inside it was a portable El Dorado."

"What were they going to do with it? It seems to me things would have been safer as they were."

"Wenzel had heard that Franz was being posted to Kahlberg. It was his idea to stash the complete loot in some hole in the wall there. It seemed an ideal hiding place, and one with which Franz was already familiar. They could always recover it after the war."

"But they couldn't..."

"No, they couldn't. But they didn't even know they were going to lose the war at that point. Wenzel didn't like the way Diamondy looked at him, so Franz took no chances. Swearing to come back to her, he kissed her goodbye and left for his new post. She was rushing to warn her family when the SS pounced. She simply disappeared. Of course Rosa was half-mad with worry. Franz took his very first opportunity to come to Rosa in search of his sweetheart. You know what a superb actor he is."

Kate felt her face turn warm, and she looked at the fire. "How did Rosa find out in the end, then?"

"After they got the story from Hannah Stein, Dov's crowd looked her up. Diamondy had wanted Stein to tell Rosa if she ever got the chance. Of course after that Rosa would have walked through hell barefoot to get Franz. Franz had let her think that he was still trying to trace Diamondy; he had asked *her* to help him out by making the run to Florida in order to avoid the scrutiny of some remote relative in the Bonn bureaucracy."

"But Sam, wouldn't Rosa see...?"

"Oh, Franz operated on the probably correct assumption that the fine points of the law were less important to Rosa than personal loyalty. Otherwise he'd have thought of something else. Franz's mind generates plots the way Niagara Falls generates electricity. But once Rosa had heard Stein's story his number was up, one way or another. He didn't have a chance."

"I still don't see. Why would Wenzel trust Franz, after all?"

"Wenzel knew Franz needed him. Wenzel was a real big shot. He knew his way around in places Franz had no access to. He'd been dealing in stolen art ever since he got a look at what was available to the conquerors of Europe, and he had friends who could help Franz no matter what happened. Conversely, they could see to it that he didn't pull any fast ones. Only thing, they couldn't figure on James Bell. He was a wild card."

"But neither could Franz! How could he know that James would fall out of the sky?"

"James was luck beyond anything Franz hoped for. When he knew Kahlberg was doomed he must have had some rough moments. He couldn't leave the object there, but it was a hell of a risk trying to take it out himself. *He couldn't just disappear.* Then it turned out that he didn't have to do a thing. James Bell made love to the employment." Kate detected a curling lip. "With all his romantic ideas, and the kind of nerve that never quite goes out of style, James was a gift from the gods. He snapped up the bait like a starving trout."

"But James might not have made it!"

"Everything was a chance. He probably wished James had both arms at that point, but if he'd had as many arms as the god Siva he couldn't have looked like a cooler hand. You know James." He paused. "Sorry, Kate. You knew James."

"James told me how the escape was managed, but not about the treasure."

"Didn't you wonder what it was all about?"

"Yes, I did. I wanted to think about it. I was all mixed up, because of the gypsy and the card and Fan. And because of the Bells."

"Kate, none of it was all that fair to you. I'm sorry about that." He looked very serious. "I tried to watch out for you, more than you realize, but I could have been kicked out of England at a moment's notice given the present British policy on Palestine."

"I understand. But *you* didn't know Tony was Franz?"

"No. I wish I had."

She looked at him and then looked away again. "Not to worry," she said in a small voice. "Rosa had my number the minute she saw me. Anyway I found out about the treasure by eavesdropping on James and Franz. Franz doesn't seem to have much luck with girls eavesdropping."

"Handsome types like James and Franz always have to watch out for girls." There was an expression on his face, but Kate couldn't make it out.

"Why don't you shave off that beard?" Then she wished she hadn't asked.

"Oh, come now, Kate. A beard was wanted. I supplied it. Did you only make two cups?"

"You're awfully fond of tea."

"Suspicious, I admit. Do me a favor, though. Don't ask around about me just yet."

"Then tell me what you've done with the diamonds."

"Turned them over to representatives of the future Jewish state. Private claims may be made by survivors of the camps or their heirs. All very quiet." He frowned.

"All right. I believe you. What about Lisa? She certainly went for *you* in a big way. What did she have in mind?"

"Okay." He jabbed the fire. "Look, Kate, I've got to take off soon. Let me finish. Lisa Dragonette was Dieter Wenzel's mistress in Paris during the Occupation. He told her about Franz, but of course she'd never seen him and his Tony act was so smooth she didn't give him a tumble. I'd thrown her a little Yiddish-style German just to see what happened and I guess she thought I might be Franz in a false beard. The Hessians may have been Hittites, after all."

"I forgot about the Hittites."

"You'd be surprised how interesting they are." He looked wistful. "Anyway Lisa, who used to be a cabaret singer named Suzie Song in the Paris days, was not without a modicum of real talent. That, combined with as much brass as the great bell of Pankor Vat, enabled her to assume — *assume* being the operative word — a new role and a career to go with it after her Nazi pals got the boot."

"But she was still Wenzel's girl? Never seeing him? She must have had a lot of faith in the Hanged Man. Why are you giving me that funny look?"

"Maybe she was in love with him. It's something they talk about on stage. It can last quite a long time, and is not dependent on the personal beauty or even the moral worth of the object."

"How come you know so much about it, Sam?" He didn't answer. "Well, what was Lisa going to do?"

"Take the Hanged Man, diamonds and all, from Florida to Brazil via one of the hundreds of illegal flights that are back in business in the Caribbean area. I suppose you knew that the only traffic between Miami and Latin America wasn't Alice Faye and Carmen Miranda? And now there's a fresh batch of unemployed hot pilots."

"Like you?"

"You don't seem to take my interest in the Hittites seriously."

"You dazzled the guard in the British Museum."

"If you want to know what happened, Kate, you'd better stick with the story. I wouldn't want to get the crazy idea that you're interested in hearing me talk about the Hittites. Franz was already thinking Brazil — a lot of them were — so when he heard about James' Uncle Albert something went click..."

"*My* Uncle Albert..."

"Yeah. *Your* Uncle Albert. That's the key point, actually. What with your Uncle Albert, etc., there was a helluva lot that could go wrong. When Lisa got herself a hired gorilla and searched the cottage on Snake Lake she found zilch. She set out after *you* like a V-2 rocket. Everybody always goes after the heiress."

"Where is she now, then?"

"She's on her way to Wenzel with Rosa in hot pursuit. She may not even know the diamonds are missing. We hope she doesn't know that Rosa's on her tail."

"I think Rosa should get a medal! You and your friends just wound her up and sent her off. You didn't even tell her about the diamonds."

"It seemed safer not to. There was no need."

"Safer, why? Didn't you trust her?"

"As a matter of fact, I wanted to tell her. Dov's group nixed it. It's one of the rules of Intelligence that nobody knows anything unless they have to. Thank god they can't hear me talking now."

"Who sent her after Lisa? Franz is finished, after all."

"Nobody sent her. She decided she wanted to get Wenzel too."

"It's too dangerous. Your friends have to stop her."

"It's her life, Kate. She's not alone. Two of Dov's pals are right behind her. They also want Wenzel, and they want him alive. But they're going to protect Rosa."

"Maybe."

"They'll try anyway. Is there anything else you want to know before I go?" He spoke abruptly.

She tried to smile. "What about Tom Burrows? Why was *he* after Lisa? There's a limit to the number of people I'll believe are in love in any one story."

"Tom Burrows was in Paris right after the Germans left. He may have recognized Lisa and wondered if he could make use of what he knew."

"He knew James."

"It's not possible to know exactly what happened, but your friend Inspector Bucket persuaded Harry Feather to talk. James Bell stumbled into an American unit on his way out of Germany. He was beat. While he was sacked out Burrows searched him — Bell might have been a German after all — and found the Hanged Man. He asked about it. After that Bell didn't wait for an escort home. He took a powder. Burrows didn't report the incident, but he brooded. God, how he brooded. Especially after he got home and found that Captain Burrows was just plain Joe Blow from Kokomo."

"But he wasn't really a crook?"

"Not a pro. But when he finally blurted the story to Fan — you know how it is on a ship, nothing seems to carry its normal weight — she opened up a whole new world to him, what with her self-confidence and her 'connections.' Of course her 'connections' were a joke compared to Wenzel's. These guys were just babes in the wood. They didn't know what the hell they were doing. They were flying blind." Sam shook his head.

"They didn't have anything to do with the real plot, then?"

"Nope. Birdsill just suffered from congenital larceny of the heart. Burrows was a coward and none too bright. It takes all kinds to make an army. You can bet Franz didn't want to kill either of them — murders rev up the police — but they got in his way and he couldn't fool around."

"But how did Fan get in his way? The ship was a terrible place to kill her — and right off too. And what happened to the body?"

"Throw your mind back and look at it this way. Practically everybody was watching *you*, remember, but except for the Fan-Burrows axis it was every man for himself. Lisa didn't know Franz and Franz — here's another kicker — knew absolutely nothing about Lisa. Does that suggest anything to any part of your mind?"

"Wenzel hadn't been able to tell him?"

"Forget able. Somewhere down the road Wenzel was going to doublecross Franz. But in the meantime Franz had been to Titus in his Tony suit and Fan had seen him there. He just couldn't risk an explanation, especially when he was worried about who I might be. He saw her coming out of Burrows' room and he strangled her, probably with that cord he strung his monocle on later. Then he heard your footsteps and ducked into the empty cabin — he'd just left Burrows in the lounge, remember. When you ran away he dumped the corpse into Burrows' trunk."

"Oh, Sam, why didn't I just scream?"

"You did fine. You sure had a lot of faith in your mission from Rosa, hiding the Tarot card. But you did fine. You see Franz figured Tom must be in with Fan, what with her coming out of his room and his striking up an acquaintance with you. He expected the card to give Tom enough of a scare to get rid of him — but of course dumping the body on him was a better way. Tom must have been scared white when he found it — he didn't dare talk. He just got rid of it one dark night."

"It must have been soon."

"I'd guess almost at once. But it was after the first search of the lifeboats."

"He didn't stay scared, though."

"Worse luck for him. He just hung around you until Franz decided he had to deal him out. Of course James Bell had the wind up about him. Bell believed your story about being followed in the park. That's why he was so anxious to get you to Moon Croft. One reason, anyway." He threw her a glance.

"Oh, Sam. Do you remember what it was like on the ship?"

"Yeah."

"Tony was so plausible. What about Lady Tingly-ffinch?"

"She was the aunt of an old Harchester chum named Tony Smith, missing in action. It wasn't all that risky. Nobody ever heard him talking to her. He was pretty safe in Tourist Class. Geoff Weston was at Harchester, too. *You* must have noticed that he stayed away from London."

She smiled. "Uh-huh." She thought a minute. "But why was Tom going around the moors in his underwear?"

"Franz took his outerwear off to delay identification of the body by the police. The card was for any other accomplice who might be lurking around. It was rather stupid, for him. The underwear just didn't look English, but Franz was no longer English enough to realize it."

"Tom Burrows didn't search my room at the Brown Bull."

"That was Harry Feather."

"Harry Feather!" Kate was indignant.

"We're all disenchanted nowadays. He said he didn't take nothing. You never opened a peeper." Sam stood up. "That's about it. So long, Kate. Unless there's a good lamp on that bike you'd better get back to town."

"Where are you going, Sam? I still think you could have told me some of this sooner instead of letting me be scared out of a year's growth." She was trying to smile.

"I did you a favor. You're too tall anyway." He turned away.

"I might have been killed." Everything was ending too soon.

"I saved you in the nick of time."

"That was just luck."

"I guess I'm a lucky guy," he said. Then he was gone.

She watched his car from the window, two red spots getting smaller. After a while she found her scarf and blotted her face with it.

Chapter XXXI

> Or is he the hero? If I tell you that, then I seal his fate as well as yours.
>
> —Madame Sosostris

Kate was packing very very carefully. She had all evening in which to do it, and all night too for that matter. The York bus did not leave until the morning. So she folded her skirts and sweaters first one way and then another, though it made no difference at all which way she folded them. Into one elasticized pocket she put her nylon stockings, the clean ones in neat pairs at one end and the ones she had worn bunched together at the other end. Another pocket took her little padded jewel case, stuffed with fake pearls and clip-on earrings. The photograph of herself she put on the bottom, sliding it underneath everything. Outside she could hear a bus pull in. It seemed too late for the bus that had brought her from Witherton the night of the Guy Fawkes bonfire, the night she had seen Sam through the flames. The night Franz had kissed her behind the shed.

That was more of a game for me than it was for him, she thought. After all, it was important to fool me. Look at the stakes.

Jenny Ricks had been in twice — to see whether or not Kate would like a bit of roasted cheese for her supper and to see whether she wanted anything ironed or mended. Kate had turned her face away and said, "No thanks," in a discouraging manner.

Jenny's outstandingly undiscouraged knock sounded again.

"Come in."

Jenny burst in like a messenger bearing joyful tidings. "There be a gentleman to see you downstairs. I've put him into the small parlor then."

"A gentleman?"

Jenny pondered. "Well, praps not a *proper* gentleman. Not like that other one, who turned out to be a nasty spy. It's yon American."

"Do you mean the ferrety man?" Something inside Kate had got loose and was knocking against her ribs.

Jenny laughed. "I'd never be calling that one a gentleman, not was it ever so. I mean the one that had a beard."

"*Had* a beard?" asked Kate in a squeaky voice. "How do you know?"

"Well, it looks just like him — it's his hair and that old jacket and especially them eyes."

"What *eyes*?"

"You'll never tell me you've not noticed them eyes? When he looks at you you go all squishy."

"Not me," said Kate, sitting down suddenly. "How does he look in general?"

"Is he handsome, do you mean?"

"No, I mean, is he friendly?"

"Pooh."

"What do you mean, 'Pooh'?"

"Of course he's *friendly*. But if you're wanting to know is he handsome I would say no, but it doesn't matter. He looks a bit like a highwayman — you know, like in that film. Valerie Hobson was the innkeeper's daughter..."

"Oh, Jenny."

"Oooo," said Jenny. "I see, said the blind man. It's *him* you be daft over, miss."

"No, it isn't." She looked at Jenny in despair. "But I can't go down to the small parlor alone, Jenny. Are you sure he looks friendly? I don't think he likes me."

"Well, he's got a grand bunch of heather. He won't have got it on the moors, not so late in the year."

"Maybe he's on his way to call on Rosemary Broadbent. Would you say he was in a hurry?"

"Well, if he is you'd best be getting downstairs then, miss," said Jenny, giggling.

Kate rushed to the mirror. "Do I look all right?"

"I'd say you look smashing — a proper bobby-dazzler."

This was England, land of the closed door. The economy of the custom, with draughty corridors and struggling fires, was obvious. Also obvious were the more personal advantages to the insiders — the peace, the privacy. Nevertheless Kate longed for rooms that spilled their human contents into one another in a casual, non-committal fashion. The door to the small parlor was closed, and as she stood outside she wondered what percentage of the human body was, in fact, water.

Then she opened the door, entered the room, and closed the door behind her, continuing to hold on to the knob. Sam was standing beside the fireplace. He had put the heather down on the table and was reading the *Manchester Guardian*.

"Hi," she said.

"Hi," said Sam.

"You got rid of your beard in a hurry."

"I needed a disguise."

There was a silence, then Kate said, "Did you forget something?" and Sam said at the same moment, "I wondered whether you would mind..." and they smiled at each other stiffly.

After a polite interval Sam began again, "Will you be going home soon? To New York, I mean?"

"Next week."

"I wonder whether you would mind phoning my sister. Just to say you've seen me and I'm all right."

"Oh, I'd *very* happy to phone your sister. What's her name and number? I haven't anything to write with."

"I'll write it down for you. I'd like to send a small present to my niece, but..."

"Oh, I'd *love* to go to Brooklyn..."

"You wouldn't have to do that. My brother-in-law works near you. He's in sweaters."

"Oh. Well, I'd certainly be *glad* to do anything."

"Thanks."

Neither of them moved. A chorus of "On Ilkla Moor baht 'at" had started up in the bar and was audible through the wall.

"I'd also like you to thank Sumner Partridge for me," said Sam, with an air of coming to the point.

"What for?"

"Well, he was quite helpful."

"I suppose so. He didn't know he was helping you."

"I didn't want to be churlish, after all. I hope you'll both be very happy."

"What do you mean?"

"Surely he's the one who gets the girl? You seem to be running out of leading men."

It was not a very graceful thing to say, but Kate smiled happily. "Sumner Partridge is going to marry MaJa. She says I'm going to wear coral taffeta and catch the bride's bouquet."

"MaJa?"

"My best friend. Her name is really Mary Jane. She plays the harp."

"I'll say she does. She sits on a cloud and flaps her wings." Sam looked as if he had suddenly caught a glimpse of paradise.

Kate took her hand off the doorknob and rubbed it on her skirt. Sam tossed the *Manchester Guardian* onto the chair. They gazed at each other across the rolling sea of floorboards. There was really nothing left but happiness. Everything else had been used up or thrown away.

Finally Kate asked, "Is that heather, by any chance?"

He seized the bouquet. "It's for you. I didn't want you to go away from here without having some heather."

"Where did you get it?"

"Peniston Crag."

"Then it's not real. I like things to be real."

He grinned. "I drove over to Witherton after I left you and got it from the florist. He keeps it for the tourists."

"There can't be all that many tourists. The Brontës didn't come from Witherton."

"They get them mixed up."

There was another silence. Neither of them moved.

"Sam?"

"Yes, Kate?"

"I still don't understand why when…"

"Let's talk about that sometime when we're not so busy."

"Do you want to have some roasted cheese?"

"Not yet."

"It's suppertime."

"Hold it. What are you going to do about this heather?"

"I thought I'd see about that after I got it."

"Well, then. Come on over here and get it."

"That's not how it's done."

"I know how it's done."

"I'm scared, Sam."

"Ah, no." There was a soft note in his voice she had never heard before.

"How would you feel if your shadow was going to disappear? If you were going to lose your heart and not get it back? If you could never be the same as you were before?"

"Take a chance. Maybe you can walk right through me," he said, and held out his arms.

Epilogue

The Split: December 31, 1947: Sao Paolo

"Thank you for consenting to join me, madame. Why should you wait for a table? I know this café. It is always crowded."

The small elegant woman smiled inscrutably.

"It is crowded everywhere on New Year's Eve. I was last year in München. It was the same."

"Of course I know your face. You are always around. You do not search my room, why not? Perhaps you wish to assist at a lovers' meeting. You are foolish. You will have waited too long." She spoke very quietly.

"Not for me." The voice was somber.

"I am right, then. It is Wenzel you want. You, and your shadows."

"Shadows?" Dark eyes widened.

"Come, madame, I have not your years but I was not born just yesterday. You are not alone."

"They come from Sam, then." The older woman shrugged. "No matter to me."

"Ah, so. Sam. He should learn to dance." A few strings and maracas struck up "Brazil" from a small raised platform.

"What is your intention? I assure you I am willing to die."

"I propose an alternative."

"Propose it then. I don't like to be here around."

"Your friends have the diamonds, but there is still something for you...and also for me."

"You misunderstand me. I seek justice. That contents me."

A skinny waiter in flared trousers brought tiny cups of steaming coffee. The aroma was bitter as death.

"Here is justice for everyone. *Tout le monde.* I hate Dieter Wenzel."

Her companion hissed. The women leaned together in a cloud of smoke. "For what reason?"

"It is not entirely personal. I am a sometime French agent."

"Goddam."

"I said sometime. At the moment I'm on holiday. I suggest you keep your *copains* off until Wenzel sells the Hanged Man. His buyer is in place. It will be cash — green US money. A share for you, for your trouble. For Wenzel, his enemies can have him. Agreed?"

"I am thinking."

"*Alors*, it is decided. Do not crowd me." The speaker stood up and said clearly and carelessly, "My pleasure, madame. The crowds are shocking. Enjoy your visit. There is much to see in Brazil."

HILDA DUNN was born in 1925 in New York State. She attended Syracuse University, majoring in English and Journalism. After college she studied abroad in Edinburgh and Venice, then returned to the United States, eventually settling outside Boston, where she raised four children. She passed away in 1998, while on vacation in England.